BANGKOK

STEPHEN SHAIKEN

(2018 EDITION)

This is a work of fiction. Names, characters, businesses, places, events, and incidents are either the products of the author's imagination or used in a fictitious manner. Any resemblance to actual persons, living or dead, events, or locales is entirely coincidental.

Published by Stephen Shaiken
Cover design by Melody Shaiken

Visit Stephen's website at www.stephenshaiken.com.
Follow Stephen on Twitter: https://twitter.com/StephenShaiken.

First Edition: August 2018
Print ISBN: 978-1-732147416
eBook ISBN: 978-1-73214709

TABLE OF CONTENTS

1

I WAS GETTING by as a lawyer in San Francisco, but was never satisfied with my life.

I won some difficult cases, which led to referrals from the drug dealers and sex traffickers of Northern California. This brought me some money, but not much happiness.

I spent hours each day stuck in traffic, running from Point A to Point B, fueled only by fees that needed to be earned because of bills that needed to be paid.

There were plenty of those bills, most of the time more than the fees. No matter how much was earned, more was spent.

The long hours of work and the constant stress ruined every relationship I ever had. It was not clear to me then, but it is now. Overwork and stress are not good building blocks for dealing with other people. They know this in Thailand, but not in America.

My thoughts were always about the need to make money, and make it as soon as possible. That meant always chasing that one big fee that would allow me to jump off the treadmill I was trapped on. I waited and waited, but it did not arrive.

ONE NIGHT I was to meet a client in a restaurant in the East

Bay. He had picked up a federal drug charge and a forfeiture action against his home and bank accounts, and he was going to pay me a retainer of fifty thousand dollars cash. This would be the largest fee of my career. That he wanted to meet and pay me cash in the parking lot of a restaurant in a rough part of town at night did not trouble me. Such was the life of a criminal defense lawyer.

While driving across the Bay Bridge, I thought of how to avoid the reporting requirement for more than ten grand cash. My thoughts also focused on the stack of unpaid bills held together by a rubber band on the passenger seat.

While entering the parking lot, I saw my client leaving his car. He had parked far from the restaurant, in a deserted section of the lot. I aimed my car at a spot right next to him.

Before I could park, a black Land Rover came speeding into the lot. It stopped right next to my client. Suddenly the sound of gunfire came from the Land Rover. I instinctively lowered my head and pushed my seated body as low as possible.

The firing lasted a few seconds. When I lifted myself up, the black car was gone. My client lay sprawled on the ground next to his car.

I leaped out of my car and ran to my client. Blood was gushing from his body and head. I called out for help but there was no one else in the lot and I was too far from the restaurant for anyone inside to hear me.

One did not have to be a doctor to know that my client was dead. In the brightness of my headlights there were visible bits of brain and skull swimming in a pool of blood. Never having seen anyone who had been shot, my first response was nausea. It felt as if I was about to vomit, but the nausea passed. Fear gripped me like an icy hand but not strongly enough to prevent me from thinking.

The dead man grasped a small paper bag in his right hand. Hundred dollar bills spilled out onto the gravel lot. The money must have been my retainer. I reached for the paper bag, but then wondered whether it was lawful to take it. Through the open door of my car the stack of bills were directly in my line of sight. I scooped up the stray currency and stuffed them into the dead man's bag.

The door to my client's car was open, and inside on the front passenger seat was a brief case. I reached into the vehicle and pulled it out. It was light and it was locked. It may have held something important to my late client, perhaps something to do with his case. Any representation of my client expired with his demise, but I decided that a look inside the briefcase was permissible.

Our cars were at the farthest end of the parking lot. There were no vehicles anywhere near us, and the lights around the restaurant did not illuminate this spot.

No one came running from the restaurant. No cars drove into the lot.

A voice inside my head reminded me that someone may have called the police, and if so, they would be there momentarily. I did not want to explain to law enforcement my reasons for meeting a drug dealer late at night to receive a bag of cash. Or why evidence was being taken from a crime scene.

These issues weren't going to be resolved in the parking lot. After looking around the vicinity to make sure no one was watching me, I jumped back into my car and left. Two police cars with sirens on and roof lights blazing passed me as they sped in the opposite direction, heading towards the parking lot. A tingling sensation shot through my arms and legs. The police cars ignored me, and the tingling left as suddenly as it had arrived.

The fee and whatever else was in the briefcase would be protected in my office. The building had good security: surveillance cameras and an alarm system. No burglar worth their salt would try to break into this place when there were so many easier pickings.

At every red light I looked in the rear view mirror and to my sides for any sign of a pursuing vehicle. By the third light I felt confident there were none. It took me ten minutes to reach the office. The building was completely dark, but a light on in my office would not have been unusual, as lawyers are known to work very late. I knew that well, having had to do it all too often. Brutal hours had killed many relationships, my own marriage among them.

In the end, it is never worth it. It wasn't for me.

An old lawyer whom I respected retired in his late sixties as a worn and bitter man, a shell of what he once was. He had sacrificed so much to the law, not being there so many times when family or friends needed him, foregoing other interests and passions to the demands of the profession. He had been a mentor, and we had a drink on his last day as a lawyer. I still remember what he told me:

Nobody ever said on their deathbed that their only regret was not spending more time at the office.

He was dead a year later. I was one of a handful of people at the funeral.

I KEYED MYSELF into my office, locked the door and turned on the desk lamp. First I checked the paper bag. Aside from the few bills that had gotten loose when my client was shot, it was filled with hundreds held together by rubber bands. The first three packets each had fifty Ben Franklins. It seemed reasonable to assume the same for the other seven. That was my fifty thousand dollar fee. Declaring it as ten thousand or more in cash would be a problem. I couldn't give my client's social security number as I didn't know it, and there would be an IRS inquiry when they heard about this one.

Worry about that later, I told myself, and reached for the brief-case. It was a standard, old-fashioned type, which closed by pulling a leather flap down from the top and locked by a combination setting on the latch. The briefcase was stuffed and bulging.

I tried to cut the leather flap above the lock with my office scissors, but they were not sharp enough. The supply room had a few basic tools. Using them enabled me to break open the lock.

Inside were more bundles of cash, all hundreds, bound by rubber bands just like my fee. I pulled out two and counted, and each had one hundred Ben Franklins. There were sixty. They formed a pile on my desk. I stared at the stacks of money, my heart beating fast.

Six hundred thousand dollars. Six fifty counting my fee. The owner was dead and they were without question the proceeds of drug dealing.

My responsibilities were clear. A lawyer cannot facilitate or cover up a crime, nor hide or destroy evidence. The cash and the brief case were evidence of several crimes, committed both by my client and his killers.

If the rules were followed there was one course of action. Call the police, tell them what was found, and turn it over.

And explain taking fifty thousand dollars cash in a paper bag at midnight, not to mention the briefcase, and failing to call police at the scene of the shooting.

I would probably avoid any charges or bar action, but it was not assured. Certainly my name would be splashed across the papers and news broadcasts. There is a saying in the law that as long as they spell your name right, any publicity is good publicity. Experience persuaded me otherwise, having seen many instances where bad publicity ruined a career.

There was no way to legally keep any of this cash. It would be forfeited and given to whichever police and prosecutors worked the case.

I did not know what to do and did not want trouble, but this was the chance of a lifetime. All my debts and money worries would disappear.

The odds did favor me. Lawyers know the system. It was still a difficult choice. Seeing a client shot dead before my eyes made it even harder to focus on a solution.

I did what always worked back then when faced with a difficulty. I reached into my bottom left drawer, retrieved a small tin box, opened it, and pulled out a bag of weed, a pack of rolling papers, and a lighter. A joint was quickly rolled, the window opened, and the joint lit. I sucked in the smoke, held it in my lungs for a few moments, and exhaled it out the window. With each puff of released smoke I felt tension and fear escaping. When the joint began to burn the tips of my fingers, I stubbed it out on the ledge and flicked it out the window.

Alcohol never works for me the way cannabis does. I am at best indifferent to the taste, hate the hangovers, and don't like losing control. The burst of calmn that comes with a good vodka martini is enjoyable, but it is always my backup choice when a joint is not available. As it does to everyone, drinking diminishes my mental skills. Weed relaxes me and as far as I can tell, years of smoking have left my mental processes unimpaired. Drinking is for social reasons, but weed is my substance of choice.

My valuable papers and documents were kept in my little office safe. Since the divorce, I had moved often and this allowed me twenty-four-seven access and security. The safe was in my credenza. A square was cut in the bottom shelf, the safe dropped in, the top flush with the square. A heavy metal slab placed inside weighed down the safe. The top of the safe was covered with books and papers. Even if discovered it was too heavy to carry, and I was doubtful many burglars are also safecrackers.

The money went into the safe, all six hundred fifty thousand dollars. The safe was then locked and covered and the credenza closed.

It was a quick drive to my latest short-term rental. I never made it to bed and collapsed on my living room recliner. Sleep did not come easy, an hour or two at most before a burst of anxiety awakened me again. *What have I gotten myself into?* I asked in my semi-conscious state. By dawn any further thoughts of sleep were abandoned.

After a few cups of strong coffee my plan was formulated.

At eight a.m. I called my good friend Charlie. He was also a lawyer, but the kind you go to when other lawyers are unwilling to do what you ask. Some of Charlie's work would have interested prosecutors. He was very good at his trade, because despite courthouse scuttlebutt, neither he nor any clients had ever been known to have problems. Charlie somehow managed to solve them all and create none.

In spite of his shady reputation, no one had ever claimed that Charlie cheated his clients or failed to deliver as promised. Charlie had been a friend since law school, when we ran around together. We remained friends over the next fifteen years. I was fairly confident that Charlie could be trusted, to a large degree because there was information in my possession he would not want the state bar or the U.S. Attorney to know about.

"Meet me in my office at nine," I told him when he picked up his phone on the sixth ring.

"It's Saturday morning," he croaked.

"There's money for you. Lots of it," I told him.

"Can we make it ten?" he asked.

BY NOON, FUELED by more strong coffee, we had it all worked out.

"I'll get the money to you, pay off your ex, get your cases covered, sell your car, pay off your bills, close down the office and apartment. All for only ten percent plus expenses. You can trust me," Charlie said as he shut his notebook. He stuffed the keys to my office, apartment, and car into his coat pocket.

"You can be trusted only because I can cause you more trouble than you can cause me."

Charlie ignored my wisecrack.

"Just give me a call when you get to wherever you're going and I'll send you the money and an accounting." He was out the door without another word.

THE NEXT DAY my alarm woke me before seven. After guzzling down three cups of French roast I stuffed a week's change of clothes into a small duffel bag.

The cab was waiting at the curb. I made myself comfortable in the back seat and watched the streets of San Francisco pass by as the cabbie cruised just above the speed limit. It might be a long time before I saw these streets again. "What terminal?" he asked a minute into the ride.

"International," I replied.

"What airline?"

"No particular airline. Just the international terminal."

That was the extent of our conversation.

As we approached the terminal, I scanned the names of the carriers posted outside the doorways. Most meant nothing to me, some revealing their nation, others not.

As soon as the cabbie stopped in front of the main entrance, I grabbed my duffel bag and paid him, leaving a large tip.

Inside the terminal most of the ticket counters had very long lines. One had a very short line.

Thai Airways.

I got on the end of its short line and in a few minutes was speaking with a ticket agent.

"When does your next flight leave? And where is it going?"

"We have a flight leaving for Bangkok in three hours, with a stopover in Japan," the agent said as she studied the screen at her station.

"I'll take it," I told her.

A few minutes later my boarding pass was in my hand and my duffel bag checked in.

In a small dark bar along the concourse two vodka martinis were downed in quick succession. I couldn't recall the last time I had more than one, but this was a special occasion. Not as good as weed, but it does the job in a pinch. I went through screening, found my way to the gate, and fifteen minutes later boarded the plane.

I started to watch a movie once we were airborne. A meal was served, and, after eating half of it, sleep claimed me. The flight attendant gently woke me at breakfast. By the time it was finished, we were landing in Japan. It was questionable whether there was enough time to take the shuttle to my next plane. Everything at the airport happened in a blur of movement. We took off five minutes after boarding. The attendant gave me an extra cup of coffee with the meal they served to help me stay awake. It failed, and I dozed off again, waking up when we landed in Bangkok.

AFTER RETRIEVING MY duffel bag from the baggage carousel, a Thai woman in a uniform directed me to Immigration where my picture was taken and my passport stamped with a thirty-day stay. I cashed a few U.S. hundreds into Thai baht, stuffed them into my pockets, and found my way to the public taxi queue. An attendant ushered me into a cab which was soon crawling through rush hour traffic towards Bangkok, to the hotel I had seen in the airline in-flight magazine. Exhaustion prevented me from watching what was happening outside on the streets.

At the hotel, a pretty young woman at the front desk made a photocopy of my passport, gave me a form to sign, and handed me a key card. A pleasant young man took my duffel bag, and I followed him into the elevator and to my room. He showed me how to work the air conditioning, the lights, and the television.

As soon as the bellboy left, I sat on the bed and closed my eyes. Exhausted as I was, sleep was not possible. Jet lag might be one reason but leaving my old life behind and starting over eclipsed everything else. I had no idea what form my new life would take, but knew I had to get it started.

I splashed some water on my face and ventured out onto the streets of Bangkok. It was hot and the streets were teeming with people. They were moving at a quick pace but it was calmer and less hectic than San Francisco. There was a 7/11 on the same street as the hotel, where I bought a sim card and talk time. I called Charlie to inform him of my whereabouts. He asked a few questions, took my hotel address, and told me not to worry.

"Just sit tight. Around this time two days from now I'll let you know where to find your money. The accounting and some other documents will arrive by FedEx." Then he hung up.

Charlie may cut corners when it comes to ethics and rules, but he has always been a man of his word. Two days later, upon returning to the hotel after lunch, the pretty woman at the front desk said there was a package for me. She handed me a FedEx envelope.

Once in my room the package was torn open. Clipped to the sheath of papers was a letter from Charlie.

Enclosed you will find a bank transfer notice in the name of William Rawlings, a Canadian. Just bring it to the bank at the address on top. When you get to the bank, make sure to ask for Mr. Samsuk and deal with no one else. Also enclosed is a copy of your visa application in your real name, which you can sign. You will see the name and address of your legal representative at the bottom. Go there tomorrow morning with your U.S. passport and the application and by the afternoon you will have a two year business visa. There is a complete accounting enclosed. Your car is sold, your office and apartment closed, and all your cases taken over. Your ex is happy. Enjoy Thailand and don't do anything I wouldn't do.

That gives me a pretty wide berth, I thought.

The accounting was detailed to the last cent. My new net worth was about a half million dollars in cash. William Rawlings was listed as a Canadian, so no worries about the IRS snooping around foreign accounts. Canadian authorities had no idea of his existence.

I met the legal consultant in his office at ten. He provided me a Canadian passport in the Rawlings name, with my picture. A post-it advised me "For the bank only if necessary." I gave him the application Charlie had sent, plus my U.S. passport, and he assured me that it would be returned with a visa later that day. By two p.m. my American passport was returned to me at the hotel with a visa stamped in it. My next stop was the bank.

Mr. Samsuk assured me that the Canadian passport would never be necessary unless he was not around. "But I am always around," he added.

My stay in the hotel lasted a few more weeks, until a chance meeting with a real estate agent seated next to me at breakfast. He was an American married to a Thai woman and had lived in Bangkok for fifteen years. We agreed that he would show me some properties. He bristled with enthusiasm, which made being around him enjoyable.

"You'll love it here, " he assured me over coffee in the lobby of my hotel before driving around town to look at condos.

He showed me several places. None of them appealed to me very much until he showed me a condo on a quiet side street between

Thong Lor and Ekamai, two of the most desirable areas in Bangkok.

It was a two bedroom place on the tenth floor, with a balcony and a City view, a five minute walk or one minute motorcycle taxi ride to either the Thong Lor or Ekamai BTS stops. Expats quick learn the value of being near the BTS or Skytrain, as it means avoiding traffic. The BTS glides above congested Sukhumvit and Silom, two of the main arteries in Bangkok. It is better than any transit system in America.

"This is perfect," I said after ten minutes of poking around. "You can have the money in the morning."

Bangkok was a bigger mystery to me then than it is now, but the trial lawyer instincts developed over more than fifteen years told me that this was right. It was a far nicer place than any of my residences back in the States.

The agent was caught by surprise. He never thought it would be this easy. He was silent for a moment.

"You're going to love it here," he then assured me in his honey-smooth voice, "You are never going to leave."

So far he is correct. Seven years and I'm still here.

ONE OF MY most pleasurable activities is going out on the balcony, watching the lights of the city and staring at the traffic below. It is most often quiet and peaceful on the tenth floors of Bangkok.

On rare occasions over the years my thoughts have turned to whether my life would be different today had other choices been made. If I never left America, never stopped being a lawyer in California, what would it be like? My conclusion is always that life would have grown more miserable as stress and time took their onerous tolls.

Many times I asked myself if life would always be this easy and this good, so devoid of problems.

The answer would eventually be shown to be a resounding "no."

2

I COULDN'T VENTURE a guess as to how many hours I have spent at the NJA Club during my seven years in Bangkok. The place is within walking distance of my condo and offers a full menu and bar, but it is the people who congregate there that make it the center of what passes for my social life.

No one knows the true origins of the name NJA Club. It really doesn't matter. Bangkok is in many ways several cities coexisting simultaneously in the same time and place. There is Thai Bangkok, the vast portion of the metropolitan area, where few foreigners ever venture. There are expat venues and condos, often catering to a specific nationality, American, British, and German, among others. There are the Chinese and Japanese housing and businesses, worlds of their own. NJA was different. The Club was a place where people of all nationalities gathered. Thais mingled with white foreigners from all over the world, known as *farangs*, and with other Asians as well. Most regulars were pleasant to be around, people who understood and respected boundaries, but as is to be expected in any large group, there are exceptions.

PHIL FUNSTON ALWAYS sits at the same table when he has

breakfast at the Club, which he does three or four times a week. If someone is seated there, he will ask them to move. If they decline, Phil will break into his shouting routine. "This is my seat," he will exclaim. "Do you know who I am?" he will ask. This behavior is frowned upon by Thai culture and by longtime expats as well, but Funston does not care. After fifteen years in Bangkok, he still does not recognize that he is a visitor in someone else's country. He is in his early fifties, and those who knew him when he first showed up at the NJA Club shortly after his arrival in Bangkok assure the rest of us that he has not changed at all.

Phil always orders the continental breakfast, lording over his table with a cup of coffee in one hand and a folded Bangkok Post in the other. He is often at the Club in the evening, when coffee is replaced with wine or beer. He is tall, with a modest but noticeable gut. He sports a shaved head and a salt and pepper Van Dyke. His shaved head is lumpy, and that hairstyle isn't right for him. Funston has a long neck, and when he lowers his head to sip his coffee, he reminds me of a Tyrannosaurus Rex. His voice reveals his Boston origins with its unmistakable Back Bay accent. He still pronounces "car" as "cah" and "park" as "pahk."

Phil is an outstanding guitarist. I have seen him play a few times at respected venues like the Saxophone Club by Victory Monument and the Blues Club in Banglampoo, the closest neighborhood Bangkok has to New York's Greenwich Village or San Francisco's North Beach. If Phil weren't so difficult person he might have been a star.

Phil came to Bangkok fifteen years ago as the stand-in guitarist for one of the many over-the-hill rock groups that in those days did Asian tours when the West had forgotten them. The lead guitarist of this particular group had suffered an unfortunate fatal encounter with a syringe of heroin, and Phil was hired for their Far Eastern tour. The band had one night in Bangkok. They went on to the next destination but Phil is still here. No one knew the full story, but based on snippets told by Phil, it had something to do with him waking up in a short time hotel with a bargirl and missing the flight to Jakarta. When the band's manager was able to reach him, Phil cursed him out and the band found a Filipino guitarist to finish the tour.

There is much mystery surrounding Phil Funston. No one knows where he lives, or who, if anyone, he lives with. He is hired for sporadic fill-in gigs with local or touring bands, but is never asked a second time, and he has had a few students over the years. Other than that, he has no visible means of support yet he does not appear to have any financial worries. He once hinted that he had a resident card with work permission, based on a paper marriage of convenience to a Thai woman to whom he paid an annual fee, but no one has ever seen any proof.

Among the congregants at the NJA Club, there is an unwritten rule that Bangkok's fabled nightlife is not a proper topic of discussion. The bars and the women who work in them are deemed the province of short-term sex tourists, not permanent residents. If one chooses to frequent these venues, it is their own business, not ours. I never understood the attraction; it is seedy and demeaning to have to pay for companionship or sex or whatever these men hope to find. Bangkok is filled with good women with whom one could have a normal relationship. Many a man has been attracted to the ease and illusion of Bangkok prostitution when they first arrive, but few maintain interest once they settle down. There are far better attractions in Thailand. If men don't stop going to the bars they at least stop talking about it. Everyone knows these rules except Phil Funston.

Funston does not care what anyone else thinks. He is a fixture in the go-go and beer bars as well as the sexual massage parlors that dot the Sukhumvit area. When he grows tired of the same old places, he spends a weekend in Pattaya, otherwise known as Sin City. Pattaya is the worst place in Thailand. I spent one day and night there soon after my arrival in Thailand and vowed never to return. That vow has been scrupulously honored.

Phil Funston believes we respect him and wanted to hear his exploits. Nothing could be further from the truth. We listen to him only because he will not shut up.

"I've got fifty girlfriends," he once boasted. Inside me was a burning desire to tell him it wasn't a girlfriend if you had to pay. I bit my tongue instead. There is no reasoning with a guy like Funston.

"And I won't take a girl just because she wants the money," he often declares. "She has to want to sleep with me."

Doubtful there are fifty young women in Bangkok who want to sleep with a paunchy and disagreeable middle-aged foreigner with a lumpy head. In fact, I doubt there is even one. It is for the money, no matter what Phil Funston tries to convince everyone, including himself.

"I have to kung fu away dozens of beautiful girls," he exclaims. He doesn't look like the kung fu type.

My friend Rhode Island Joe once asked Funston why he has to pay if he is so desired by Thai women.

"It's not a commercial transaction," Funston said with condescension. "It's just taking care of the lady for that night. If you guys think it is nothing more than sex for money, you don't understand Thailand."

In my years in Thailand, I have encountered many men who were caught up in the delusions of the sex industry. They either wised up or wound up going down in flames. The fact that Funston is none the worse and still solvent is unusual. Give the devil his due.

The only women I see Funston interact with are Noi, a Club regular, and the staff. If they are representative, Phil is not the charmer he believes himself to be.

The Club has two waitresses, Joy and Mai. Joy is short, dark and thin, and we all guess her age as somewhere in her thirties. She is quiet and always smiling. She comes from Isan in the Northeast, like Noi and many working people in Bangkok. She goes home for visits at every opportunity. She lives with a cousin in an apartment in Dindaeng, a section of Bangkok with few foreign residents. Her English is serviceable.

Mai is tall, full bodied, and lighter skinned than Joy. She too is somewhere in her thirties but could pass for younger. She was born in Chiang Mai, Thailand's second city, in the North, but grew up in Bangkok. She is talkative and often interjects her opinion even when unsolicited, unusual for a Thai. No one ever seems to mind. I enjoy speaking with her, and we chat overtime when we see each other. Rhode Island Joe suspects she was open to becoming more than my waitress, and indeed he is on to something, but I never considered it. The Club is of great value to me, and a failed relationship with a staff person might jeopardize my status or tranquility, and is out of the question. I already have enough failed relationships to last me a while. Thai women are wonderful, but the end of a relationship with a Thai woman can be an ordeal. Remember that old Neal Sedaka song "Breaking Up Is Hard to Do"? He must have had a Thai girlfriend.

Both waitresses dislike Funston, and even Thai reserve cannot conceal their feelings. He has made lewd suggestions to them several times a week, and always complains about their service.

"Why do I always get my food and drinks last?" he asked to no response.

"You know a man could do quite well for himself in Cambodia," he once railed when the waitresses ignored his entreaties to bring him his food. "It's my Plan B."

"Then go there," Rhode Island Joe told him.

After all these years, Funston has no close friends at NJA. Maybe he doesn't want any. Perhaps he is happy with his fifty girlfriends and his guitar. He shows little interest in the rest of us and is enamored with himself, believing we are as well. If he understood that no one likes him, he never lets on. I consider him an embarrassment to America and hope he opts for Plan B.

3

NO ONE WAS certain of Noi's age. Asian women age differently than white women, and even a seasoned expat cannot always tell how old a Thai woman might be. Asian women don't develop the wrinkles, lines, neck folds, and sagging skin that are so common in the West. Often the best guess is somewhere between late twenties and early forties. Somewhere in her thirties was the best I could guess about Noi, based on her figure and her clear and smooth face. No one at the Club knew Noi's real name. In Thailand, last names are almost never used, and like all Thais, she went by a nickname. Foreigners don't automatically get nicknames, and most of the time are known by their given name. Thais refer to me as Mr. Glenn or *Khun* Glenn.

Noi was attractive, tall for a Thai, willowy, with long smooth black hair, and a curvaceous body. She almost always flashed a bright smile and her eyes sparkled when she laughed. She spoke English well enough so that communication was never a problem.

Noi said she came from Udon Thani, in the Northeast region known as Isan. She gave no further details, and I never asked. Isan has about a quarter of the Thai population, and is also the poorest region in the Kingdom. Many Isan people feel mistreated and discriminated, left out of Thailand's progress. It remains agricultural, not caught up in the tourism or high tech booms that have benefitted the Bangkok region. After living in Thailand for several years, it became clear that their grievances were true. Isan people were hard working, honorable and decent. In my opinion they also had the most beautiful and charming women. Not everyone in Thailand feels the same. Certainly not the rich and the elite of Thailand, who look down on the people of Isan.

When we first met about three years ago, Noi was living with an Englishman in an apartment two blocks from the Club. They came by together almost every night. One day the English guy stopped showing up but Noi continued to be a regular.

"Have no boyfriend now but I have English," was the only comment she ever made on the ending of the relationship.

No one knew how Noi supported herself. She never mentioned work and never seemed in need of money. She often took off for a few days or a week, sometimes saying she was visiting her village, sometimes not saying anything.

"I don't ask you where you get money," she would snap at Phil Funston, the only one rude enough to inquire about her finances. He asked many times, and always received the same answer.

One day when we were sharing a table, Noi went to the ladies room and left her phone on the table. It rang and the caller's number was from the U.S.

Maybe an overseas sponsor was my thought, some lovestruck fool who sends her money. There was no evidence, but that often tells the story. She had not been seen with a man since the Englishman disappeared, but no one was with her around the clock. It was unclear where she really went when she told us she was visiting her village in Isan. I did not push the matter. We all have our secrets.

Noi loved jazz and blues as much as I, and we sometimes went out to listen to music. The Saxophone Club over by Victory Monument and the Sunday afternoon jazz session at Check Inn 99 were our favorites, and every so often we dressed up and listened to the Russian jazz combo in the bar at the Oriental Hotel, right at the

Chao Phraya River, where a martini costs as much as in America. The thought that almost a century ago the great English writer Somerset Maugham sat where we were, listening to jazz, added even more character to the brass, marble, and hardwood that graced the fabled hotel.

Noi embodied all of the traits of Thai people that appealed so much to me. She was kind and generous, friendly, tolerant, not judgmental, always willing to listen, and always there for a friend.

Noi was charming, and exotic, and at the same time understanding. I could unburden myself to her about anything I wanted to talk about. As we grew closer, there was no denying that I was falling in love with her. The feelings could not be contained despite the danger. Love had failed me more than once in Bangkok and it should not be allowed to happen again, but it felt out of my control. Only her lack of interest had prevented disaster.

None of this prevented me from trying to create a romantic relationship, always without success. Physical contact and offers to travel were firmly though gently rebuffed.

"We are friends," she would say with that bright smile. "Friends are better than lovers," she would add.

She was right. Having a female Thai friend was indeed beneficial to me. Noi could explain the strange ways of Thailand and could handle problems where my minimal Thai was deficient. She would never refuse to translate, but chided me for my lack of language skill.

"How long you gonna live in Thailand but speak only *farang* Thai?" she once asked only partly in jest.

"Until you become my live-in teacher," was my reply and we both laughed. In my case it wasn't sincere laughter.

Noi was always there when I needed someone to talk to. She walked me through two breakups, several arguments with guys at NJA, and the rare occasions when homesickness for America emerged out of nowhere. She listened quietly, spoke few words, but all were meaningful. She never asked for more information than I divulged, and never revealed any problems of her own.

My feelings for Noi seemed like love to me, but I really don't know much about love and understand it even less. My ex-wife in America and my three former girlfriends in Thailand can vouch for that.

Phil Funston complained that Noi was a "stuck up bitch" because when he came on to her in his crude manner, she ignored him. He complained about this on several occasions.

"Sounds like she has some class," was my response.

One time Funston went too far, even by his irreverent standards. With few glasses of wine under his belt, he yelled out to Noi.

"Bet you haven't gotten any since Prince Charles sailed home," he taunted. "Maybe you ought to let me give you some. An act of mercy."

This was a terrible insult to any woman, but more so to a Thai woman whose culture places great value on face. It's difficult to provide an exact description of the term to Americans, because our perspectives are so different. The best description to come my way was that face means preventing embarrassment to anyone, including yourself. So you don't do it to others and they don't do it to you. A boorish *farang* like Funston probably didn't exhibit proper behavior in America, so why would he do so overseas?

Rhode Island Joe, seated at the bar, hoisted up his six foot, two hundred pound frame and hauled it in front of Funston. Holding up a hamsized fist, he addressed him. Funston's eyes widened and his face reddened.

"You leave the lady alone and don't ever speak that way again, to any woman," Joe said in a soft voice.

"If you do, you'll be hearing from me," he added. Joe turned around and went back to his seat at the bar.

Funston never repeated this behavior with Noi. He sometimes

cast lecherous glances her way, but he never again insulted her.

JOE, BORN JOSEPH Potowski, was called Rhode Island Joe, after his home state. This distinguished him from another Club regular, Sleepy Joe. When only one was present, we could refer to them as Joe, otherwise the nickname was required. Rhode Island Joe was beefy, carrying a few pounds too many, but not enough to be considered fat. His arms were thick and roped with muscle though he was never known to exercise. In a climate where short sleeve shirts are prevalent, his strength was clear to all. No one picked fights with Rhode Island Joe, at least not when sober.

Joe had driven a beer delivery truck back home, and after twenty years, like so many Americans, found himself exerting much effort but going nowhere. One day as he was getting out of his truck, he was run over by a speeding Porsche. Joe spent three months in the hospital. His suffering was rewarded with a handsome legal settlement. He made a full recovery except for a few aches every now and then. A diet might solve most of them, but Joe was not interested in any diet other than one calling for several pints of beer a day.

When Joe came home from the hospital he discovered that his wife had been cheating on him while he was healing. He found several pairs of another man's underwear in his dresser drawer. When he confronted his wife, she admitted to the affair with one of his fishing buddies.

"He did me a favor," he told me years after the fact.

He paid his divorce lawyer, got his decree, took his share of the assets and left Rhode Island. He showed up at the NJA Club one rainy day not long after my arrival. Joe claims he wandered into the Club because it was the closest tavern to his apartment.

There was no particular reason for Joe coming to Bangkok, and he never suggested any. He did nothing except eat, drink, and complain, which he could have done anywhere. Like me, he avoids Bangkok's renowned sex industry. In my case it is revulsion, but in Joe's case it is because it requires more effort than he is willing to expend to make his way to any of Bangkok's three red light districts.

Joe is a good listener, a rare virtue among *farangs* at the NJA Club. An air of mystery surrounds all of the regulars except for Rhode Island Joe. Everyone but him seems to have some unspoken and hidden detail about their lives before they came to Bangkok, something they do not want the others to know. The Club, like so many Bangkok venues, is filled with expats hiding something in their past. In Bangkok, everyone gets the chance to start over. Some take advantage of this option but others do not. These mysteries and vagaries from the past often linger like traces of aftershave long after the razor is used. Not so with Rhode Island Joe. His life story is an open book, boring but open. What you see is what you get. I came to learn over the years that what you get is a loyal and caring friend, not the oaf one might perceive upon first meeting him. Joe became one of my best friends in Bangkok. I have come to appreciate that as a blessing, because everyone needs friends, especially *farangs* in Bangkok.

~

IT WAS A mystery why Noi chose to spend so much time surrounded by *farang* men in whom she had no romantic interest, but it gladdened me that she was here. Noi was a true friend in every way. The NJA crowd was a family, with Noi and the two Joes my close blood relatives, even if I was amenable to incest with Noi.

4

THERE WERE MANY reasons for living in Thailand so many years, but as time passed it became clear the main reason was the Thai people. The most important character trait to a Thai is *jai dii* or good heart, which means many things and describes them well. They are kind, generous, and slow to anger—but if they do, be careful. Thais have patience, tolerance and balance. They have what we in the West would call manners. It still amazes me how Thais line up quietly for a crowded Skytrain. In America we would see fistfights, shoving, and trampling at rush hour.

Many expats say it is difficult to make Thai friends. That is their choice, not a rule. I have had several Thai friends over the years, not counting girlfriends. Thais are indeed mysterious to the foreigner, but that is part of their attraction.

Noi was not the sole Thai to frequent the Club. We also have the General. Like Noi, he became my friend.

He retired at least ten years ago. His military background is obvious from his trim and fit military bearing and the deference he receives from other Thais. He has been coming to the Club since retirement. We never learned why he picked NJA of all the places in Bangkok, or why he chose to associate with *farangs*, not typical of retired Thai generals. He is at the Club almost every day between one and five in the afternoon, drinking dry martinis or imported beer. Martinis at the club are as strong and as good as the best places in San Francisco. The General, like me, appreciates a good one, but he drinks more than my usual limit of one per day. It was doubtful he prefers weed to spirits as I do, and it is a subject we never broach.

We regulars never know what the General does when he isn't at the Club. He makes it clear to me that he spent considerable time with his most current young *mia noi*, or minor wife. In English we call them mistresses. The General changes them quite often. He sometimes shows me photos of the latest one, with pride. He does not hide the fact that he is married and has grown children.

"My right as a man," he once proclaimed without a hint of shame when he showed me his latest paramour. "My son has a *mia noi* too," he told me with paternal pride.

Many times the General has offered me dalliances with beautiful young women. Tempting as the offers may have be, they are declined. My life is not like my law practice, which relied upon referrals. In matters of the heart, or of rank passion, one must find their own way. Maybe some voice deep inside me, the trial lawyer's instinct, is warning me to beware of retired Thai generals bearing gifts.

The General speaks fluent English, having studied warfare at Fort Benning, Georgia and serving as a military adjutant in Washington D.C. He likes Americans, and feels quite comfortable around them. He is more pro- American than most of us Yanks.

"I cannot understand why any American would criticize his own country," he will comment when he hears Americans criticize their homeland. "Greatest country in the world, after Thailand."

The General is very wealthy. He comes from a Thai-Chinese family that has lived in Bangkok for many generations, but he never speaks of family wealth or businesses. He owns several properties throughout the Green Belt, where most foreigners live. He also owns a private security company, a few restaurants, and a string of 7/11 stores. How he became rich on a military salary is a subject of great speculation at the Club, but not when the General is around.

"Payoffs," Phil Funston has opined. "Massage parlors, go-go bars, gambling rings."

"Drug smuggling," someone else will counter.

"Maybe he married rich," is Rhode Island Joe's take.

One irrepressible rumor is that the General is the owner of the NJA Club. No one knows who pays the staff and buys the booze and food, or whose name is on the deed or the business registration. We expats have all learned that in Thailand, one does not ask such questions. Since no one knew who did own the place, the rumors thrived.

"People think you own this place," I once told the General after a strong vodka martini.

"People say everything," he said softly. "People say Elvis is alive. People say spacemen crashed in Nevada. Don't listen to people."

That struck me as a friendly suggestion and the topic never came up again. It made me think maybe the rumors were true.

The General does have his eccentricities.

He lives in fear of an imminent civil uprising, and goes around Bangkok in an armored Hummer, accompanied by two of his armed security employees. When he comes to the Club, one waits in the vehicle outside the Club, and the other stands or sits behind him. It was at first discomforting to have an armed guard hovering about, but as it became normal for us, we came to appreciate that we were the safest *farangs* in the Kingdom.

The General has an obsession with fresh eggs. He explained to us that in one of his apartment buildings, he constructed a state of the art chicken coop, complete with incubators. Every few days he has a guard carry in a basket of organic eggs which are offered to patrons. According to Noi, they are as good as any farm eggs in Isan. I took her word for this but never took any. There was a small stove in my condo but I wouldn't know how to turn it on. Brewing coffee is a passion which I indulge in each morning, but that was the extent of my culinary skills.

The General is less reserved than most Thai men of his stature in society, though by Western standards, he would be seen as a man who plays his cards close to the vest. Not at all aloof, and not the least bit unpleasant, but a man of few words. With me he is a relative chatterbox. He regales me with tales of adventure with his young consorts, passes on the latest bits of political gossip, along with his theories of where Thailand is heading, never pleasant predictions. He has hinted several times that if I ever had a serious problem, he could help. He is not as open with other *farangs* at the Club. He isn't even that casual with Thais. For the most part he ignores Noi, and is courteous but not expansive with the waitresses Mai and Joy. He does enjoy chatting with Wang, the cook who spent most of his time in the kitchen.

"I'm not the kind of *farang* who has problems here," were my words when he suggested he could help, but I felt grateful for the offer and flattered that he thought of me as a friend.

"You are a lawyer," Noi had once told me, explaining why the General chose me as his confident among all the Club regulars. "You dress well. And you have some money. He thinks you are high class."

"Boy, is he wrong," I said.

5

"A PLACE IS only as good as the staff," Rhode Island Joe proclaimed on numerous occasions.

"Starts with the bartender," he would elaborate.

Joe had no restaurant experience at all, aside from eating in many, but he was right. It was often the case that Joe is right about matters of which he did not appear to have any knowledge.

The bar at the Club starts about twenty feet in from the door, and runs almost the entire length of the wall. It is all hardwood and brass, with a wall mirror running its full length and facing barstools. The Club offers an excellent selection of alcohol. I am gratified that it stocks my favorite vodka, Tito's, made in Austin, Texas and distilled six times. Vodka is tasteless, and imbibing Tito's is like drinking water. Vodka is the perfect alcoholic beverage for people like me who do not like the taste of alcohol.

There are two bartenders working at NJA. Daytime bar is kept by Yik, a stocky Thai woman of indeterminate age. She has a permanent wan smile and a small scar on her right cheek. Yik was on duty on my first visit. No one knows how she came by the scar, nor does anyone ask. Yik speaks with customers as little as possible. She is very efficient and polite, but reserved in that unfathomable Thai way. As a daytime barkeep, her job is to mix good cocktails, pour cold beer, and make sure they get to the drinkers. She performs well.

Phil Funston is of course as rude and insulting to Yik as he is with everyone. She generally ignores him, but once he made a nasty comment about her looks, and she smacked him in the head so hard he fell of his chair and spilled a glass of red wine all over his white shirt. The entire Club broke into a sustained applause. Rhode Island Joe bought drinks for the house.

Evenings, the bar is the province of Ray, a beefy Irishman with traces of red in his graying hair and a smile that would make a Thai proud. Old timers say Ray must have tended bar in Ireland as he knew everything there is to know about mixology. He came to the NJA Club nine years ago when his predecessor, a fellow Irishman, died of a heart attack at age seventy-two while consorting with a prostitute in a short time hotel. The legend goes that some of the NJA crowd moved the body elsewhere so his Thai wife would not find out.

Sleepy Joe was on Khao San Road scoring weed when the Grim Reaper caused this problematic coitus interruptus.

"I didn't help move him, but do remember it well," Sleepy Joe later revealed. "Helped pay off the cops and the medical examiner."

Ray is a storyteller of the highest order. He recycles every tale he has heard and makes them better. Every variation on a *farang* being ruined by a Thai woman, every tale of crooked cops hosing foreigners, every explanation of how a foreigner found success in business, or won a lottery or wound up in the wilds of Isan is channeled through Ray. We never tire of hearing his stories even when we can predict the endings. It is Ray, not the story, that captivates.

Each evening, Ray holds court behind the bar. All stools are filled and there are always half a dozen standees, and anyone within reach of Ray's voice clings to his every word.

In his big, baritone brogue, Ray opines on the day's events and weaves his stories between this commentary. Sometimes the stories are relevant to the discussion, other times not. They are all good stories.

When he hears a shouting match, Ray brings down the temperature with a withering look, and if that fails, with a growling command to lower the volume. I couldn't tell you what people argued about, having learned years ago not to pay attention.

I allow myself a single martini each day. If I smoke weed at home beforehand, the martini is a nice complement, and if not, it loosens me enough to enjoy the Club and Ray's stories even more.

Upon my arrival, Ray unfailingly notices me, mixes my martini and has it brought to my table or awaiting me at the bar.

It is always a fine martini. Dry, with an olive. Vodka, of course. Gin is for Englishmen. Shaken, as well. After one martini, it is water or soft drinks.

Ray never speaks about his life before arriving in the Kingdom. Some say he was a fugitive from justice; others argue he is just creating a mystery around himself.

As a former criminal defense lawyer, there is no doubt in my mind that Ray is hiding something. Criminal lawyers develop a special radar that detects hidden details. Everyone is hiding something, some people hiding darker and deeper secrets than others. What Ray is hiding may be a mystery to me but not one we dwell upon.

As long as the stories are good, it doesn't matter.

6

EVERY MORNING, MY day starts by boiling water for coffee. Good coffee is my passion and a grinder, electric kettle, and a French press my heaven. Such is the extent of my culinary activities. Bangkok overflows with a cornucopia of restaurants, street food, and delivery services, so there is no reason for *farang* men to slave over a hot stove.

Two former girlfriends sometimes cooked meals at my place. The last one threatened suicide with a carving knife when I broke up with her, creating wariness about allowing another in my kitchen. On the infrequent occasions when a woman visits my apartment, we order food or dine out.

Special occasions might bring me to dine elsewhere, but the Club enjoys the lion's share of my business. The food at NJA is good, although it is not what draws me. The Club is more than just a place to eat and drink. It is my family and my community.

Wang the cook lords over the kitchen in the rear of the Club. There is a large opening in the wall through which orders are passed. Wang has worked at the Club for ten years and speaks some English. His hair is short and black and muscles press against his t-shirt sleeves. He looks like he is in his early forties, but this estimate could be off by ten years. Wang says he served in the Thai army, ending his career as a sergeant and a cook, confirmed by the General. It doesn't seem likely that Thai generals keep track of every cook in the army, so I suspected Wang may have had other duties.

Wang works from eight in the morning, when breakfast starts, until the last dinner orders are taken just before nine p.m., six days a week. He sometimes exchanges pleasantries with regular customers through the window but most of the time he is busy cooking. During his breaks, he smokes a cigarette or drinks a beer in the alley behind the Club. We all know to leave him alone when he is on break, but the General can intrude on his private time. Sometimes the two of them are seen drinking beer outside during Wang's break.

We have not spoken much over the years, but Wang always smiles or nods when he sees me arrive at the Club. Until recently, my impression of Wang was of a quiet and passive man who blends into the background and remains there. He cooks, takes breaks, smiles and keeps the customers happy.

That perception changed in mid-November of last year, just after *Loi Krathong*, the Thai holiday when boats are set loose on rivers and the skies are filled with fireworks and burning hollow paper balls.

I WAS AT the bar that day enjoying Ray's skills as a raconteur. He was regaling the regulars with a story about an adventure he had in Singapore some decades ago involving cards, whiskey, and women. No one within twenty feet of Ray uttered a word while he held court. His lilting Irish brogue, delivered in a stentorian tone, entranced us. My friend Edward, another Club regular, sat with a handsome young Thai man at a table along the wall. Ray's audience was engrossed in the bartender's every word, but Edward was focused only on his companion. He paid no attention to the tale of a young Irish traveler dragged into a rigged card game by an off-duty prostitute.

Edward was the NJA Club's resident Englishman. Since Noi's

boyfriend vanished, we have not had another permanent limey on site. We have the occasional drop-in, but none beside Edward is rooted in our garden of foreigners.

It is a mystery why a bar filled with English speaking expats does not attract more Brits. Rhode Island Joe thinks most English are just too boring for our group. Phil Funston thinks they have their own special places, English pubs transplanted to Bangkok. Sleepy Joe says the Club is a tad too expensive for the cost-conscious English. The General insists that Brits don't feel comfortable in a place dominated by Americans and Australians.

"You are too loud and too pushy for the English," the General explained.

At least we had Edward.

Edward had been an accountant and auditor for the Crown in England. He was actually Welsh but had been educated and employed in the British capitol. His job with the government was to uncover British citizens hiding money overseas. He reached the highest attainable civil service level and found the work boring and pointless. Seven or eight years back, when he turned fifty, after returning from a two week vacation in Thailand, he quit his job, packed his bags, and has been here ever since.

Edward found work as an advisor to a Bangkok financial services firm with a large foreign clientele. He rents an apartment a few blocks from upscale Ekamai, near the Club. For several years he had lived with his partner Kiet, a quiet fellow from Chiang Rai Province in the North. They had separated the month before, and Edward was living alone and unhappy. The young Thai fellow seemed like a replacement prospect.

"Even when a relationship is going bad, it still beats having no one around," Edward had told me a few days earlier.

I disagreed.

"Getting divorced was far more pleasant than living in Hell," I retorted.

Edward stared back and said in exasperation, "You Americans."

He was prone to say this whenever a Yank contradicted him.

Edward was a walking tax compendium who knew how to avoid taxation for a half dozen nationalities. He knew which nearby countries never reported foreign accounts and what to do with money earned by trading gold or quick real estate turnovers.

"What you are avoiding is discovery, not compliance," I once told him. "They still have the obligation to report, and by not doing so, they might find themselves in some serious criminal trouble."

"Well aren't you the lawyer?" he snapped back. "You are absolutely correct. They are big boys and I give them options and the rest is up to them.

"You might be tempted to do the same if you all of a sudden found yourself with heaps of cash," he said.

"Not me," I replied.

On that November evening, it did not look as if Edward and the young Thai fellow were discussing finances. Edward wore a dreamy, love-struck look on his face. Seemed like he was getting over Kiet.

As Edward was romancing the young man, three beefy men walked through the front door of the club, dressed in tight black t-shirts and jeans. Their biceps were well developed and their dirty blonde hair closecropped. Scowls formed on their faces when they saw no empty table.

In my previous life I had represented enough hard men to know them when I saw them. These three guys looked like they were on the diamond scale of hardness.

The biggest of them approached Edward and in heavily Russian accented English, demanded that he and his companion yield their table.

"Get up, faggot," the Russian said as his two friends glared at Edward.

"Fuck off," was Edward's reply.

The big Russian turned to his friends and muttered something in their language, and it didn't sound like he was pleased. He lunged for Edward, grabbed him under his armpits, lifted him, and threw him against the wall. There was a loud thud and a few pictures that had decorated the walls since my first days at the Club fell to the floor.

The General's ever-present body guard reached under his shirt for a gun but one of the Russians reached behind his back and pulled out a pistol before the guard could draw his weapon. The Russian pointed the gun at the bodyguard. The other Russian was pointing a gun straight ahead while sweeping the room with his eyes. No one in the Club uttered a word.

The lead Russian walked over to where Edward lie crumpled on the floor, a growing stream of blood pouring from a gash on his forehead.

"Out now while you live," he barked.

The big Russian was about to deliver a kick to Edward's head when Wang appeared without warning and interjected himself between the Russian and the fallen Edward. Wang had nothing in his open hands and a small smile crossed his expressionless face.

"You and your friends must go now," he said in English in a soft but firm voice. "No table for you tonight. Or ever." He stared up at the Russian, who stood a head and a half taller. The Russian stared at Wang and spoke in a loud and angry voice.

"We kill you and everyone here," he yelled out.

"Some of you will die too," Wang said. "My friend will kill one or two for sure," he added, gesturing with his left hand towards the General's bodyguard, who had managed to withdraw his pistol after Edward had been thrown against the wall and the Russians had cast their gazes towards his prone body. The guard had his weapon pointed at one of the armed Russians.

The huge Russian leader glanced at the bodyguard.

"You too must die," he responded. "If not today, tomorrow. You know who I am?" he asked.

"Yes," Wang answered. "But do you know who I am?"

"A dead man," the Russian said.

"I don't think so," Wang said as he stared at the Russian. Their eyes remained locked for what was no more than seconds but seemed like an eternity. My bladder had become unbearably uncomfortable but there was no chance of going to the restroom with two armed men facing off. My legs would not have moved had I commanded them to do so.

This is what fear feels like, I thought.

"Tell your friend to put the gun away," Wang said to the Russians' leader.

"I don't want to kill him," he added in a voice so soft it was difficult to hear. As he spoke he continued to stare at the big man.

The Russian squawked in his own language. His companion tucked his weapon back in his rear waistband. Wang nodded to the General's bodyguard, who put away his own weapon. Wang continued to stare, and the big Russian looked nervous. His eyes were rapidly blinking. His body was rigid and his back arched slightly. He said something to his friends and they all turned towards the door to leave.

"Like I said, fuck you, you Slavic shitballs," Edward shouted as he picked himself off the floor. His young friend had come over to him with a glass of water and a napkin and was wiping the blood from Edward's face and forehead.

One of the Russians turned to Edward and snarled something we did not understand. A quick glance from Wang and the Russian turned back towards the door and in a moment all three were gone.

The General, who had sat in stony silence throughout the incident, addressed the cook.

"*Dii maak, puuyyan khrup*," he told Wang. (Very good, friend.)

Wang bowed slightly to the General with a wai, his hands in prayer at his chest, and returned to the kitchen. Edward and the young man returned to their tables.

"Drinks on the house," Ray shouted and the members of the NJA Club clamored to place their orders.

"What the hell just happened?" I asked the General after my free martini arrived and I joined him and his bodyguard at their table.

"One of our Russian friends just received an education," the General replied.

"Can you educate me?" I asked.

"Sometimes a cook is not just a cook," he replied. "That's all you need to know right now."

A FEW DAYS after this armed confrontation I found myself enjoying a late afternoon martini with the General. He was hungry and both waitresses were busy. The General waved his hand and Wang the cook emerged from the kitchen. The General gave his order. Soon afterward Wang returned with the General's food.

"Now that's what I call service," I remarked.

The General tasted his dish and smiled.

"Wang and I are indebted to each other. That's how it should always be."

"How are you indebted to the cook? Because of yesterday?" It seemed impossible in Thailand that a General owed a cook. If that were the case, what was the cook getting out of it? The General paused. A look of contemplation was stamped on his face, one he had not shown before. The General could be gregarious, or imperious, but never before had he appeared reflective.

"It was during the war against the communists," he began.

IN THE MID 1970s, the General was a young captain in the Royal Thai Army, a few years out of Chulachomklao Royal Military Academy. Since he was a young boy he had dreamed of being a soldier. He devoured every book on Thai military histories and revered the various Kings who had battled the Burmese, the Cambodians and each other. He ignored his parents' entreaties to study law. His heart was set on being a soldier and someday a general.

He received his commission when the Kingdom was embroiled in the midst of an eighteen-year communist insurgency. Assisted by Thailand's many communist neighbors—China, Vietnam, Laos and Cambodia—the insurgents maintained a long and deadly campaign mostly in the Northeast, where people were poor and the border was porous.

The young captain commanded a unit within the Second Army, which was responsible for the Northeast. He led his men into the forests searching for communist rebels who were attacking the army and seizing remote villages.

"There was incredible violence and cruelty on both sides," the General said. "The communists were worse, inhumane. They tortured any soldier they found alive and massacred innocent villagers as warnings not to help us.

"Most of the rebels and most of the enlisted men were from up there in Isan. A lot of bad blood between the two sides, and you know Isan people are a violent lot to begin with," the General added.

I knew that was not true and I suspect the General knew it as well, but like most rich and powerful Thais, he felt compelled to demean the people of the Northeast. The people of Isan were largely farmers, and they spoke a different dialect than the Thai heard in Bangkok and Central Thailand. There was also a widespread belief that they were darker, which is a negative in Thailand. Whatever reasons may have existed for these attitudes, none of them rang true to me.

"We patrolled the forests near the Lao border," the General recounted. "Looking to shut down supply routes and catch and kill some Reds.

"Wang was an enlisted men. Barely an adult, maybe eighteen. Scrawny boy out of Isan. What a soldier he was. Tracker, scout, sniper, tactician. Brave as any man I've ever seen.

"He always knew what was going on around him. Just sensed it somehow. He was a lowly private, but I made him my adjutant, my right hand man. No connected guy would do, I wanted Wang. Some of my superiors questioned my decision.

"But soon they understood why."

It was difficult to reconcile the urbane sixty-year-old man before me with a young captain fighting guerrillas in the forest. But his passion could not be mistaken as he waxed on with enthusiasm stamped on his face, and he gesticulated with his hands ever so slightly as he spoke. I hung on to his every word.

"Wang saved my life on more than one occasion," the General said. "And I helped him when he served. Those are the mutual debts I told you about.

"That's all that needs to be said."

The General had seen in Wang those many years ago what the Russian thugs had just seen the night before. I had observed the results but what the General and the Russians saw was still hazy to me.

"No wonder you like it here so much. Must feel safe with Wang around."

"Not to overlook that I get to spend all this time with you," the General said. "And Ray makes a hell of a martini."

The General had revealed much about himself. He had admitted a debt of honor to a man far beneath him in social stature, unusual for one who placed such emphasis on status. The General was not a man not expected to give proper due to others, especially those he deemed his inferiors, which included Isan people. He made an exception for Wang.

"I have told you something very personal about my beginning as a soldier, so it is fair that you tell me something about your beginnings as a lawyer. Then my eyes will see you as yours have just seen me."

"THIS WAS THE first felony case I ever tried. Back in New York, before my move to San Francisco. I was a public defender assigned to defend a transgender woman who was busted in a sting. She was a recovering heroin addict who got methadone from a clinic. The methadone did not get her high but it satisfied the craving from her years of addiction. The cops set up a sting to arrest people who sold their methadone to addicts because, if you weren't a regular user, methadone would work like heroin.

"What's a transgender?" the General asked. "We hear it a lot but not sure what it means."

"A lot of people are confused about transgenders," I replied. "It has to do with the gender one identifies with, not the one they were born with, which aren't always the same. It's not something a person chooses or can change."

"So these are guys that go around in dresses?" the General asked.

"Maybe, but not just because they like dresses. Some might decide to dress and hold themselves out as the gender they identify with, others don't. It could be women who identify as men, but right now we're talking about men who identify as women. Some of these men who have the money get hormone treatment or surgery. My client dressed as a woman and was hoping to have hormone treatment and surgery when she could afford it."

"Are they *katoys*?" the General asked, using the Thai term for people foreigners call "ladyboys."

"I'm not an expert but it appears some are. Phil Funston may know more about this than me."

"I don't want to talk to him," the General said. "Especially not about katoys."

The General seemed interested in the challenge of defending a man who planned to appear in court dressed as a woman. He listened intently as I explained that our defense was entrapment, meaning my client had no criminal intent or predisposition to sell methadone to the undercover cop. She did it because they kept begging her to sell it for a sick friend, overcoming her will as the law says. That was what the case was about, not her gender. At least that's how we wanted it to be.

"We had a good defense, all things considered," I said. "Any New York jury would have suspicions about cops and might not like the idea of them going around trying to snare law abiding citizens instead of chasing down real bad guys. After all, my client was off heroin and was taking methadone under medical supervision. The jury was never going to hear about her old prostitution arrests."

"So in New York, like in Bangkok there are men who want ladyboys?" he asked with incredulity.

"Some. Just like here, not all of them know."

The decision to have my client testify was the key to the case. It wasn't predictable how the jury would feel about a street smart, sassy transgender person who admitted she sold methadone to an undercover cop, claiming the legal equivalent of "the devil made me do it."

"In the end my decision to put my client on the stand was not hard to make. Without her, there was no way to prove entrapment.

I believed her story about being pressured by the cops. It was rare for me to believe most of my clients, but this time it was easy."

Recounting the story drew me back into that long-forgotten courtroom. I could see the judge, a friendly old Italian politician who retired to the safe sinecure of a judgeship, and the assistant district attorney, an earnest young man with a prep school background and a stick up his behind. Not one juror's face was recalled; as with every one of my trials, they dissipate into obscurity after the verdict. My career included fifty felony cases tried to verdict. That's six hundred souls on juries, and not a single face is remembered. Yet during trial, those faces were the objects of my intense focus, gauging what effect evidence was having on them.

"Honesty was the best tactic," I explained. "My client was going to come to court dressed as a woman and we insisted that she be referred to by her female name. Even a new lawyer like me knew the strong reluctance of defense lawyers to place their client on the stand, subject to cross-examination, but I decided from the start of my representation that this was going to be different.

"My client was a likable person with a compelling story. She was struggling with addiction recovery and the problems of being transgender in the early 1990s. No one was talking about protecting their rights back then. So she showed up in court every day in a different dress, showed a well styled permanent, and was referred to as "Miss." Of course her true gender would be revealed. Even those jurors who could not see her large hands and Adam's apple would hear that her methadone prescription was in a man's name and that was the name she gave when booked. Also the name on the indictment. But when she met with the cops she was dressed as a woman and used her female name. If we tried to hide the truth it would make us look bad when the jury figured things out."

The General was incredulous.

"You mean you were just going to allow the jury to find out she was a katoy? Maybe they wouldn't figure it out."

"Believe me, General, at least one person on a New York City jury would have figured it out during jury selection. Wouldn't take long before all twelve knew. If we tried to cover it up, the whole idea of being straight with them was out the window. I let them know about her being transgender in my opening statement.

The General considered this for a moment. "I see," he said, but it was not clear he did.

"Things started off well," I said. It was clear from the police reports that they had asked my client to sell methadone on three occasions, which both undercovers had to admit on the stand or be contradicted by their own reports. But they denied that they pleaded with her to help their sick friend and that was not in the reports. That was my whole defense and if the jury did not believe it my client was going to prison."

The General was surprised at all the efforts put into this prosecution.

"To prison for something that small? Selling a legal prescription drug to a cop who was making up crimes? Why?"

"New York had the Rockefeller Laws. Toughest in the nation. Really only punished the little guy, not the big fish. Cops can make believe they're really fighting drugs."

The General nodded in agreement. "Works here that way too," he said. "Fortunately," he added and then smiled.

"She was on the stand for a whole day," I continued. "On my direct examination she told her life story, raised by a single mother, being transgender, how she turned to heroin, and how she sought treatment. She was taking methadone and had not used heroin in over two years. Studying to be a hairstylist as well. She said the third time the cops gave the story about helping a sick friend she felt so bad she agreed and swigged half a bottle and sold the rest for ten dollars."

"Ten dollars?" the General exclaimed. "They made such a big thing over a ten dollar deal? That's crazy!"

"Kept me employed."

My narrative continued.

"She stood up well under cross examination. The prosecutor with the stick up his ass was not lovable to New York City jury. He asked my client why she became a heroin addict if she loved her mother so much. My client replied, 'What's that got to do with anything?' The jury laughed. I can still hear them laughing."

The General smiled and gave me his full attention.

"My client also testified that the first time the cops approached her she had no idea they were looking to buy drugs. She said they didn't seem seedy enough to be users."

"Then the DA did something really stupid, a real rookie mistake."

"What was that?" the General inquired.

"Never ask a question to which you don't know the answer. He asked my client what she thought they wanted from her.

"Without batting an eyelash, she said, 'I figured they wanted a BJ.' The prosecutor looks puzzled and in a sarcastic voice asked 'And what, may I ask, is a BJ?' to which my client replies with a cackle, 'A blow job, young man, ain't you ever had one? Might do you some good.' The poor fellow turned red as a beet as the entire courtroom erupted into laughter, the jury, the court staff, and even the judge.

"In my closing argument, the jury was told that the case was about honesty. My client could have come to court in a suit and tie and used her birth name. She could have relied on her Constitutional right not to testify. But she wanted the jury to know who she was and to hear what happened right from her mouth. The police on the other hand were admitted liars who pretended to be someone they were not just so they could arrest her."

"So what happened?" the General asked.

"Took the jury an hour to come back with not guilty verdict.

They liked my client. They didn't like cops going around creating crimes and trapping innocent people. They didn't like the prosecutor either."

"I think they liked you," the General said.

"Not as much as they liked my client."

The General had a question for me.

"Glenn, you had many cases much more important than this one. White collar cases, big time drug dealers, murders. You could have told me about any one of those. Why did you choose such a minor case?

"It wasn't minor," I replied. "The story is not about the seriousness of the crime. It's about being real and honest. My client won over the jury because she hid nothing and everything was an open book. She was what politicians like to call authentic. Somebody else telling the same story might have been laughed out of court. I played it straight just like my client, telling the jury right up front who my client was, and that she did in fact sell to the cops. They respected me for that.

"That was an invaluable lesson to learn right away, early in my career. Being honest, not hiding the ball is what gets people to trust and believe you. A lesson learned from that lady."

"And she wasn't even really a lady," the General said.

"That's where you're wrong, General. She was as much a woman as we are men."

7

SLEEPY JOE HAD the thickest Aussie accent I have ever heard. Sometimes it isn't clear that he is speaking English. I still cannot distinguish his pronunciation of "NJA" from "energy." The first time he said the word "can't" I thought he was using a crude term for female genitals.

He was almost always stoned, causing him to slur his words, making him even more difficult to understand. After several years, deciphering his speech became easier but was still a chore. Careful attention is required to understand Sleepy Joe.

Joe had blown into the Club one windy day during the rainy season ten years ago, three years before my arrival, and he has been planted at a rear table near ever since. It is a rare occurrence when he is missing from the Club for more than a few hours. There is always either a beer or a coffee in front of him.

Joe is the resident contact for weed, highly illicit in Thailand, but he is able to obtain it without fail. I never know who else is a customer, and I never ask.

The unspoken rule required that Joe never bring anything into the Club. On his way to the Club. He will make home or office deliveries to people he knows. Joe shows up like clockwork every morning at eleven. He wears rumpled clothes that look like he slept in them, and sometimes wears sunglasses indoors. His unkempt graying hair is long and stringy and often tied into a ponytail. He almost always needs a shave.

I am one of Sleepy Joe's most loyal customers. Departing America meant leaving almost everything behind me except my love of weed and coffee. The first few months in Bangkok were spent without the former, as I had no idea where to find it. That all changed when the winds of fortune blew me in the direction of Sleepy Joe.

When we first met, shortly after my discovery of the Club, he was dressed in worn jeans tattered at the cuffs, a rumpled shirt, with his long stringy hair hanging over much of his face. The smell of grass was all over him. I sensed that my problem could be solved.

"Is that the smell of weed?" I asked him quietly as we sipped beers at a table. I was making it a point to get to know everyone at the Club, and invited myself to sit beside him. We had been bantering about where we came from, how long we had been in Thailand, the usual expat introductions. When I smelled weed seeping from every pore of his body, it was as titillating as if I were sniffing the finest perfume on a beautiful woman.

Soon Sleepy Joe was my regular and sole weed contact. Discretion as well as quality are his promised virtues, and Sleepy Joe is a man of his word. It might be difficult to understand his word, but he abides by it. He has never told a soul about our dealings.

When he speaks, he is brief and to the point. His favorite topics are music and cinema, both areas of his expertise. It always felt that he was showing just the tip of an iceberg-sized knowledge.

There is good money to be made betting that Joe can name any rock group and their songs from 1955 through 1990, and any film with its director and stars from 1930 to the present. Sleepy Joe is proof that cannabis does not adversely affect brain tissue.

"Music sucked after ninety but not film," was how he explains the different cutoff dates.

Once a month, Joe drops by my condo with my order. He also comes by a few times just to hang out. We roll a joint, smoke it while listening to classic American rock, jazz or blues, and often watch a movie on my big screen television. When the music or movie ends, we saunter over to the Club, floating along the streets of Bangkok. Joe's stuff is always top of the line.

Sometimes we catch a film on the big screen, usually on Wednesdays, when Bangkok theaters show week-old releases at half price, or at the old Lido at Siam Square, where the tickets are always only 100 baht. We can afford to pay any price, but a few years in Thailand gets a *farang* thinking like a Thai, taking advantage of genuine bargains.

Joe claims to be forty-nine but looks older with his straggly, long gray hair and usual two-day stubble. He has claimed to have been in the Australian army for ten years, and when he decided not to re-enlist, he found himself with little money and even less marketable skills. He had heard that one could live cheaply in Thailand, so he decided to give it a chance.

Joe had been a pothead all his life, even in the military. He had no trouble tracking down old army buddies who had settled in Thailand, and they kept him in weed, and after some time introduced him to their connections. Whoever those connections might be, Joe keeps that information to himself.

Joe once let on to me that he had one prime customer, a foreigner, who bought a kilo every month and paid a very inflated price. That sale took care of most of his financial needs and allowed him plenty of time to smoke, indulge his passions for music and cinema, and park himself at the Club.

I do worry about him, fearing that he might be arrested someday and find himself in deep trouble. Maybe a customer facing some problems of their own would decide to give Joe up. No doubt it happened in Thailand just like it happened in America. Many years as a criminal defense lawyer taught me that snitching was a fact of life, and no reason to believe it was not an international phenomenon. Wherever there are people facing the hammer of the law, there will be some seeking to avoid the blow.

The General once told me not to worry, that Joe was paying off someone. That would not have surprised me. Things work that way in Thailand.

It was a delight to have a friend who could sell me weed and also discuss every film by Kubrick, Tarantino, the Coen Brothers, and Scorsese, and educate me about more obscure directors.

Joe may look like he is always half asleep, but I had represented too many dealers to believe that to be true. For a *farang* to survive in Thailand, let alone a dealer, they must remain alert and think quickly ontheir feet. So Joe had to be sharper than he appeared.

Goes to show you can't judge a book by its cover, or a maybe a joint by its rolling paper.

8

OLIVER IS LARGER than life. Much larger.

He is the center of attention whenever he is at the Club, several hours every day when in town. He keeps no fixed schedule and can appear at any time. He takes control the moment he arrives.

Oliver manages to do this without infringing on Ray the bartender's authority, and the two together entertain us for hours, alternating their storytelling artistry.

"Now, here's what I think," Oliver booms when a topic catches his fancy, and whoever else is speaking yields the floor, with one exception. He never interrupts Ray and always allows him to finish what he is saying before picking up the charge.

Oliver is a big Australian, loud but not at all unpleasant. He is the polar opposite of his countryman, Sleepy Joe. Oliver stands six feet one, a solid two hundred pounds, and ever since he had a stomach bypass and lost fifty pounds, his body ripples with muscles instead of flab. He wears tailored clothes to emphasize his restored physique.

"Man's got to look the role," he informed me when he came home from Bangkok Hospital with his new physique.

He certainly looks the role though it is a role he created.

Oliver is in his mid-fifties, based on what accounts of his life he has provided. He has never given his exact age, and with his head and face shaved smooth, it is hard to be more precise. Unlike Phil Funston, Oliver's head is a perfect sphere, free from lumps. He once revealed that he had come into a fair amount of money when he was thirty. He hinted that he had started one of the first chains of computer stores in Australia and had sold it for a handsome profit a few years later. He had been living in Bangkok, traveling and enjoying life ever since.

I knew the feeling.

"Why work when you can have a good time?" he is fond of saying. I silently agree.

Oliver lives with a beautiful young Thai woman whom he occasionally brought to the Club. She speaks not a word of English, and like most foreigners, Oliver speaks no more than a fist-full of Thai. I have a better command of the language, and that's not saying much. He could perhaps count to ten, on many days only up to five or six. I have no idea how they communicate, assuming they do.

Oliver sometimes shows up at the Club with other beautiful young Thai woman with whom he also lacks a common language. I noticed that except for his live-in, he never brought any of the others a second time.

"I have you guys to talk to," he explains when anyone questions the viability of such non-verbal relationships.

"They know what I want and I know what they want," he will add. He made clear what he thought they want without breaking any of our rules.

"You sell yourself short," I once told Oliver. "With you it's not just money. You're a fascinating guy, smart and successful. You can even be a nice guy at times," I added.

"Not that any of that matters to these gals," he replied.

Oliver is an authority on innumerable topics: Bangkok real estate, where to meet women, best street food in Bangkok, how to find parking, what it takes to bribe a cop in a given situation, dealing with crooked cabbies, where to find good tailors, the best beaches, how to obtain any kind of visa. He chooses the subject, either one that is under discussion or one he wants to opine upon, and no one dares resist. Listening to Oliver is entertaining and informative, as no matter what the subject, he actually knows what he is talking about. I had no idea where he obtained his information, or even if it was true, but it always sounded right to me.

If someone needs a private consultation to solve a problem, Oliver is available. He always knows what to do in any situation. As is the case with his knowledge, his judgment is impeccable. With Oliver's guidance, Club regulars have found apartments, solved visa problems, or worked their way through touchy breakups with Thai girlfriends. Over the years that I have known Oliver, he has helped me get out of a relationship that went South—literally and figuratively—as well as a few that went North or Northeast.

As the years passed, I found myself spending more and more time with Oliver. We have taken a few trips to the islands. Oliver loves them, especially Koh Phangan, and he is forever talking about moving there.

"You and me, Yank, we should ditch the City and go island," he told me one day over drinks. "We could have really nice lives."

"I already have a really nice life," I replied.

"It would just keep getting better," he countered.

"I'm a city boy," I explained. "And Bangkok is a great city."

Lately Oliver spends increasingly more time in Koh Phangan. From what he lets on, he has a woman and a business interest on the island. He is often gone for a week or two. Each time he leaves I fervently pray for his quick return. I hope he never realizes his thoughts of moving there full time.

The NJA Club just wouldn't be the same without him. Neither

would I.

9

MY CELL PHONE rang a half dozen times before I grabbed it off the nightstand. My phone has no ring limit or voicemail. The screen told me it was three fifteen in the morning.

A Thai speaker was on the other end of the line. When it was clear this *farang* was Thai-deficient, he asked me to wait a minute. After five minutes an English-speaking woman came on the line.

"Your friend *Khun* Joe asked to call you. He is in jail in the Thong Lor Station. He wants you to come now."

"Will they let me see him?" I asked as the shock melted into realization.

"If the Desk Sergeant feels happy, no problem," she said.

Even the most naive *farang* knows what that means.

Seven years living in Thailand had never required me to face the daunting task of dealing with hostile officials. Everything had been made easy for me by Charlie. My call to his consultant every two years resulted in a business visa renewal. My money and caution led me to feel insulated from the difficulties so many *farangs* report. Now, out of nowhere, a real problem was staring me hard in the face. At three fifteen in the morning no less. Without a game plan based on experience, this had to be played by ear. A hot flash coursed through my body, and my stomach tightened as I forced myself awake. There was no choice. This was Sleepy Joe in trouble. There wasn't time to worry.

I pulled on a pair of pants and put on a respectable white long-sleeve shirt, made sure my California State Bar card was with me, and stuck my U.S. passport in a pants pocket. Several one thousand baht notes were peeled from the roll in my desk drawer and stuck in the other pocket. From everything the newspapers and other foreigners had said about dealing with Thai police, the baht was necessary.

The Thong Lor station was a few blocks from my condo, a ten minute walk. But an orange vested driver standing by his bike at the motorcycle taxi stand had me there in less than three.

At the station I forced a smile and asked the cop at the front desk for the shift sergeant.

"That's me," he said in English.

After figuring out my reason for being there, he asked to see some identification. Praying he could not detect my nervousness from my fumbling hands, I showed him my passport and Bar card. Sticking out from the passport were the top edges of three one thousand baht notes. Surely the sergeant had to split this with his shift captain, and the jail guard and the female translator would get something as well. Bribing a Thai cop is not against the law, I kept assuring myself. At least not the laws they follow. If my intuition was wrong, Sleepy Joe would soon have a cellmate.

"Sit here," the sergeant said, pointing to a row of empty seats behind me. A few minutes later he called me, pointed to a door and directed me to walk through it. On the other side, a cop met me and escorted me to a small room. He opened the door to let me in. Sleepy Joe was inside, seated at a small table. I sat on the other chair in the room.

Joe looked like a man who had just stuck his finger into an electric socket. His eyes were red but not the red of a stoner. Those eyes blazed with the redness of fear. His long stringy hair stuck out from the sides of his head as if blown by a wind.

"Get me out of here," he croaked.

His appearance frightened me at first, but the criminal lawyer in me took charge for the moment. If there was any place in this world where I felt at home, it was in a holding cell with an accused criminal.

"Have you said anything?"

"Not that stupid," Sleepy Joe said.

"Have you been abused in any way?"

"Unless you count being handcuffed and stuck in a hellhole and being fed rice and water, the answer is no."

"Did they tell you what the charges were all about," I asked.

"They didn't have to," Sleepy Joe said. "They broke down my door and said they found a kilo."

Joe was indeed smart enough to play along and never admit to anything while managing to tell me the important facts. This was a set-up. The question was how to use that knowledge and get him out of jail as soon as possible. This wasn't California, where a lawyer could call a bail bondsman when bail was set. Or if there was no bail yet, a court clerk to get bail set right away. Those people were far away in miles and years. I told Joe to just sit there while the situation filtered through my mind, grasping for a plan. One dawned on me. Not a sure thing, but the only serviceable option. I let Sleepy Joe know we had something to work with.

"There's someone who can help. Just don't say a word to anyone about anything."

"I can't spend another night here," he cried.

"You'll be out today one way or another," was my lawyerly advice to my client.

I hoped my word could be kept.

THE GENERAL LIVED in a fine modern freestanding home on a halfacre on one of the small hidden lanes off *Soi* 16, a redoubt of the affluent.

At four in the morning, the streets of Bangkok are at their quietest. Most late night activities are over by two a.m. and except for the twenty-four hour convenience stores, everything is closed. There are no vendors and few pedestrians. Traffic is very light. It is much cooler than later in the day when the sun rises and the people and the vehicles venture forth.

I knew where to find all-night motorcycle taxis and even regular cabs but decided to walk. I knew from our many discussions that the General arises at four thirty a.m. and enjoys his coffee before venturing out to care for his chickens. When asking for a favor, waking him up earlier than he liked was a bad way to start.

It was still and quiet at this predawn hour. Other than a few men sleeping in doorways or under the trestles supporting the Skytrain, there was no one but me on the streets. A few taxis and cars passed by and an occasional delivery truck rattled along Sukhumvit. Several street vendors' carts and furniture were covered by tarps and pulled up against the buildings. The street cleaners had not yet started working, and stray bits of paper and debris lay scattered about. It was cool for Bangkok, not much over seventy degrees Fahrenheit. Not enough to make me sweat, more likely Sleepy Joe's predicament would do that.

It was just about four thirty when I reached the gates protecting the General's home. I pressed the intercom button and waited a minute before ringing it again. A voice speaking Thai crackled through the small speaker. I did not recognize the voice through the crackle but it had to be one of his regular security guards, all of whom knew me well. This one recognized my name and in English, asked me to wait five minutes. My reply was "certainly," as if there was a choice.

Exactly five minutes later a tired looking young man who regularly came to the Club as one of the General's bodyguards let me in and told me to follow him. He seemed upset at being aroused so early. While passing through the gate a knot started forming in my stomach.

A minute later, we were in the General's library. The shelves on the walls were lined with books in English and Thai. A pot of coffee with milk, sugar, and two cups sat on a tray on the table. The General was already seated, with one of the cups filled with steaming brew set before him. He motioned for me to sit.

"Did you just happen to be in the area for an early morning stroll, or is there something I can do for you?" he asked without a trace of emotion. "It must be rather important if you did not even call," he added.

The General accepted my explanation that knowing he arose this time every day, it would have been rude to awaken him earlier. The knot in my stomach lessened slightly upon seeing his smile. Then again, everyone smiles all the time in Thailand. I poured myself some coffee and then explained the reason for showing up unexpectedly.

"Sleepy Joe is in custody at the Thong Lor station. He was arrested in his condo right after a one kilo ganja transaction."

"How is he?" the General asked.

"He says he hasn't been abused in any way. He's just frightened out of his mind."

"Sleepy Joe has been out of his mind for a long time," the General said. "They haven't tried to beat any confession out of him and they allowed you to see him with a modest payment. No threats were made to you or him. This tells me that the entire matter can be resolved with the appropriate financial resolutions."

"In other words, a bribe?" I asked.

"Let us just say that in our criminal justice system, every possible option carries a cost. In this case it may well be only monetary."

I downed more coffee. It was necessary because after being roused out of bed at a quarter past three, adrenaline alone would not fuel me. Worry and fear had sapped what strength could be mustered at that hour. The caffeine surged through me, awakening body and mind. It enabled me to tell the General what I needed from him.

"I came to you for advice. Who would know better than you how to help our friend?" The General had in the past led me to believe he could help me if ever needed, and now we would find out if he really meant it.

"Allow me to make a few calls," the General said as he put down his coffee cup, rose from his chair and walked through the library door. I poured myself more coffee and drank it while waiting.

AFTER HALF AN HOUR and three cups of coffee, the General returned. He sat down and looked at me.

"Your friend crossed some powerful people," he explained. "He thought he could do better by buying his products from an unauthorized distributor."

"Didn't realize there were authorized ganja dealers," I cracked before my better instincts seized control. This was no laughing matter.

"He learned his lesson now," I said. "Can we get him out of this as soon as possible?"

"It can be done," he began. "But it will not be cheap."

"How much is not cheap?"

"One million baht," the General said

A million baht is a great deal of money in Thailand. It was slightly less than thirty thousand U.S. dollars, no small amount to most Americans.

I was not like most Americans, being set for life in Thailand.

Sleepy Joe would repay me, but even if he did not, the money would not make much difference in how I lived. The truth was that most years my money earned more than my expenses. All for Mr. Rawlings of Canada, of course. The money part was the easy part of this adventure. Not developing an ulcer or suffering a heart attack or a stroke were the harder parts. But Joe was my friend.

It had not not been a pleasant feeling to be a foreigner at the Thong Lor police station trying to free a drug dealer through bribery. Being with the General was not unpleasant in that same way, but it too caused a strong sense of unease which could evolve into a chilling fear. I could not put my finger on exactly what caused this discomfort, but it was without question present. I was outside my usual orbit and I didn't like it one bit.

The General seemed pleased that the money would be available by ten that morning. He told me to put the cash in a small satchel which his guard would give me. He told me to take a cab from the bank to the Thong Lor station and ask for Captain Kasiton. Sleepy Joe would then be turned over to me and there would be no record of the arrest.

This called for more than just a thank you. Never having learned the proper rules for the wai, it seemed best to just place my hand over my heart as while expressing my gratitude. I rose from my chair and was about to depart when the General spoke.

"And of course, Glenn, out of respect for this favor, I will someday expect a favor from you." The General was polite but firm, in a tone he had never used with me before.

The uneasy feeling reemerged in my stomach and it was not because of the many cups of strong coffee. If it were only a matter of money, it would not have concerned me very much, but being in the General's debt in a non-monetary way was something that had never passed through my mind.

"What kind of a favor?" I asked.

"You will be told when it is needed," the General said.

"Any idea when that will be?"

"None whatsoever," the General replied. "But rest assured the day will come, and I am confident you will graciously comply."

I nodded in assent. There was no other option. In Thailand the *farang* always pays. Or, to paraphrase the great Joe Louis, pays and leaves a hell of a tip.

At the gate, the surly guard handed me a small satchel. It bore an uncanny resemblance to a briefcase full of money that had brought me here those seven years ago.

It was six thirty in the morning. The bank would not open until ten. Four cups of strong coffee had provided more energy than needed. Walking back to my apartment worked off much of the caffeine surge. By the time I reached the Ekamai area it was only seven fifteen. Fortunately there was a good movie just starting on television, the latest remake of *King Kong*, and when it ended it was time to leave for the bank.

AT THE STATION the desk sergeant was expecting me.

"*Khun* Glenn?" he asked before a word came out of my mouth.

"*Chai*," I responded, more than a little concerned that the General had given my real name.

The sergeant motioned me to walk down a hallway. At the end a middle-aged police officer wearing what looked like a custom-tailored uniform greeted me with a salute. He identified himself as Captain Kasiton and led me into his office where we sat at a small table.

"Give me your bag," he said. He was neither threatening nor hostile.

He snapped open the satchel and looked under the flap. Satisfied, he put the bag down beside him.

"You may wait outside," he said. "Your friend will join you very soon.

Would you like a cup of coffee?"

The offer was graciously accepted. It was the most expensive cup of coffee I would ever drink.

TEN MINUTES LATER, Sleepy Joe walked through the door. Aside from looking tired, he was none the worse for his ordeal. In fact he looked neater and better groomed than usual.

"They let me have a shower and even gave me some real shampoo," he told me as we walked out into the street. "A razor and shaving cream as well."

"Let's grab some breakfast," I suggested and Joe nodded in agreement. We walked the few blocks to a nearby restaurant that served a credible American breakfast.

In between forkfuls of eggs, bites of toast, and slugs of yet more coffee, we worked out repayment. For the next five years, Joe would provide me with one ounce of top-flight buds a month without charge, and with each delivery would also give me ten thousand baht, until the debt was repaid. Of course there was no interest.

"Jews aren't allowed to charge each other interest," I told him. "In this case you are an honorary Jew."

"Didn't you know my maternal grandfather was Jewish?" he asked as he wiped some yolk off his upper lip.

"No wonder I always liked you," I replied.

"Do you think it's too early to go to your place, roll one, and watch a movie?" he asked.

"No," I said.

THREE DAYS LATER I sat at a table at the Club mid morning talking with Oliver. Aside from two corporate types a few table away, we were the only ones in the place.

"Word is our friend Sleepy Joe had a little problem and you got him out from under it," he said.

"How the hell did you find out?"

Oliver looked at me and smiled. His shaved head and smooth face reminded me of a large billiard ball.

"Never told you that my game is information? The guy that knows just about everything. What little I don't know can easily be found out."

"Actually, you never told me that."

"Well now you know," Oliver said.

This should not have been a surprise. Oliver was the master of stories. He must have collected hundreds of them. Collecting information takes many forms.

Oliver listened to my account of what had happened to Sleepy Joe. The part about the General insisting on a favor to be called in at an unspecified future date was omitted.

"The old pirate sure raked you," he said with a chuckle. "Tacked on a hefty fee for his services and to make up for lost revenue. Joe shouldn't have tried to give him the runaround just to save a few bucks per kilo."

"Are you telling me the General is his supplier?" I asked in astonishment.

Oliver smiled again.

"I'm just telling you that anything like that goes on in this part of town, the General is sure to get a piece. He guarantees protection. But only through him.

"If you had come straight to me we would have gotten it done for no more than two hundred fifty thousand baht," he added. The cops would have tossed the General some of it out of respect and everyone would have been happy."

"I'll keep that in mind if there's ever a next time, Oliver." Hopefully there would be no next time.

"And just make sure you keep all of this between us," Oliver said.

"Who else?" I asked.

10

WEDNESDAYS MEANS BRUNCH with my friend Charles, a retired political scientist from New York University, when we enjoy the bagels and lox with cream cheese over at Au Bon Pan on Ekamai, while discussing the state of the world. All other breakfasts are at the Club. This was one of those days.

The Bangkok Post and a cup of acceptable coffee occupied me while waiting for Mai to bring my eggs over easy with toast. The Club serves a decent breakfast and allows me to substitute the choice of bacon, ham, or sausage with a second cup of coffee. Glenn Murray Cohen may not be the best Jew in the world, not even in Thailand—Chabad takes that honor—but pig meat will never slide down my gullet. The Club gets the better end of that deal. Their coffee is middle-of-the-road, good enough to wash down eggs and toast but often not usually compelling enough for a second cup.

Mai chatted with me when she took the order. She was more flirtatious than usual that morning, confirming my belief that she contemplated a relationship with me. There was a question as to whether her interest was in me as a person or my money and status as a lawyer. It was my feeling that she liked me because I am a good man, but my record on judging the feelings of Thai women is abysmal.

"You are number one guy around here," she told me more than once with an inviting smile. "You are high class, *jing ka*."

Of course, up against guys like Rhode Island Joe, Sleepy Joe, and Phil Funston, high class and number one were not difficult plateaus to reach.

If my heart were not set on Noi, Mai might have had a chance of persuading me to abandon my fear of a relationship with a Club employee. She fit my vision of the ideal Thai woman: hard working, honest and with *jai dii* or good heart that matters most in Thai culture. Many fellow expats were deluded and thought that the sex industry workers of Pattaya, *Soi* Nana, or Cowboy represented Thai women. Perhaps those women were normal when not on the job, but while working they were playing a fantasy role designed to pry money from fools like Phil Funston. Nothing Thai about it. My policy of never setting foot in any of those venues made me even more appealing to Mai and to myself as well.

I was deep into an article about artificial intelligence, where noted scientists in the field debated whether robots would ever be able to experience the full range of human emotions. Questions were raised as to whether "artificial humans" were capable of having genuine emotions.

I often ask the same question about myself.

My reading so absorbed me that I did not notice Noi seat herself beside me until she rested her hand on my forearm. My attention was distracted from the ethics of robotics by the touch of the beautiful woman at my side.

"Can I ask you for a favor?" she asked.

"You can ask me for anything."

"You are a lawyer, right?" she queried.

"I was a lawyer in America and keep my license current but haven't worked in what, seven years? And I am not a lawyer in Thailand."

"But you are smart," she countered.

I put down the newspaper as she lifted her hand from my arm.

"Not smart enough to win your heart."

"That's feelings, not brains," she said.

I took a quick sip of coffee and asked what kind of a problem she had.

"I would have to show you some papers. Can we meet at your place in half an hour?" she asked.

"My pleasure," I said.

It was a few blocks from the Club to my condominium and during the walk I imagined that this time things would end up as they were supposed to, but recognized that those thoughts had to be suppressed. Noi was correct, and our friendship was worth more than anything else. My life in America had lacked true friends like Noi, or Sleepy Joe and Rhode Island Joe. Most of the people I knew back in America were lawyers and they were colleagues, not real friends. These genuine friendships I now enjoyed made Bangkok my true home.

Lek, the doorman at my condo, greeted me in the lobby.

"Good morning *Khun* Glenn," he called to me as I walked to the elevator. "Your magazine come yesterday but don't see." He handed me a flat packet.

It was the latest copy of the *New Yorker*, at least the latest to arrive. Deliveries were always few issues behind, thanks to the mail systems of the U.S. and Thailand, but with the *New Yorker*, that never matters. Their articles and fiction can be read well after the issue date. My hands greedily grasped the magazine.

Every *Songkran*, the Thai New Year, my gift to Lek is an envelope containing several thousand baht. He probably would like me anyway, but that earned me his undying loyalty. On several occasions when a relationship ended with the lady storming out of my condo in a rage, Lek calmed her down and put her in a cab. I considered authorizing him to take deliveries from Sleepy Joe if he came by with my monthly packet while I was out, but decided it was unfair to place Lek at risk.

Like many of the working people in Bangkok, Lek came from Isan, the Northeast region of the country. As a rule these were hard-working, honorable and amiable people. Lek often told me of the achievements of his two young children, both outstanding students. He and his wife, a restaurant worker, had decided against the common practice of leaving the children with the grandparents in the province while the parents worked in the city and sent money home.

"Children belong with parents," he intoned and I agreed with him, despite knowing nothing about raising children.

I had just settled into my easy chair and started in on the political section of the *New Yorker* when the intercom squawked and Lek informed me of the arrival of "Miss Noi."

A whiff of her perfume greeted me as soon as the door was opened. My sense of smell is sharp and informs me when Noi changes brands. She wore a smart pants suit and looked like a real estate or insurance agent meeting a *farang* client. She carried a large bag over her shoulder.

I invited her to sit on the couch opposite me and asked her what problem she needed to discuss.

"Look at this," she said as she reached into her bag for a sheath of papers, which she handed me.

Some of the papers were in Thai, which I do not read. The rest were in English and enabled me to determine what this was all about.

"It seems that the American government has asked to see your bank accounts and looks like the Thai government has agreed to allow this."

"That's what I thought," she said. She gripped a sheaf of papers tightly in one hand. Her right leg was moving up and down as she lifted her heel off the floor. "The Thai papers say that the bank will turn everything over in ten days unless there is an appeal in some court."

"Then that's what we will do. First we need to find a good lawyer.

But in Thailand, that won't be easy."

"Can't we just pay someone?" Noi asked.

"If it were just the Thai government people, yes, but not with the Americans involved." After the Sleepy Joe incident I considered myself an authority on bribing Thai law enforcement.

"You are an American lawyer," she said with a trace of desperation. "Can you help me?"

"Up to a point. First we need to deal with the Thai end of this."

"Maybe it's time we talk to the General," she said.

I wondered why she was bringing up the General.

"No, I've got someone else in mind."

OLIVER WAS HOME when I called and he agreed to be at my condo in half an hour.

An hour later the big Australian was sitting next to Noi on my couch, studying the papers. It was a surprise to see him reading Thai.

When Oliver was finished he put the papers down on the little table in front of the couch.

"Let's defer to Glenn on the American legal stuff," he genially remarked. "As for the Thai end, we need to hire this young lady a sharp lawyer to halt the release of her records."

"Do you know of any?" I asked.

"I know both of the honest lawyers in Thailand," he said with a smile.

I explained to Oliver and Noi that the American legal papers said that "for good cause showing" the Americans were asking the Thais to issue a subpoena for the bank records and to turn them over to the U.S. Embassy. Based on my experience this meant that in the opinion of the U.S. Department of Justice, there was probable cause to believe that the documents would contain evidence of some criminal activity by Noi or someone else.

Noi said not a word nor did her face reveal any emotion.

Oliver added that the Thai documents acknowledged the American request and that it all seemed proper but it did not tell the complete story.

"No doubt there have been some off-the-record discussions between the two governments.

"First thing we need to know is what the hell is really going on. Noi needs to tell you everything she can," he said, turning to me, indicating it was my turn to speak.

"I am still a licensed American lawyer and this does involve an American legal issue. Whatever Noi tells me will be honored as within the attorney-client privilege. But that does not apply to you, Oliver."

"I don't squeal so don't worry about me," Oliver said. The scowl on his face signaled his indignation.

"There's no fear of you opening your big trap. But Thai and American law enforcement could question or even subpoena you if they knew you were helping us. They could keep you in jail until you testified.

"If we bring you on board as my investigator you're within the privilege." I pulled a wad of bank notes from my pocket, counted off a few one thousand baht notes and handed them to Oliver. "You can start working for us right now. Make your calls and tell us what you learn. Then Noi will tell us what she has to say."

Noi followed me into the kitchen where I prepared a pot of coffee. As an extreme coffee afficionado, morning means the ritual of grinding beans, placing the grounds and boiling water into a French press, waiting exactly four minutes before pushing down the plunger and then enjoying a cup or two of first rate brew. The coffee at NJA is potable but is nothing compared to what is brewed in my condo.

I once invited the staff of the NJA Club over to my condo to celebrate the King's Birthday and served them coffee and cake. After sampling my brew, Mai told me we should open a fancy coffee shop.

"I'll be your manager," she said.

"But how could the Club get along without you?" I asked.

"They will find somebody," she replied.

THIS WAS MY second brew of the day, the best way to pass time while Oliver gathered background.

It is my delight to breathe in freshly brewed black coffee before adding sweetener or lightener. The tendrils of steam creeping up my nostrils are as much a part of the coffee experience as the taste of the beverage. Noi added milk and sugar immediately.

"I'm worried," Noi said.

"No need to be," I replied, not knowing if in truth that was the case.

"You are going to have to come clean with me and Oliver. Otherwise we can't help you."

She stared at me with her dark, mysterious eyes.

"You know Thais don't like to talk about unpleasant things. Especially to *farangs*."

"We're not just *farangs*. We are Glenn and Oliver,"

"Still *farangs*," she said.

Once a *farang*, always a *farang*, as they say around here.

We drank the rest of our coffee in silence. Five minutes passed. Oliver called to us from the living room. Noi and I returned to where he sat.

Oliver told us that he had arranged for a partner of his personal Thai lawyer to file an appeal and delay the disclosure of the bank records.

"His name is Panchen Solderwanterkan and he is one of the best criminal defense lawyers in Thailand. Has gotten a few government officials and mob bosses out from some serious trouble."

"Not that there is any significant difference between the two," he added with a hearty laugh.

"He isn't cheap, but worth every penny."

"Don't worry about money. It's covered," I assured Noi.

"Thanks but I can afford *Khun* Panchen," she replied.

"I know the name and he is very good," she added.

This was not the time to ask her how she came to know the names of criminal lawyers.

"Also made a quick call to a contact of mine in the Ministry of Justice," Oliver said.

"He says they came across Noi as part of an American investigation into money laundering. They believe Americans are making big money overseas, most assuredly by illegal activities, and bringing it into countries that do not comply with the American requirement to inform them about all accounts and transactions. Laos for example."

I focused my best courtroom-withering gaze at Noi's face. She looked down for a moment and then spoke.

"Let me tell you about it," she said softly.

THE ENGLISH BOYFRIEND had shown her how to do it before he ran afoul of a certain Thai gangster and was forced to depart the Kingdom without even a fare thee well to Noi.

"Do not miss him for a minute," she assured us.

The boyfriend had been operating a lucrative racket running

money earned questionably by Americans into neighboring Laos.

"Trying to get around FATCA," I explained. "Foreign Asset Transaction Compliance Act. When an American opens a bank account overseas and runs more than ten thousand bucks through the account in a year, that foreign bank has to report all transactions to the IRS. If they don't, they can get fined and even worse, be barred from using the U.S. banking system."

"Laos has little concerns about that," Oliver chimed in. "There is so little commerce between the U.S. and Laos that the poor little country gets overlooked. They do far better laundering money than with imports."

So all of those trips to her village and the unexplained absences were for the most part bunk. Noi had been carting currency across the border and depositing it into banks in Vientiane. Maybe she did stop of and see her family in Isan, but that was not the real purpose of her frequent travels.

"They were paying me a percentage," she revealed. "I have become a rich woman by Thai standards."

The clientele were Americans, most involved in the sordid night businesses, some drug dealers, a sprinkling of boiler room scam artists and a handful of legitimate businessman seeking to avoid taxes. Noi would change the baht into dollars, earn a nice chunk of change on the transactions, and then shuttle it off to Laos earning even more.

"So you must own that condo you live in," I said.

"Plus two others that are rented," she replied. "And the big house in Isan I built for my family."

Noi had gotten her post-boyfriend start in the money laundering business after a conversation with Edward. She suspected that the former Welsh accountant was doing something akin to her missing boyfriend's business, and when she revealed the absent man's work to him, each knew they had found a partner. Laos was less than an hour drive from Noi's hometown in Isan. She soon became the best runner Edward and his associates employed. As value added, she bought the dollars without leaving any records. She had friends in Chinatown.

"Edward told me I was perfect," she said. "Speak Thai and Isan, hometown close to Lao, have a good reason for going up their all the time, and am honest."

"Honest meaning he knew you won't steal," I added, prompting her first smile of the day.

It was easy for me to understand how Noi's Americans felt. I was lucky and had Charlie to make things easy for me.

AFTER NOI LEFT, Oliver remained and we drank several cups of coffee, smoked a fat joint, and listened to Art Blakey and the Jazz Messengers as background. "Night in Tunisia," the 1961 release featuring Blakey on drums, Wayne Shorter on tenor sax, Jymie Merritt on bass, Bobby Timmons on piano, Lee Morgan on trumpet. Oliver was another friend who enjoyed jazz.

"Can you help?" I asked while stubbing out the end of the joint.

"I can get you any information you need," he replied. "At a price. The young lady can likely afford it and if she can't, there's you."

Oliver would first find out if there was any action being taken against Edward or others involved in this scheme and would set up a meeting with Attorney Panchen as soon as possible.

"Get back to you in a few hours," he said as he rose from his chair.

"This meeting is free. I'll bill Noi for the calls about Edward."

"Send all bills to me. I'm handling the U.S. side of this as her personal attorney."

"No doubt you would like to make that very personal," Oliver said as he opened the door and left.

Another example of Oliver's information always being right.

OLIVER CALLED ME several hours later just as he had promised.

"Crazy as it sounds, Noi is the only one either government is looking at."

I had an idea as to why.

"Maybe they're starting at the bottom, hoping to build a case against the people at the top. That happens all the time in America."

"We're not in America," Oliver said.

PANCHEN'S OFFICE WAS in a high rise building a short walk from the Sala Dang BTS stop, in Silom, one of Bangkok's commercial and business centers. Many Thai and multinational corporations have offices there and Silom Road, the main street, offers a choice selection of Western style restaurants and bars. Off on a few side streets sits Patpong, the original nightlife district, established for the recreational needs of American soldiers during the Vietnam War. I rarely visited Silom, and never at night, when hordes of Thai men follow me down the street offering young girls or "ping pong shows," both of which repulse me. I have always believed myself capable of forming meaningful relationships with normal women, despite all evidence to the contrary.

Noi and I were served coffee by an attractive assistant as we sat in the waiting room of Panchen's office on the fifteenth floor. The windows opposite us provided a view of the Chao Phraya River. Boats glided in both directions: commuter boats, tour boats, private longboats with dragon heads on the prow and fins on the side, immense commercial ships and barges. Wat Arun, across the river was fully visible. Due to my interest in Thai history, I knew that the wat or temple already existed when King Taksin established Thonburi as the capital of the Kingdom in 1767, after the fall of Ayutthaya to the Burmese. Thonburi, where today millions of people live their lives peacefully and never have to worry about multigovernmental investigations.

After we finished our coffee the assistant led us down a carpeted hallway into Panchen's office. It was large, with a view similar to the waiting room. A small Buddhist shrine sat on a table in one corner of the room. A portrait of King Rama IX hung behind the attorney, who was seated at a sleek modern desk that was little more than a glass table. Panchen was several years older than me, so we both gave a respectful wai, though Noi's was better than mine. To my surprise, the lawyer extended his hand and we shook American style. He simply nodded at Noi.

Panchen's face was smooth and impassive. He wore round wire rimmed glasses. His eyes were focused on me as he spoke. He was balding and wore his remaining hair cut short. His teeth were gleaming white and perfect.

"I have had a chance to review your papers and make a few calls to friends in the prosecutor's office," he began, speaking in very lightly accented English that sounded almost American. With his well tailored suit and expensive tie and self-assured tone, he would have been right at home in a law office in San Francisco. I had been a lawyer long enough to size up a colleague, even in Thailand, and suspected he was as good as his reputation, which is not always the case.

"To be quite frank, Mr. Cohen, I find it strange that your country is expending this much energy on what appears to me to be a rather modest case.

"I have seen money laundering cases where the amount is in the tens of millions. Here it looks like if we added up all of the deposits Miss Noi has made, it perhaps comes to a few million dollars. Hardly worth the effort it seems."

"Well then this should be an easy one to resolve," I replied.

"One would think so," Panchen said, fingering an expensive pen between his fine, well-manicured fingers. "But every one of my contacts told me the same thing. This case cannot be discussed and cannot be settled. It must play out, whatever that is supposed to mean."

"Are you telling me that we can't buy or deal our way out of this?"

"Exactly," the lawyer replied. Light gleamed off the lens of his glasses. "There is something going on here, something I suspect is not really about Miss Noi and her little game," he said with a tinge of disrespect, as if he were embarrassed to be representing such an inconsequential criminal.

"This does not appear to be about what is at most a comparatively minor breach of American reporting rules," he added. "Something else is going on. Experience suggests that we will eventually learn the truth. Until then, stay calm and let me find out what I can. An appeal has been filed, arguing that the affidavits from your American government are insufficient to violate the privacy of Miss Noi's Thai bank records. We may force the two governments to reveal more than they wish. Until the appeal is resolved the records will not be provided. And it is not out of the question that we win."

Panchen showed a slight grin.

"But of course, there is little doubt that the U.S. government has already obtained whatever they want. Or they can get it any time they wish. This process seems to be undertaken to send a message of what is coming."

"And what is coming?" I inquired.

"We will find out," he said. "That is certain."

THE GOOD NEWS was that Panchen was not as expensive as feared. It would be my bill to pay, as Panchen warned that the two governments' interest in Noi's bank records meant we didn't want any paper trail showing how she was paying her lawyers. Panchen wanted a retainer of two hundred thousand baht, which at the exchange rate was a little over five thousand U.S. dollars. That was less than my retainer fee would have been for the same type of case back in the U.S, and my office was nowhere as impressive as his. I probably wasn't as good as him, certainly not as affluent.

"He's a very good lawyer," I assured Noi as we walked up the BTS steps. At midday it takes forever to get from Silom to the NJA Club over in Wattana by cab. I was a regular on this impressive elevated rail system and always carried a fare card with plenty of baht on it so I could just swipe it at the turnstile and avoid the lines at the ticket kiosks. Fortunately Noi had one as well. The BTS calls to mind what BART could be if it were well maintained, clean, and safe.

"Are you sure about that?" Noi asked as we reached the platform, up a long flight of steps.

"Yes. He speaks excellent English, has what seems to be a well-run office, and from what I can see, he knows what he is talking about. This is the not the first time he has dealt with requests from the U.S. government. He was honest about the case and he seems to have connections even if he is not being open about them, which makes sense. He was recommended by Oliver and that carries a lot of weight with me."

"*Khun* Glenn is a better *tinai kwaam*," Noi said with a smile as she touched my arm, using the Thai word for lawyer. "Lucky to have you," she added.

No need to tell her my thoughts. She already knew.

11

I SAT ON my terrace watching the sun go down over the part of Bangkok known as the Greenbelt. It is a stretch of the City running from the night entertainment venues of Nana and *Soi* Cowboy, places I never set foot in, to the middle class high rises of Phra Khanon and On Nut. There was no more consensus as to how this area was named than on the origins of the NJA Club. Some say the Greenbelt was so titled because foreigners live there with their green money. Others claim the name comes from the many trees lining the streets and even the roofs of buildings, or the two large parks within the area. Suffice it to say someone along the way came up with the name and it stuck.

My cell phone rang. It was Charlie. He was still listed as a contact after all these years and his name was written across the screen.

There had been no contact with Charlie since I arrived in Thailand, aside from the quick call to tell him I made it here. In the next seven years there had been no reason for us to speak. Departing America meant leaving behind my life as a lawyer, along with my former colleagues.

"How's it going, old buddy?" he cheerfully inquired, as if we had just spoken the day before. Maybe in Charlie's world that was how it worked, but not in mine.

"It's going great." I was wary, knowing he would not call unless he wanted or needed something. That was how guys like Charlie operate.

"It's been a while," he said. "Last time we met, you had just come into a ton of money and I helped you figure out how to enjoy it painlessly."

"And for that I am eternally grateful. But you're not calling to chew over old times."

"That's right," he said. "I'm calling to make you even more money."

There was a pause before my response.

"Charlie, I don't want or need any more money, especially if it means dealing with you.

"Nothing personal, but your services are the kind a person wants once in a lifetime. And only once." Emphasis was on the last word.

"Lightning does strike twice," Charlie countered. "No matter what the old wives' tales might be.

"And I've got a deal you can't say no to."

"Just watch me," I said.

"We're talking about some serious money here," Charlie said. "One million dollars, in cash, tax free.

"And the best thing about it is that the U.S. government is paying."

It was intriguing, but dangerous to take Charlie's bait.

"I don't need money and certainly don't need the government sniffing around me. If you recall, some of the things you did for me might not pass their muster."

Charlie was undeterred.

"Rest assured they don't know and never will know about the bank accounts and the Canadian passport," he said. "They wouldn't even care. And you would be doing them a big favor, for which they would be indebted, on top of the million they would be paying us."

"Us? So this is really about you making money, isn't it?"

"I'm not going to mislead you," Charlie said. "Of course a fair share should be paid to me for my facilitation and talents."

"Is that supposed to be reassuring?"

"Yes it is," Charlie replied. "Ten percent is quite reasonable."

"Let me tell you a little about what you'll be doing," he continued, before I could stop him.

"There's this Russian gangster living in Pattaya, about two hours from Bangkok," Charlie began.

I interrupted him.

"You'll never get me to that garbage dump, not even for the chance to meet a Russian gangster,"

"Get off your high horse," he countered. "No one is asking you to take a girl from a go-go bar." He knew me well even after all these years.

Apparently he also knew Pattaya. It seems like everyone in America knows about Pattaya, the urban swamp we call Sin City. My one and only trip there ended with the vow never to return.

"God forbid you ever have a good time with a woman with no strings attached," he continued. "But it's not necessary for this job."

Charlie kept talking. My desire was for the call to end. It couldn't happen soon enough for me.

"This fellow is wanted in America for everything under the sun, from gunrunning to money laundering to conspiracy to murder federal agents.

"Wouldn't surprise me if he even had a few unpaid parking tickets," he added. A forced chuckle followed.

"Well, Charlie, isn't this a job for the CIA or the FBI or somebody besides a former criminal defense lawyer living in Bangkok with an illegal bank account you set up? Not to mention a fake Canadian passport and a fake business visa?"

"I already told you nobody knows about your deal. Do you question the efficacy of my work?" he asked, a trace of hurt in his voice.

"Not at all. But that doesn't mean there's a need to go looking for trouble."

"Anyway," Charlie continued, ignoring my comment, "the U.S. government cannot be directly involved. If you recall, there was a big to-do a few years back when Thailand extradited another Russian gunrunning gangster to the U.S. Caused quite a kerfuffle between Thailand and Russia. And with all those Russians coming to Thailand, your adopted country can hardly afford to piss off Putin and the boys."

"I can assure you, Charlie, if every Russian in Thailand was shipped off to Vladivostok tomorrow, the Thai people would hold a week long celebration."

Again Charlie breezed past my comment and kept talking.

"The idea is for you to snag this bastard and ship him to America without any official Thai or American involvement. So it requires people with no government connections. People off the intelligence grid so to speak. Led by someone with brains and guts. Someone who can think on their feet. Someone nobody would ever suspect of being a U.S agent on a covert operation. Who is better suited than an American lawyer living in Thailand who knows the country like the back of his hand?"

I paused for a moment to absorb what Charlie was saying and looked at the back of my hand. Charlie has a grossly inflated idea of my knowledge of Thailand. My Thai was at best good enough to carry on a conversation with a two-year-old. My past relationships with Thai women were not much more impressive, my dreams of Noi were going nowhere and I had just been played by the General. So much for Mr. Thailand Expert.

"And even if we assume that somehow the U.S. government wanted me on their team, why would on earth would they go through you?"

Charlie had a ready answer.

"Remember my old college roommate Billy Sloane?" he asked.

"Never heard the name."

"Well that's good because Billy's line of work is not one that benefits by publicity. Billy joined the CIA right out of college, and today he heads up a unit that tracks down dangerous people when normal law enforcement can't get the job done. Deals with them as necessary. We've been friends forever."

"Sort of does for the CIA what you do for the legal system."

"You're more or less right," Charlie said. "Billy knows two things about me. One, as a man who can be trusted to keep my mouth shut, and two, a guy who will always get the job done. Something you too know quite well.

"Billy asked me if I could help out my country in this situation and assured me that everyone involved would be well compensated for their troubles. And as soon as he mentioned Thailand, guess who came to mind?"

"Are you expecting me to become a kidnapper? If so, you've come to the wrong guy. My old job was to defend criminals, not imitate them."

"Well, that's not entirely true," Charlie, responded.

"True or not, include me out. Tell your friends I am not interested."

"That won't be possible," Charlie replied. "I've already told them you were in. You'll be hearing from Billy."

"We'll be in touch," he said as he ended the call.

I THOUGHT ABOUT calling Charlie back and telling him to drop dead, but that would accomplish nothing. He wouldn't even answer his phone.

No doubt that what Charlie told me was true, at least as Charlie understood truth. One had to admit that Charlie was honorable in the way that there is honor among thieves. It was also certain that he withheld as much information as he provided. He was telling me only the best parts and they didn't sound all that good, the million dollars notwithstanding. What good was a million dollars if a Russian gangster killed you before you could spend it?

A desire to talk with someone wise burned within me, but could not done because it would mean revealing things best kept secret. This problem would have to be dealt with on my own. A cloak of worry wrapped itself tightly around me. Life was suddenly not as easy as before.

I rolled and smoked a joint and then headed off to the NJA Club for one of Ray's signature martinis. Of all my options, that seemed the best.

AS SOON AS he saw me walk through the door, Ray reached for the bottle of Tito's and poured it into the shaker with just a touch of vermouth and some ice cubes. I love the sound of the ice rattling against the metal of the shaker, and the sound almost tastes like a martini.

The martini was drained quickly, as Ray delighted in recounting the latest indignity to befall Phil Funston.

"The General came in earlier today with some European friends," Ray said with a grin.

"One was a rather attractive lady, if I say so myself, might have been in her forties but quite classy looking, way above Funston. But then again, isn't everyone?

"Funston starts yelling something out in French," Ray continued. "Tommy tells me it was the worst French he has ever heard but there was something about her breasts." Tommy was a New Zealander who spoke French.

"French lady stands up, stares at Funston, and says in perfect English, 'Fuck off, asshole, I once had a dog with a face like yours. Shaved his ass and had him walk backwards.'

"You should have seen Funston," Ray went on. "His big old bald head redder than a tomato and about to explode.

"Gave the lady's table drinks on the house.

"Sorry to talk like this about your countryman," Ray concluded.

"You're forgiven," I told him, pointing to my empty martini glass. He promptly prepared the refill. Ray knew that a rare second martini meant trouble. In the past he knew me to have more than one right after a breakup.

"One of those days?' he asked. I nodded yes.

Two vodka martinis and one large joint of Sleepy Joe's top-flight buds almost permitted me to forget the disturbing conversation with Charlie. My name being bandied about by CIA agents was enough to throw me into a maelstrom of worry. The worry escalated to outright panic upon considering that the CIA was trying to recruit me for a life-threatening task.

I slid off my bar stool and headed to the men's room. After emptying my bladder, I spied Oliver seated at a table with a plate of food and a pint of Foster's before him. He waved me over to the empty chair at his table.

Being with Oliver snapped me out of the deep funk that had overtaken me. No need to weather this hurricane alone when there was a trusted friend who could be counted on for good advice. If there was anyone who might find some answers to my questions, it was he.

I practically fell into the chair.

"Oliver, I need to talk to you. Privately. It's really serious. Maybe better at your place." He lived in a condo even closer to the Club than mine, and not walking any more than was necessary seemed like a good idea.

Oliver finished chewing on a forkful of *pad thai.*

"Soon as I finish my dinner, mate. Can I buy you a drink while you wait?"

"Why not?" I answered. Oliver caught Ray's attention, pointed a thumb my way, and Ray reached for the Tito's. He'd never before served me three in one day. Nobody ever had.

"Must be a hell of a day," he said as he brought the martini to life.

12

OLIVER'S CONDO WAS only three blocks away, but in my condition it took us fifteen minutes to walk there. It required great effort to proceed in a straight line without falling down. My mind was functioning almost as usual, but my body had become far less reliable. I was frightened and drunk. It brought to mind all the reasons for favoring smoking weed over drinking and my reason for the one martini per day limit.

None of this escaped Oliver.

"You're just not yourself, mate," he said as he watched me stumble along the *soi* leading to his building. "Never seen you drunk before. Looks like you broke your one drink rule."

"I'm not drunk. Just legally under the influence."

The *soi* was lined with food vendors. Bangkok has the best street food in the world. The scent of chicken grilling outside attracts me like honey attracts bears, and more often than not my discipline and diet yield to my desire, and the result is a piece of chicken on a stick for twenty baht. Sometimes I add sticky rice. That afternoon, the smell of street food made me nauseous.

The security guard at the gate greeted Oliver with a smile and let us inside. We walked through the small courtyard into the lobby. An attendant handed Oliver some mail as we walked to the elevator. The ride made me dizzy.

Oliver's place was on the sixth floor. His balcony had a better view than mine despite the lower floor, and the apartment was bigger and had nicer furniture. No one was home when we arrived.

"Girlfriend went off to Isan for week. Family business. Soon as we're done someone is coming over so let's get down to business," he said jovially.

"So you're meeting your *gik*," I replied, using the Thai slang for a relationship in addition to one already existing, like spouse or someone you lived with. Essentially a form of cheating. Someone like me could not have a *gik* as one first needs the principal relationship to violate. One cannot cheat on someone who doesn't yet exist. Oliver ignored my attempt to seem more experienced than in reality.

"But first let me brew you some coffee," he said

"Good idea," I croaked as he went to his kitchen. The coffee might jolt me enough to function.

While Oliver was brewing the coffee, I spied that day's issue of the Bangkok Post lying on the edge of the small table in front of the couch. I picked it up and skimmed the headlines. The military government running Thailand announced that there would be legislative elections at some unspecified date in the future, but first there would be a straight up or down vote on the new constitution they were proposing. People would be allowed to vote as they pleased, but they would not be able to campaign against the document. Democracy, Thai style. Then it struck me that when I came to Thailand, America was governed by a president who came to office after losing the popular vote. He won an electoral college vote only after the Supreme Court, controlled by his party, decided to stop a state recount in Florida where he was a few hundred votes ahead, in effect appointing him President. Thousands of ballots for his opponent were questionably disqualified. The Florida governor just happened to be the new president's brother. So it's not just Thailand.

Oliver brewed his coffee strong, like me. He was almost as fanatic about the bean. He carried a tray with two steaming mugs, a small beaker of milk and a few packets of real and fake sugar. I grabbed a mug and stirred in a packet of the fake stuff. This time milk was omitted to keep it as strong as possible. Oliver turned the television to the Australian news channel and kept the volume at a level just enough to hear without giving me a headache. We drank our coffee as the newscaster discussed the latest twists and turns in the leadership of the Australian Labour Party, a subject of little interest to me. I followed American politics up to a point, but Aussie politics was not on my radar screen. Oliver, a staunch supporter of the Australian conservatives, took it quite seriously, and he sporadically muttered obscenities about each of the Labour Party contenders.

When my cup was drained, Oliver turned off the television.

"So now maybe you can tell me what has driven a one martini man into drunkenness," he said with some concern in his voice.

I told him all, describing in detail the call from Charlie and filling him in on my own secrets. It was the first this had been discussed this with anyone except Charlie, and part of me felt uneasy but another part felt relieved. If Oliver did not know everything, he would not be able to give me the advice desperately needed. I trusted Oliver. He did not give any indication of what he thought of my finances or visa and since that day he has never brought up the subject.

When my account was concluded, Oliver closed his eyes for a moment and tented his hands on his lap. He sat that way for ten or fifteen seconds and then opened his eyes and relaxed his hands.

"We can believe your mate Charlie is on the level with you," he said. "It's a matter of record that Thailand did extradite a Russian gun runner and the Russians were none too pleased about that. It is also a matter of record, though maybe not public, that he was not the only one of his kind in this fair Kingdom.

"You know as well as any expat that someone with money can buy all sorts of protection around here. You in fact know that as well as anyone."

"Do you know anything about this specific Russian?" I asked. "And do you think there is any danger if the U.S. government starts looking at me?"

Oliver smiled.

"Mate, your man Charlie is several steps ahead of them, and when he assures you they will never find out about your bank accounts and Canadian passport, he's quite right. As for your Thai business visa, that's been bought and paid for and it's none of America's business. Hell, even the Thai government can't get that information."

My mug was empty. Oliver saw me peering into the empty vessel.

"How about if we brew two more cups while I make a few calls," he said with a smile.

"Sounds good to me," I replied as Oliver hoisted his large frame from the sofa and walked towards his kitchen.

Oliver did not seem to consider the possibility that he might not reach whomever he was trying to call. In his line of work, one always knows how to reach people.

He proved that right.

Ten minutes later, Oliver reentered the living room, carrying a freshly filled mug in each hand. He placed one before me as he sat down.

"It's all on the level," Oliver said as he stirred his own mug.

"My contact is never wrong and he tells me that the U.S. has a real hard-on for this guy. Name is Polinov. Viktor Polinov. His nickname is Alexi, don't ask why. The CIA swears that he has sold every type of weapon imaginable to any terrorist group with the money to pay. Some of these weapons have been used to kill Americans in uniform as well as American agents and their foreign assets. And it seems to be going on with the full knowledge and approval of Mr. Vladimir Putin, who has no love lost for you Yanks."

"They've asked the Thais to arrest him and extradite him," he continued, "but so far not even a response.

"Can't quite blame the Thais," he added. "They've got their own problems down South as you know, and it seems as if the Polinov fellow will not allow any arms to get to the jihadists down there so long as the Thais leave him alone.

"Thailand is in no position to take on Putin," he added.

"And I am?"

Oliver gently placed his mug on the coffee table and turned his gaze to mine.

"Glenn, my mate, the U.S. government didn't just pick your name out of a hat."

"What is that supposed to mean?"

"It means two things," Oliver replied. "First, they are convinced that you can handle the job, and believe it or not, despite your apparent lack of qualifications or experience, one cannot disagree with them."

"You think I can handle a shootout with a gunrunning Russian mobster?"

"Not at all, Oliver replied. "And your government does not think it would ever get to that. Your brains and your charm are your skill set, not to mention seven years living in this mysterious place.

"They want you to trick Polinov so you can disable him and deliver him into the hands of some rather covert operatives who will spirit him out of here. The Russians will howl, the Thais will feign ignorance, the American government will jump for joy, and you will lug mounds of money to the bank."

"I appreciate the faith they have in me, but still not interested."

"Allow me to address the second point," he instructed.

"And what might that be?"

Oliver paused, took a sip of coffee, and replied.

"They believe that despite your current obstinacy, they will get you to change your mind and do the job they ask," he said.

"What are they going to do?" I asked. "Waterboard me? Apply

electrical shocks to my genitals?"

Oliver smiled.

"You've been reading too many newspaper stories," he said. "There are no secrets they want from you. These guys are experts in getting people to do things they never thought they would do, and they don't have to lay finger on a person to get them to act as they want. Everyone has something that matters to them and is enough to force them do as the government asks. For some it may be the money, for others it might be something else."

"And what could I want that they could use as leverage?"

Oliver smiled again.

"That my friend, is what you will soon find out."

13

IT HAD BEEN a pleasant walk from the Club to my condo. The temperature was mild for Bangkok, not a degree above eighty. There was a modest breeze. While strolling home my mind replayed the scene of Mai insulting Phil Funston after another of his lewd comments a half hour earlier.

"Phil, you look like ladyboy," she had told him in a voice just loud enough to be heard by everyone present. "Put on wig and look for guys, not ladies. But you so fat you look pregnant and maybe guys will not like you."

Funston had cursed and snarled as the Club erupted in laughter. What Mai said wasn't even all that funny but we enjoyed any opportunity to embarrass Funston. It was necessary to explain to Thais and *farangs* from other countries that Funston did not represent Americans. My resentment towards him was constantly growing.

Once in the vestibule of my apartment, I sensed something was amiss. Light was coming from the living room. It was my diligent practice to turn off all lights and air conditioner upon leaving. It's the least one can do for the environment.

I walked slowly towards the living room. Two men were sitting on my couch. A lamp was switched on. They stood as I entered.

I assumed the defensive posture learned in *Muay Thai* class. Five years of study did not prepare me for this. I had not felt such fear since the day my client was shot dead before me in the parking lot in the East Bay. This was not the vague fear of the unknown, felt at the police station when helping Sleepy Joe. This was the fear of death.

The fellow on the left was a white man about my age, somewhere between his late forties and early fifties, with medium-length dirty blond hair, an inch taller than me, slightly overweight, wearing a long sleeve white shirt and khakis. His companion was much younger, no more than thirty, African-American, with close-cropped hair. He wore a black t-shirt and jeans. He was lean and muscular and, at five-foot-ten, was as tall as me.

The older man spoke first. He had a deep Southern accent that flowed like syrup.

"You don't have to be afraid, Glenn. We're not here to harm you. Actually, we are here to help you."

Something about the way he spoke calmed my fear enough to allow me to think. His voice was smooth and slow. The same instincts that had guided me in picking juries and deciding when to believe clients told me they were not here to do me physical harm.

The younger man spoke, with no discernible accent, in what broadcasters call standard American English.

"You can put down your guard," he said. "I'm black belt in taekwondo and karate," he added. "You're doing it all wrong anyway."

My hands dropped to my sides. He was right about doing it all wrong.

"Who are you?" I asked. "Why are you here and how did you get in?"

The older man smiled. He flashed a billfold with a bright badge. It said CIA.

"My name is Billy Sloane and my colleague is Rodney Snapp. And as for how we got in, let's just say we go where we want and nothing stops us." He sat down again and motioned for Snapp and me to do the same. Snapp sat on the couch next to Billy Sloane with me on the reclining chair.

"No doubt you recognize my name," Sloane said after we were all seated.

I said nothing.

"Charlie said you were a cool customer and looks like he was right."

Again, silence from me.

"Glenn, if I may call you that," Sloane continued, "we have things to talk about and it will be difficult if you don't open your mouth."

"How about you guys get out of my apartment," I shouted while rising from my chair. "And don't let the door bang your asses on your way out."

"Just sit down, Glenn," Billy Sloane said in a friendly but firm voice. "We came here to help you. Make you some money along the way. You were a lawyer after all, so that means you probably did a lot worse than we're asking of you."

"I don't want your money. And don't want you in my house. So get out now."

Sloane went on talking, ignoring me.

"And on top of the money, you get our help," he said looking into my eyes.

"I don't need your help either."

Sloane slowly shook his head.

"No, you're right. Maybe you don't need our help. But your girlfriend might."

"My girlfriend?" I stammered.

"The one you call Noi, though doubtful that's her real name," Sloane replied. "But whatever, we can help her out of her jam," he said with a smile.

My fear was almost gone. The vacuum it left was filling with anger. My thoughts turned to violence against Billy Sloane. And then Charlie.

"Did you have anything to do with what's happening to Noi?"

My words were shouted at Sloane. "If you did, you're going to need your buddy's black belts."

Rodney Snapp rose and walked to me, placing a hand on my shoulder. His touch was as gentle as his voice. He was not at all threatening.

"Just take it easy, Glenn. No one is here to fight. Like Billy said, we are here to help."

"Then why not call me or e-mail me or do something other than breaking into my house like burglars?"

"Because you would have ignored us," Rodney said in a voice just above a whisper.

"Please have a seat and hear us out," he added.

I stood still for a moment and then did as he requested. There was no better option.

~

RODNEY SNAPP'S VOICE was soft and confident.

"Billy and I are in a dangerous business because we live in a dangerous world. Every day we wake up knowing that if we don't do something to stop the bad guys, innocent people are going to get hurt. We have to stop as many as we can. Sometimes that means we can't play by the rules. But playing outside the rules has its own set of rules."

"I think I understand what you're saying. But why me? There must be professionals. Soldiers of fortunes, Mercenaries. Private eyes. Anyone but me. You couldn't make a worse choice." How could they be serious about talking to me about covert CIA operations?

Billy Sloane broke in.

"That's exactly why we're here, Glenn. These Russians would spot any of those people right off the bat. Miles away. They're trained to do it. They develop a sixth sense. Just like we do. We never underestimate the enemy. They're tough and they're smart.

"And my sixth sense tells me you are right for this. No one is going to think you are any kind of agent but you have the smarts to do what it takes. We want this guy alive and you can get him to us."

Rodney Snapp took the lead again.

"Glenn, we know this must sound crazy to you. Like something out of a cheap novel. But it's not. This is how things have to be done sometimes.

"Now we believe you don't care about money, and we believe you doubt your own capabilities." Rodney pressed his palms together and pointed the finger tips upward just above his lap, tilted his head ever so slightly, then sat upright and looked at me.

"Glenn, it doesn't matter why your dear friend Noi is in trouble and it doesn't matter who had anything to do with it. What matters now is that you can make it all go away and earn some serious money for you and your friends. You may not care about money but some of your friends might."

The reference to my friends did not sound ominous as did the reference to Noi. Snapp explained what he meant.

"You're not going to do this all alone. You are going to need a few friends along with you. They must be friends, because you need to trust them, and they are going to become rich thanks to you. They all have to be like you, below anybody's radar screen, especially the Russian mob's radar screen. And the minute you say yes, we take care of Noi's problems. Forever. As long as you take the job. Results required for the cash but not for helping Noi."

"You mean before I even do anything, she's in the clear? All charges dropped?"

"That's what the man said," Billy Sloane barked. The syrup was gone from his voice.

"How do you know you can trust me? How can you be so sure I

won't flake out on you after you take care of Noi?"

Billy Sloane smiled in the way a crocodile smiles. A smile that can make one shiver even in the tropics.

"Glenn, you may be many things, but you ain't stupid as the saying goes. You know that the hand than giveth can taketh away," he said through that chilling smile. He was back to the syrupy drawl. He could switch moods effortlessly.

"And besides," Rodney Snapp interjected, "You're a man of your word. You're the guy who keeps his promises no matter how painful. A rare quality these days. We respect that in a man."

"Rodney here is a trained profiler, among his other good points," Sloane said. "And what our pal Charlie said about you has been confirmed. Thinks the world of you, by the way."

Rodney Snapp resumed talking.

"You're also a guy who does the right thing. You showed that when you helped Sleepy Joe and then Noi. There was nothing in it for you except your own sense of what's right.

"We know you were scared when you went to that police station and when you called on the General," Rodney Snapp continued. "But you overcame your fear and did what needed to be done. You learned on the job and you did so quickly. And you succeeded."

"Just the kind of fellow for a job like this," Billy Sloane interjected.

They weren't going to get the pleasure of my asking how they knew these things. And they were not learning from me that saving Sleepy Joe also saved my supply of weed. No sense in telling them what little they did not already know.

"Let's figure something out," Rodney said. I nodded in agreement.

BILLY SLOANE CONCEDED there was danger but assured me it could be minimized.

"We're not looking to have you get yourselves involved in a shootout with Polinov and his Russian thugs," he explained. "That's just what we're trying to avoid. A shootout and your dead body won't help us one bit. We're looking to do this without anyone getting hurt. Unless we have to save your life. You won't have firearms anyway, so you won't start a shootout by mistake.

"You're going to be doing this with your brains," he continued. "That's why we picked you. You don't know how to use a gun anyway."

We were sipping beers in my living room. Once they had my agreement to do what they wanted, they were easy to be with. They could almost be called nice guys, but they were CIA special operatives so that couldn't be true. Not with Billy Sloane for certain. As a lawyer my cases had brought me across people like him before. Something about Billy, despite his mostly good-ole-boy Southern style, warned me that he was a dangerous and amoral man. I couldn't put my finger on exactly why. It was that trial lawyer's instinct rising within me again.

Rodney Snapp laid out the details. Oliver was right; the Russian was named Viktor Polinov but he liked to be called Alexi. In person he might seem likable, even sociable and generous but he was a man who peddled death and destruction without a thought to the victims.

He explained that Polinov was supplying deadly weapons to terrorists throughout the Middle East and to Russian proxy troops in Ukraine. He had sold to terrorists who had killed Americans. He was under indictment in the U.S. but after the diplomatic tiff between Thailand and Russia the last time the Kingdom extradited a Russian gangster to America, the Thais wanted nothing to do with this and made this known to America in no uncertain terms. There were still many Russians in the country and they were a source of cash. As long as Polinov wasn't selling to Muslim terrorists in the South of Thailand or to Thai gangsters, the government did not want to roil the waters with Russia again.

The Thais were shrewd diplomats. They have made an art out of balancing interests between America and the West, Russia and China. They did not want to upset this delicate ballet. They discretely let the Americans know that Thailand would not lodge protests if Mr. Polinov were to be removed without official American government involvement. Under American law, it would not matter how Polinov was brought to the U.S., so long as he was there. So if the U.S. could get him out of Thailand without leaving their own fingerprints, everyone except Polinov and Russia would be happy and there wouldn't be much the latter could do.

Rodney explained that Polinov had his own intelligence and security resources as well those of the Russian government, and his people would identify any American agent, official or unofficial.

"But you're off the radar screen, not possibly in their data base. Same with the people you use. We think you know what this means," Rodney said.

"Since there is no record of Sleepy Joe's arrest, he is off their radar as well?" I asked.

"Exactly," Rodney replied. "Same as it will be with Noi. No record for her because of what you are doing for your country."

"Let's keep Noi out of this," I snapped, sensing another implied threat of danger to her.

Rodney looked at Sloane and then turned to me.

"In case you have forgotten, she's about as in as in can be. You're getting her out."

RODNEY SNAPP AND Billy Sloane made it sound easy. Without doubt that was their intention. As a trial lawyer, it had been my task to persuade reasonable jurors to reach unreasonable conclusions. Trying to persuade me that I could snatch a Russian gunrunner was more difficult but the tactic the same. They were good but they still didn't make me believe it was going to be as easy as they made it sound.

"Basically all you're doing is leading this guy on to follow you, then disable him and deliver him to us," Billy Sloane began, as if he were merely giving directions to a restaurant. "We'll give you something to put the bastard to sleep."

"Aren't these guys guarded? Aren't they trained to spot thing like this?" I asked.

"Generally yes," Rodney Snapp replied. "But like everything else in life, they go by markers. Familiar signs. Indications that something they are expecting is about to happen. They have ideas in their mind as to who might be wanting to do them harm. But no one is going to look at you or your crew and think danger or kidnap. They'll think you're a bunch of sex tourists just gawking at things they don't see back home."

It was not pleasant hearing that they expected me to act like Phil Funston or his ilk. That could not be my greatest concern but it was certainly disagreeable.

"How on earth am I supposed to get this gangster away from his bodyguards and carry him off like a sack of potatoes?"

"That's what we're paying you a million bucks to accomplish," Billy Sloane answered. "But don't worry, we're going to help you as much as we can."

We spent another hour in which they provided me background, educating me about Polinov and his criminal organization, and where he liked to go to take a break from the busy life of a crime boss. How he could be friendly, and even engaging when it suited him, and how he enjoyed living in and hanging out in Pattaya, eating and drinking at some of the fanciest bars and restaurants, and sometimes visiting one of the brothels that specialized in Eastern European women. He mostly kept to venues owned by or populated by Russians but occasionally dined at popular restaurants that were not Russian owned.

"Knows he can trust Russian joints, because everyone in those places has family that Polinov can reach. He doesn't trust the Thais because he has no holds on them."

"We'll wait until he is someplace not Russian," Sloane interjected.

When our chat time ended, the two of them rose in unison and extended their hands. I shook each quickly. Rodney's grip was strong. Sloane's was weak and his hand brought to mind what a dead eel must feel like.

"Rodney will be calling you tomorrow to meet and then go on to the next step," Billy Sloane said as they walked to the door. When he calls, you just go where he tells you," he added with that crocodile smile.

Then they were gone. Their presence, however, remained in my apartment for days.

14

WHEN I ARRIVED at the restaurant, Sleepy Joe was already seated at a table upstairs by the edge of the veranda, looking out on the *soi*. We were in a quiet stretch of the upscale Ekamai neighborhood, a few hundred meters down from Sukhumvit, the main road. But for the high-rise condos looming over us, one would never think we were in the midst of a densely populated metropolis. At this time of day the restaurant was empty.

Sleepy Joe was nursing a pint of Chang beer. This restaurant sold it for 90 baht, the cheapest in the Green Belt. Many *farangs* turn down their noses at Chang, claiming it to be far worse than the ubiquitous Singha or the trendier Leo. I find all Thai beers weak and tasteless, and the foreign brands sold here are no better, just more expensive. Then again, I'm not a serious beer drinker and only occasionally touch the stuff. Chang was fine with me, and having learned to drink it with ice like the Thais, it hardly tasted like beer, which is also fine with me. On that day weak Thai beer seemed a wiser choice than my daily martini. Doubtful this restaurant could match Ray anyway.

A pretty, young waitress came for our orders. My choice was a favorite, vegetarian *pad thai*, along with a pint of Chang. Sleepy Joe had the spicy papaya salad known as *som tum thai*. That was also a favorite dish of mine, but my appetite just wasn't for highly spiced food that day. It requires a certain state of mind to focus on the intense conversation about to start, and there was no room for distraction by the fire of my food.

My pint was set before me almost immediately as was Joe's second. We spoke as we worked our way through our beers.

"So what's so important that you had to drag me away from my favorite masseuse?" he asked.

"A chance to help your dear friend Glenn and make a ton of money along the way." With Sleepy Joe both points would score.

"I'm all ears," he said, though in truth his ears were hidden by his greasy and unkempt shoulder length hair. He looked like General Custer after a long slog through Indian country.

Sleepy Joe listened carefully to everything about the kidnap scheme, even the part about Noi. My two Joes in Bangkok could be trusted with anything, including my life.

When I was done, Sleepy Joe took a gargantuan slug of beer, draining almost half the second pint in one swill.

"You mean to say all I got to do is watch your back in Pattaya and walk away with a cool hundred fifty thousand U.S.?"

"You're there more as a lookout. Joe Potowski is supplying the muscle we need."

Sleepy Joe looked downcast and hurt when he heard this. He frowned.

"No offense to Rhode Island," he said. "But when it comes to the rough stuff, you're looking at the man."

"I know you were Aussie Army once upon a time," I replied. "But that was some time ago and to be honest, right now you don't look all that threatening."

"Not just Army. Special Forces! A Commando!" he exclaimed as he leaned towards me

"Sorry, no offense intended," I said putting up my hands, palms facing him.

"You're going to learn something about me you never knew,"

Sleepy Joe said.

He stood up and placed his hands behind his back, grasping his left wrist with his right hand. He tilted his head and cocked it just a bit to the left.

"Take your best shot," he ordered. "Full force. Let's see that powerful right hook you lawyers must all possess."

I laughed while looking at this disheveled scarecrow of a man inviting a punch from a guy who works out in his condo gym five days a week and had studied *Muay Thai* for years.

"Sorry if I insulted you but no way I could never harm to as good a friend as you."

"Don't worry," Joe said. "You couldn't hurt me if you tried. Come on, just one good punch. That's all that's being asked of you."

It was crazy. His pride had been hurt and needed fixing. The solution was to throw a punch just hard enough to make him feel it but which would not break anything.

I stood up and faced him within my arm reach.

"Okay, but don't send me any dental bills."

I lifted my right arm, fist tightly clenched, pulled it back, and threw what turned out to be a harder blow than wanted. Before regret set in everything disappeared from sight and I was immobile.

I never saw how or when he did it, but Sleepy Joe had pushed me face down on the table, one hand on my neck with the elbow pressing down on my left arm, the other hand pushing by right arm up towards my neck in a strong lock. He stood right behind me, pressed up against my torso. Not a single part of my body was free to move and I could barely breathe.

"Like I told you, Special Forces." he said as he released me from his hold.

I sat down and caught my breath. All the air had gone out of me when he pushed me down. Joe remained standing.

"Wow, who would have ever dreamed this?" I said when my lungs were back to normal.

"Never fear when with me," he said with a lopsided grin.

"But what if someone pulls a gun on us?"

"You have no faith in me, do you?" he asked. He threw up his hands in exasperation.

"Here is another little trick," he said. Pick up that fork and point it at me as if it were a gun," he ordered.

"Come on, Joe, this is ridiculous, " I said, but did stand up and hold my fork as if it were a gun, the tines pointed at Joe's chest.

"Threaten me like a gunman would," he commanded.

"Okay, you dirty rat," I called out in my best James Cagney voice. "Eat lead!"

That was about all I was able to say before the fork was knocked out of my hand onto the floor, and my forearm started to hurt something fierce. I never saw Joe move a hand.

"You had your eyes on your gun, my face, looking around, all the wrong places, not on my hands. Don't feel bad, everyone is like that."

Joe had that lopsided grin spread across his thin face. He sat down and motioned for me to do the same.

"Once Aussie Special Forces, always Aussie Special Forces," he said.

"With guys like you on our side it's a wonder we lost in Vietnam." I said upon recovering my composure.

"They didn't allow five year olds to enlist," he replied.

"Just to let you know, we are going to be unarmed. No guns for us. But the Russians can have as many as they want."

"You've just seen what this Aussie can do," Sleepy Joe said. "Do you really think we need guns?

"Besides, brains can be a lot more dangerous than a gun."

"I guess that means you're in," I said.

"Of course. Where's a bloke like me to come up with a hundred fifty thousand U.S. dollars?"

We finished our beers in silence. When we left the restaurant my mind was a lot more at ease than since I agreed to take on Polinov.

15

OLIVER WOULD OPERATE on a strictly cash basis, billing me by the task. He was willing to wait until the CIA paid me.

"You can afford my bill even if something goes wrong, and I know you would pay," he told me as we ate lunch amidst the bustle of one of my favorite restaurants, an Isan place on Ekamai *Soi* 10, set in a huge barn like structure. It was a favorite of the many Isan natives living in Bangkok, an assurance that it was good. Spicy Isan food is not for every *farang*, but it works for me and the noise of the crowd provided cover for my discussion with Oliver. After my meeting with Sleepy Joe, indulging in my passion for three-alarm cuisine seemed like a fair reward for signing such a recruit.

"How soon can you have more background and some suggestions for me?"

Oliver thought for a moment and then replied.

"If all goes well and everyone gets back to me quickly, you should have something by tomorrow around this time," he said.

"And that includes helping me figure out a plan?"

"We'll talk after you mastered the background materials they give you and have your team in place. And after your two fellow Yanks share their further thoughts with you. Rest assured they will have a few suggestions. That's what they do, after all. Recruit people to do their dirty work. I'll help you fine tune and tailor the plan and provide you with details you might find helpful," Oliver told me.

"Most of my job is to make sure you know whatever you need to know. There are things I know better than the CIA. No way they have access to the same information as me in Thailand. They could never match my connections."

We each finished a large Singha with our lunch. I was grasping for anything which would make me feel less tense, even if it were Thai beer. I felt the effects of the alcohol in the middle of the day, and Oliver, recalling my last bout of drinking, waved off the waitress when she motioned for a refill. I was drinking too much alcohol these days and really ought to stick with weed.

"You worried, mate?" Oliver asked after draining his glass. "Wouldn't blame you one bit. Never did anything like this before, am I right?"

"Couldn't be more right," I replied.

"Look, mate," Oliver said as he pushed his plate and glass aside, "I'm not going to kid you. These are some rough characters you're going up against. They kill and maim people as a matter of course. But you have the element of surprise. No one is suspecting someone like you. You could pass Polinov close enough to bite him on the ass and you wouldn't be made as an American agent. Especially when you look like just another horny *farang* with a rent-a-girlfriend half his age. Besides, right now our friend Polinov is more worried about rival Russian gangs than he is about an American operation. The competition smells blood with him being wanted by you Yanks. They would be praying for your success if they knew. With his own security, and the Thai cops on his payroll, Polinov feels somewhat protected here against other Russians but knows that could change at any time. Those other Russians and the U.S. government are his main concerns. He's not worrying about sex starved sleazeballs."

"Just what I always wanted the world to think of me. My mother would be so proud if she were still alive."

We paid the bill and each went our separate way. I started walking home and Oliver went off to the Club. We agreed to meet there later. On the way home what Oliver had called me rang through my mind.

An American agent.

WHILE TURNING THE corner onto Sukhumvit Road my cell phone rang. I recognized Rodney Snapp's voice as soon as he spoke.

"Terminal 21 food court, far left side. Ten minutes." Then he hung up.

I entered the Thong Lor BTS Station right there on Sukhumvit and got off at Asoke and the Terminal 21 mall. Rodney was seated in the food court where he said he would be. He was wearing a New York Yankees baseball cap.

"Giants fan," I said while sliding into the seat opposite him.

"Red Sox," he replied. "But this is the hat they gave me."

"I must tell you," I began, "my respect for the U.S. government has not increased, knowing that they think the best person for a dangerous covert action is me."

"Nor has mine," Rodney said with a smile. "But as the saying goes, 'it is what it is.'"

"That saying makes no sense now, does it?"

Rodney paid no attention to my comment and pulled a manila envelope from his side and placed it in the middle of our table.

"Inside are several pictures of Polinov," Rodney explained. "We've had him under surveillance for months. The two big guys hanging around him are his bodyguards. Consider them armed and dangerous. Former Russian intelligence.

"The best in their business," Rodney added. The professional admiration in his voice could not be missed.

"There is also a brief background report on Polinov. His criminal history, personal history, likes and dislikes, his modus operandi in committing crimes, and any personality traits we know about. Will help you figure him out and know what to do in a given situation. Make sure you read it well and absorb every bit. If it wasn't important it wouldn't be in there.

"There's also a map of Pattaya, with the important streets highlighted," Rodney continued. "We expect you to memorize those streets and have that map in your head at all times."

"How about a surveillance trip down there first?" I asked, trying to sound like someone who knew what they were talking about.

"Absolutely not," Rodney replied. His voice was firm and his tone dismissive. "We can't take any chance that you would be noticed by Polinov's people if you show up more than once. Remember what I told you. These guys are good.

"And finally," Rodney added, "you will see two phone numbers. The first one is the number you use if you need to contact me before leaving Bangkok. The other number is the one you call on the day of the operation. When you've got Polinov under control. Only then."

He handed me the envelope.

"We will tell you when the day arrives and it will be soon," Rodney said. "And you will be expected to deliver us one live Polinov, for which you will be paid one million dollars in cash and needless to say, the government of the United States will be most appreciative."

"But no one has told me how to catch this guy," I countered.

"We will tell you where to go to find Polinov," Rodney explained. "A bar or restaurant or some other public place. It won't be Russian. You and your crew will arrive separately, you with a lady and the others on their own. They won't acknowledge you at all.

"He's never going to suspect you," Rodney explained. "He's going to see another middle aged sexpat in Pattaya with a bar girl half his age. Living in Sin City, Polinov won't raise an eyebrow. He sees guys like that all the time. They're a dime a dozen down there."

"And where am I supposed to get the young lady?"

Rodney gave me a strange look.

"Don't know if anybody has ever clued you in on this, Glenn, he said, "but that's about the easiest thing in the world in Pattaya."

"You mean you expect me to walk into some sleazy bar and walk out with a hooker, like some degenerate loser?"

"Exactly," Rodney responded. "Didn't take you long to figure that one out now, did it?

"The good news is you don't have to actually engage her services," he explained. "Get rid of her right before you make your move on Polinov."

I bit my tongue to hold it in place until the urge to scream profanities subsided, then probed him on what to do after arrangements were made with the woman to be named later.

"How am I supposed to grab this tough guy with the two bodyguards you say are the best in the business?"

"You're going to use your wit, your charm, your feigned sleaziness, whatever it takes, to get next to Polinov and neutralize his bodyguards. Your friends will be helping with this part. Your friend Sleepy Joe was made for this sort of thing. A man with your experience should be able to strike up a conversation with Polinov and that's what you aim for. Makes it easier to get close enough to him to do what is needed. After he is engrossed and not paying much attention to anything but you, disable him with the chemical spray which will be provided when you get to Pattaya. Then you drag his sorry ass to our rendezvous spot and hand him over to us."

Rodney offered to get us some food. I pointed him in the direction of my favorite stand and told him what to bring me. He left me alone with my thoughts.

There is no way this is going to work. This is crazy, makes no sense. Why is it the government can grab Polinov from me and sneak him out of Thailand, but can't snatch him themselves? How does bringing in a bunch of amateurs help things? Oliver would tell me. There would never be a straight answer from Rodney Snapp or Billy Sloane.

Rodney returned and I worked my way through a plate of *pad thai* with steamed mussels and vegetables. Rodney even brought over little dishes of spices. Rodney pushed his food onto his spoon with his fork, Thai style. He struck me as the kind of man who always did things correctly.

"How do you put up with that idiot Sloane?" I asked

"Billy's not half so bad," Rodney said. "He's a true believer, lost close friends in the field. Think of him as a real patriot, risking his life and still having to worry about paying the bills."

"Sounds like this time it's my life he's risking," I retorted.

THE NEXT HOUR was spent listening to Rodney. Over plates of more *pad thai*, morning glory with garlic, and diced chicken with basil, he explained how to detect if one was being followed and what to do to lose the tail. He told me how to look at a person and know if they are armed, and what to say and do if exposed or confronted. He made it sound easy, but in my gut I knew he was only putting on a gloss, trying to calm my fears.

"I'll be checking in with you regularly over the next two weeks," Rodney told me as we got up from the table. "By then we should be ready to go to work."

It was at relief to learn that my future dealings would be with Rodney and not Billy Sloane, and I let Rodney know.

He laughed before he spoke.

"Like I said, Billy can be a piece of work, but he is the real thing when it comes to patriotism, and let me assure you, whatever you might think, he's got your back covered every inch of the way. Billy takes care of his people. Every promise will be kept, and you can be assured of that."

Our meeting was over to my relief, as neither my stomach nor my brain had room for anything more.

We parted outside the restaurant. I headed back to my condo. Where did Rodney go? Did he live in Bangkok? He seemed so at home here. Then I decided intelligence gathering was Snapp and Sloane's game, not mine, so those thoughts were abandoned.

After leaving the air conditioned Terminal 21 for the sultry streets of Sukhumvit Road, the heat and humidity grabbed me like a mugger overpowering a victim on the streets of New York City circa 1980. Despite the steamy weather, my choice was to walk back to Ekamai, a good mile away. The walk was needed to burn off all the food consumed during my meeting with Rodney.

During daytime, the streets of Bangkok teem with life and commerce. All manner of food, goods and services are available on the streets: grilled meats, rice, noodles, fruit, also clothing, music, housewares, lottery tickets, shoe repair, seamstresses, watch batteries, Viagra. A consumer could live their whole life in Bangkok without setting foot in a regular store.

Ten blocks into my trek, the heat and walk forced me to take a break. I bought a bottle of water from a makeshift convenience stand that looked like it was once a one-car garage with the front open to the street. As the water poured down my gullet, someone called my name.

It was Panchen, the lawyer. He was wearing a well-tailored suit and a silk tie, not the same ones he had worn during our office visit. He carried a small thin leather briefcase.

"What a coincidence it is, meeting you like this," he said. "I was just on my way back to the office from a meeting. I planned to call you this evening."

"About what?"

"Let me buy you a drink and we can talk," he replied.

I followed Panchen a short way along Sukhumvit then down a numbered *soi* onto a smaller side street. A few meters down we went through a nondescript doorway and were inside a bar. Panchen lead the way to a table.

"This place may not look like much, but it is a favorite of many powerful people," he assured me as we sat down.

Panchen ordered a scotch on the rocks and I had a diet Coke. My vow to never again exceed my one martini a day alcohol limit was being strictly enforced.

"First let me tell you the good news about Noi," Panchen said after the waitress left. "The subpoena has been withdrawn. Neither government has any further interest in her. I was going to refund most of your retainer," he added.

"No need for that. You were paid for your availability and counsel and that was what we got. Your appeal got us the time needed for them to see things straight."

"I've never seen anything like this before," Panchen said after our drinks arrived. "First they go after her with everything they have and then the case is dropped without explanation. Somebody is going to be in trouble over this."

"You got that right," I replied wondering who was in trouble and hoping it wasn't me.

"If I may change the subject, why did you stop being a lawyer?" Panchen asked.

"Too much stress, too much running around. It stopped being fun and was making me crazy." That was no lie.

"We lawyers over here have our own stress factors," Panchen said, "just different than what you have in the U.S."

"You seem to know a bit about the U.S. and you speak English with an American touch," I told him.

"I spent three years getting a Ph.D in political science at the University of Michigan," he informed me.

"I was going to be a lawyer in the Foreign Ministry," he explained. "Specializing in America," he added.

"So what happened?

"The money is a lot better working in the private sector. But let's focus on the current state of affairs. My understanding of America and my specialized skills and studies have informed me that there is more here than meets the eye."

"That's what we hired you to find out," I responded, deflecting his obvious probe.

"Not exactly," the lawyer parried. "You hired me to delay the process and defend Noi's privacy rights under Thai law," he explained. "The underlying facts can be discovered from many sources, the most accessible being the client."

"I'm not the client, only the guy who paid the fee and as you know, that and twenty-five baht will get me on the BTS."

Panchen smiled and looked at me.

"You are holding something back, *Khun* Glenn. Every cell in my lawyer body detects that simple truth. You may choose to keep it to yourself, but I know you are hiding something important."

I had sized Panchen up perfectly upon first meeting him. A fine lawyer with a natural ability to see beyond the obvious and the known, instinctively feeling what others do not. Such lawyers detect something in the most minimal body or facial gestures, signs the rest of the world fails to perceive. Great lawyers understand that the way a person answers a question is more revealing than the answer itself. This innate ability can be developed but not taught. One is born with it or else does not have it. Lawyers who possess this gift can predict the effect of evidence on a jury, arguments to a judge, and the impact of questions asked from a witness. In this proceeding, the witness was me and Panchen was cross-examining me in a bar as skillfully as if we were in a courtroom. Panchen had this intuitive talent and had developed it to a very high degree. I believed myself to have been a very good lawyer, with the same gift, but Panchen had taken his to higher levels.

"Why do you need to know, assuming there is anything to know?" The desperation in my voice was obvious even to me.

"*Khun* Glenn, in my twenty-five years of practice, I have never lost a client to death and don't intend to start now. And that extends to people who pay the client's fees."

"Do you think Noi or I are in danger? Sounds like you think one of us is."

"Not Noi," he replied. "I will watch out for my client. But you believe yourself to be in a dangerous situation. The criminal lawyer within you is giving you a warning. Why is that? Maybe you should listen to your inner being, The one every good lawyer possesses."

That highly developed instinct of Panchen's revealed my fears to him.

A rush of that fear surged through my body. By slowly breathing as I had been taught in meditation class, I calmed myself as best as possible and sat quietly for a moment, hoping my mind would clear itself. That often worked, but this time it yielded minimal relief.

I told Panchen I had to leave to meet an old friend. It was true. Rhode Island Joe had to be spoken with and brought on board. In difficult times, having a good friend at your side can make all the difference in the world. These times were certainly difficult.

"Call me when you want to talk," Panchen said as we rose to leave. "Hopefully sooner not later." He emphasized "sooner."

"One more thing," he added as we walked onto the street. "Occasionally in my practice, questions about American law and procedure arise, often in your former area of criminal law. Perhaps you could assist as a legal advisor in such matters. You would of course be compensated for your time and effort," he added.

"I haven't practiced in seven years. My knowledge is surely out of date."

"We both know that your real talents do not depend on current knowledge of the law," he replied. We shook hands, American style.

"Be careful," he said as we parted. Panchen walked briskly and reached Sukhumvit ahead of me.

We went our separate ways. My eyes gazed at his figure until it was swallowed up by the sea of people on Sukhumvit and he disappeared into the horde.

WAS IT REALLY coincidence that Panchen had met me on the street? That area was not known for law or business offices. What was the meaning of his offer to employ me, and more importantly, what was he warning me about? Over the past few days enough had happened to require a scorecard to figure out which threat was being faced at any given moment.

I am not one who believes in conspiracies or far-fetched theories when there are simple explanations. Sudden circumstances outside my control had pulled me into a world I had not known and hit me with full force in the face. My friend the General had exploited our friendship for personal gain and revenge, and my own government had threatened the woman I loved in order to force me into a dangerous and harebrained scheme that could get me killed. Against that backdrop, meeting Noi's lawyer on the street had to be considered suspicious.

What was Panchen trying to accomplish? He had asked me to call him "when I wanted to talk" but he said it should be soon. That meant to call him right away. Then he warned me to be careful. But of what?

My own trial lawyer's instincts told me that meeting Panchen was no coincidence and his request to talk was to inform me of some danger facing me. This meant he had to be called the next morning after time to mull things over. Of course the mulling could only be accomplished after smoking a joint. Heading back to my condo, another question echoed in my mind: when things would return to normal?

RHODE ISLAND JOE was easy. Upon being told him he was needed on an adventure with me that could be rewarding but dangerous, he said to cut him in before there was even a chance to explain any details. Exactly what role he might play was undecided, but just having my good friend Rhode Island Joe with me in such times would be comforting. His size, courage, and loyalty were always welcome.

Rhode Island was not moved by the money.

"Got enough to last me to age ninety and probably won't be drinking as much beer by then," he advised me when told there was over a hundred grand in it for him.

"That's what I told the agents," I said. "But they got me another way."

Joe also had another reason having nothing to do with money.

"This will be the most exciting thing I've done since I caught a child molester back in Rhode Island."

"You caught a child molester?" This was news to me.

"I'll tell you about it," he replied. "Maybe even show you the newspaper article if you're nice."

"How did you do it?" I asked.

"It was really simple," Rhode Island Joe explained between bites of hamburger. He almost never ate Thai food.

"There was some perv hanging around the local Catholic school, flashing himself, even touching some kids in places he had no business going. Couple times tried to get a kid to go for a car ride. The cops were doing nothing except listening to complaints, so someone had to act."

"Couldn't the school have done something?"

Rhode Island Joe laughed so hard I thought he would explode.

"You kidding?" he asked. "I've been a good Catholic all my life and love the Church, but between you and me, most of these priests are no better than that perv."

It was news to me that Joe considered himself devout. There are several Catholic churches in Bangkok and any Filipino can guide you to them. Rhode Island Joe had never mentioned attending church services and to the best of my knowledge he never did. Then again, there are synagogues in Bangkok and they have never seen me, but I consider myself as Jewish as the day of my circumcision.

"Anyway," Joe continued, "Took a few days off from work, dressed myself up in gray chinos and workbooks and set a tool box next to me. Made believe I was fixing something in a lamp post."

"Weren't you afraid the cops might check you out?

Joe sneered.

"A cop doing an honest day's work? You don't know Rhode Island."

"So how did you catch him?"

"Had a pair of binoculars with me, the ones I used for duck hunting," he explained. "Made it seem like I was looking at power lines, swept the area and kept an eye out for anyone who might be in the school yard or hanging around the school when they shouldn't be there.

"On day two, about five minutes before school let out, there's a lone guy hanging out by himself about fifty feet from where all the mothers were waiting to pick up their kids. Guy was wearing a suit and tie, pretty strange for a working class neighborhood, especially on a super hot day in late May. He kept looking at his watch, then the ground, then his watch again. Believe me, he wasn't some father waiting for his kid. Just felt it in my bones. And that was before the Porsche whacked me and I started feeling things in my bones all the time.

"When I saw him go up to a kid leaving school and start talking, it was time to make my move. I charged over to him and grabbed him by the neck. The kid didn't know the perv from Adam and when I asked the sicko what he was doing hanging around a schoolyard all he could do was mumble.

"I called the cops on my cell phone. He tried to get away but I caught with a flying tackle, pinned him to the ground, and held him till the squad car arrived.

"Sat on him to keep him from running again," he added. Then he laughed, a hearty, sonorous laugh, the kind that warms you inside.

"Three kids he flashed picked this guy out of a lineup. He's doing ten to twenty as we sit here."

We shook hands, and Rhode Island Joe was on the team. It was to my great relief that he accepted and from here on in would be in awe of him for the exploit he had revealed.

Rhode Island Joe could be more helpful than anyone imagined. The way he caught that pervert showed street smarts and intelligence he had been hiding from me. Probably hiding it from himself as well.

~

OLIVER CALLED ME the next day as he had promised. First I filled him in on what was learned from Rodney.

"What your friends told you about Polinov is on the up and up," he said when I was done. "Not much different from what I told you the other day. Guy is an amoral bastard but he can be friendly and charming at times. There are sealed indictments in the States. They want his ass something bad. But he's protected here long as he doesn't sell to folks the Thais don't want him to deal with. It's a sure thing he greases the right palms. Last time the Thais turned a Russian over to your country they had all kinds of problems with Moscow. But if you Yanks can get Polinov off Thai soil without it being tied to your government, they're not going to get too bent out of shape. It's not like they're happy having him here.

"He's brazen enough to wander around Pattaya. No doubt your government is keeping an eye on him. My people say he has on occasion spotted his watchers and played pretty rough with them. Explains why they want a total amateur like you, someone who looks too dumb be taken for a tail."

"Thanks for the compliment," I said.

I FELL ASLEEP earlier than usual that night, far more tired than usual after smoking an extra joint for good measure. As soon as my head touched the pillow, I was in slumberland.

Sleep is for me one of the best refuges from stress and the trials and tribulations of life. Some people say that you can't really enjoy the act because you don't really know you are sleeping. I dispute such a claim. Whether dreaming or not, sleep is almost always pleasurable. There are however, some exceptions. That night was one of them and it was because of the dream.

It was the same dream that came once or twice a year after coming to Thailand. The dream stopped without notice two or three years ago and I didn't miss it. That it returned during such troubling times for me made its reappearance even more chilling. Could it be an omen?

The details changed with each dream, but the theme was always the same. While having lunch with friends back in California, it would suddenly dawn on me that I had a court appearance in ten or fifteen minutes, always in the Redwood City courthouse, my least favorite in Northern California. There was no way to make it to the courthouse in time, even with me dashing to my car and driving like a maniac down Highway 101.

The courthouse always looked like a war zone, ringed by a barbed wire fence and surrounded by armed troops. I always managed to find a way past the fence and wander through a maze of paths, yards, and building hallways. The outside and the interior of the courthouse were always the same, a surreal version of a real American Hall of Justice. In the dream version, staircases went nowhere, elevators stopped at eerie and deserted floors, strange and mysterious people appeared out of nowhere delivering cryptic and unsettling message which could never be recalled after awakening. By the time I made it to the right dreamland courtroom, it was always too late. The doors were locked and there was no one around. Strange and frightening sounds could be heard coming from inside the locked room. When attempting to leave the building, I always found myself trapped there, struggling to find an exit, and when one finally was found and led me outside, my car was never where I parked it.

I always woke up in a sweat, my fists clenched and my neck aching. It was no different this time. It took several minutes before I was certain it was all a dream. As always, the rest of my day was unpleasant, a queasy feeling in my stomach and a vague sense that something ominous was lurking out there.

16

I WAS ENJOYING "Paraphernalia," my favorite cut on my most-beloved Miles Davis album, *Miles in the Sky*, recorded in 1968. Miles on trumpet, Wayne Shorter on tenor sax, Herbie Hancock on piano, Ron Carter on bass, George Benson on electric guitar. Miles had made the full transition from bebop to jazz-rock fusion, which disappointed some fans but delights me. My mind became lost in the music and I momentarily forgot the sudden turmoil in my life. The cut followed up with "Country Son," my second favorite track, and when that number ended, it was timeto start working.

Panchen's words sounded in my mind once the cocoon of the music had lifted.

"I have never lost a client to death and don't intend to start now. And that extends to people who pay the client's fees," the lawyer had said."Call me when you have time," he had urged.

I dialed his office and identified myself, and his secretary remembered me as Noi's American lawyer. I told her that Panchen had asked me to call him to discuss Miss Noi's case. She put me on hold and then informed me that *Khun* Panchen had not come to the office that morning. When asked if he had called in ill she told me that they had not heard from him that day. After being pressed she said me that he did not have any court appearances or meetings on his calendar.

"*Khun* Panchen always tells where he will be," she said.

Something did not seem right. In fact it seemed quite wrong. Panchen spots me on the street, supposedly a coincidence, and the next morning he fails to show up at the office with no explanation. Every cell in my body knew something was amiss.

I thanked her, made sure she had my number, and told her to call me when Panchen was available. She promised she would.

OLIVER ANSWERED MY call less than a minute later. He said he would get me Panchen's home address and put it on the tab.

Ten minutes later he texted me Panchen's home address. The attorney lived in Sathorn, near Lumpini Park in what Oliver described as a luxury high-rise. The apartment was on the twentieth floor.

"Good security, so use your brains," Oliver advised in the text.

After a shower and a shave, I put on my lightweight grey suit, white shirt, and tie and slipped my feet into fancy Italian leather loafers, which looked as new as the day they were purchased several years ago. My prayer that it not be one of the worst steaming hot and humid Bangkok days was answered. It was only a normal Bangkok day, hot and humid but not quite life threatening to a *farang* in a suit and tie.

Oliver was right, the high rise implied luxury. Sweeping curved driveway, high glass lobby windows, lots of polished brass and marble everywhere.

The uniformed guard at the lobby desk called Panchen to announce my arrival. He told me there was no answer but he could take a message.

"I'm from the U.S. Embassy and *Khun* Panchen is handling an important legal matter for us," I said in Thai. "He did not show up for a meeting with the ambassador. The ambassador sent me here to make sure he is okay." My primitive Thai was intended to impress the guard.

"Let me see some identification," the guard replied in English.

He took my California State Bar card and my California driver's license. He looked at the photos and then at me, and satisfied that they were all the same person, handed them back to me.

"Wait for the assistant manager to take you to condo," he told me. "Can sit while you wait."

A few minutes later a young woman came through a door behind where the guard sat and approached me. She held a key card in her hand. She identified herself as Wassana. I told her my name was Glenn. First names are all that matter in Thailand.

"Come with me," she said and I followed her. She wore a short black skirt and a tight white blouse, her long black hair contrasting with the white cotton. We took the elevator to the twentieth floor.

"So you work with U.S. Embassy?" she inquired as the elevator rose.

"Yes," was my answer, feeling that in a general sense, this was now true.

"Can you help a Thai get a visa to America?" she asked as we stopped on the twentieth floor.

"Yes, for a friend," I replied as we exited the elevator car. She handed me her business card.

"*Khab Khun ka*," she said, thanking me with a smile. "Hope we are friends." I noticed for the first time how very pretty she was.

Panchen's condo was at the end of the floor. Wassana rang the bell to no response. After knocking several times there was still no answer.

Wassana used the key card to open the door and we entered a long hallway. At the end was a living room with a window running full length along one wall, displaying a panoramic view of the City. The furniture was minimal but expensive: black leather couch and chairs, shelves lined with Thai statuettes and small sculptures, a shrine on a corner table. There was no sign of a female touch. Panchen must have lived alone.

Without saying a word, I walked from the living room down a short hallway leading to a closed door that would be the bedroom. The door was unlocked.

The room was dark. The heavy curtains were drawn and all lights were out. My hand felt for a light switch. The room lit up and the outline of a body could be seen under the covers on the large bed. I hurried to the bedside and pulled the covers aside.

Panchen was on his back, his face frozen in a grin, his eyes open. His body was stiff and cold. I stepped back as the room briefly swirled around me and the floor moved like the sea. Wassana was gasping in shock, her hand covering her mouth.

"What has happened to *Khun* Panchen?" she asked when we recovered somewhat. "He is such good man."

"I don't know. But we will find out." In my shock I did not consider how difficult that might be.

"We must call the police," she said. The shock and sorrow in her voice were obvious as she struggled to speak and almost choked on her words.

"No," I replied. "This is not a normal police matter. This is a U.S. Embassy problem. Our security will deal with the police." To my surprise, lying came quite easily to me.

"But the condo management must be notified," she said. There was worry in her voice, revealed by her stammering as she forced out the words.

"Not now. Everyone will be informed in due time. And your kind cooperation will be noted by our visa section."

Wassana said nothing more as I pulled out my phone and called Oliver.

"Put on a suit and tie and get over to the address you gave me as soon as humanly possible," I said the instant he answered. "Tell the guards downstairs to call Panchen's apartment." Hopefully Oliver had a suit that fit his new body. "They are expecting another representative from the U.S. Embassy."

Wassana called the guard downstairs and let him know that my colleague would soon be arriving.

We returned to the living room and sat on the couch.

"You knew right away *Khun* Panchen was dead," she said as a fact and not a question.

"Stiff and cold, no other possibility."

We sat in silence for five minutes. What thoughts Wassana had she kept to herself. It seemed like the wrong time to speak with her. My own thoughts returned to the dead man in the next room. My mind struggled with the idea that there was a connection between Panchen meeting me and his sudden death. Our silence was interrupted by the phone ringing. Wassana rose and answered it. After brief conversation in Thai, she returned and sat next to me.

"Your colleague from the embassy is on his way up," she said.

Minutes later, Oliver stood in the doorway, dapper in light gray pinstriped suit, electric blue tie, and Panama hat. He introduced himself to Wassana as Mr. Gordon Brand. He sounded more Canadian than American, but it was good enough for Wassana. She told him her name and title of Assistant Manager.

"Show me the body," Oliver ordered and Wassana pointed to the bedroom. We all went in.

Oliver put on a pair of disposable rubber gloves. "You shouldn't touch anything." he said to Wassana. She nodded her assent.

Oliver felt Panchen's pulse, carotid artery, and heart. He pulled a magnifier from a pocket and scrutinized the dead lawyer's head, neck, shoulders, face, arms, and upper body. With the scissors on a Swiss Army knife he snipped some hairs from the side of the balding man's head. He then clipped the top off a fingernail. He dropped the samples into small plastic bags just like on crime shows. He continued his examination on Panchen's lower body. He took several photos with his cell phone. Wassana turned away.

Oliver checked the drawers in Panchen's dresser and rummaged through the closets. Wassana watched him with awe, her eyes wide and following his every move. When he had exhausted his search of the bedroom, he went into the bathroom. We heard doors opening and closing and items clinking against each other.

Oliver finished up in the living room, scrutinizing the contents of the little desk in a corner and the bookshelves. When he was done, he motioned for Wassana and me to sit on the couch. He pulled up a chair and faced us.

"Our lawyer and friend, *Khun* Panchen, is of course dead," he began. "There is no doubt he was murdered. But not for reasons of theft."

"Why do you say that?" Wassana asked. Her face showed the blankness of shock.

"Couldn't he have died a natural death?" I asked.

"I have reason to believe he was poisoned and I'll share my reasons with *Khun* Glenn later," Oliver said. "In the meantime, let me point out some other facts to you."

"Nothing was taken from this condo. Not his expensive watches or the jewelry sitting in plain view on his dresser, not the stash of gold coins in the closet, not the stack of thousand baht notes in the living room desk. Didn't even take his brand new iPhone.

"No sign of forced entry," Oliver continued. "So whoever did this was let in by Panchen or was able to enter without doing damage."

"In other words, whoever did this had a key card?" I asked.

"Quite possible," Oliver answered. "These condo doors lock automatically as a security measure. If a tenant locks themselves out, they call security downstairs to let them in. If Panchen did not allow them in, unless whoever did this can walk through walls, there is no other explanation."

"Is there a master key card?"

"Let's ask your friend," Oliver suggested.

"Who besides you and *Khun* Panchen had a key card to this apartment?" I asked Wassana.

"Beside me, only the manager," she replied. "They are master cards that can open every door."

"Do either of you ever lend out the key to anyone else?" Oliver asked.

"No, sir, we are not allowed to do that," Wassana answered. Her frown told us she was offended to even be asked.

"Where are these key cards kept?" I inquired.

"We keep them with us at all times," she replied.

"Have you or the manager lost or misplaced your card over the past few weeks?" Oliver asked her.

She told us that no keys had been lost during the two years she had been the assistant manager.

"I would know. We would have to reset every key card."

Oliver asked Wassana for her business card. She handed him one and asked for ours. Having none, my explanation was that the nature of my work did not allow for cards but that her number was now on my phone as I took it from her card and we would discuss the visa some other time.

Oliver gave her a business card. "My colleague will be the person to contact you," he added. My eyes caught the seal of the U.S. government on the card as it passed before me.

"May I please be excused?" Wassana asked. The worried look on her face told me that she was not comfortable being in the condo with a dead man and two *farangs*.

"Of course you may," Oliver said in a pleasant voice. "We ask only that you be very careful. We don't want to frighten you, but until we know for sure who did this and why, the United States wants to make certain nothing happens to you. *Khun* Glenn, one of our most experienced security agents, will see that you are safe at all times. But if you talk, we cannot protect you."

"And we will be in touch about that visa," I told her.

"*Khab Khun ka*," she said, followed by a *wai*.

I watched her leave the apartment, her body gently swaying on her high heels. The door locked behind her.

"You owe me one, mate," Oliver said. "Handing you the opportunity of a lifetime. What a classy lady. Above your pay grade. But sounds like she wants a visa, so who knows, maybe you have a chance."

The door to Panchen's room remained open. An uneasy feeling passed through at the thought of what was on the other side. My gaze avoided that doorway.

"Oliver, we have a murder on our hands and the victim just happens to be Noi's lawyer. When he bumped into me on the street yesterday he said he wanted to meet with me. Then he's dead. And all you can think about is Wassana?"

"Oh no, Oliver replied. "But I'd wager that in a few hours when this shock wears off all you will be able to think about is Wassana."

"Can we please deal with the dead man we have in the next room?" I asked. "First tell me how you know how to act like a character from CSI and then how you happen to have a U. S. Embassy card at the ready."

"Easy," Oliver said. "For the card, you ever hear of printers? Takes a few seconds. As for the medical exam, just pick up the phone, call the Central Institute of Forensic Science, get the chief forensic pathologist on the line, and they walk you right through the whole process."

"You have friends everywhere, it seems," Good for me that he did.

"I have few friends besides you and Ray," Oliver said. "Those are contacts, not friends. It's business. You'll see it on the bill."

Oliver need not concern himself with his bill. If alive to pay it, doing so would be a pleasure. Right now we had to concern ourselves with Panchen. Oliver's cocksure attitude about Panchen being poisoned raised question he would hopefully answer.

"You sound so sure it was murder. By poison. Surely you don't consider yourself qualified to state a cause of death just by looking at a body?"

Oliver shot me a withering look as he shook his head.

"Of course not. That's why we have forensic pathologists. Just sent mine the photos of Panchen and my observations.

"We can be quite certain the preliminary findings will be poison," Oliver added. "Take a look at this photo of the left side of his neck. See the little dot about halfway down? Looks like a needle did it."

Sure enough, on the photo that Oliver enlarged on his phone, there was a tiny black mark right where he said it would be.

"Can't think of any reason for Panchen to inject himself in the neck," Oliver said. "My contact will make certain that the hair and nail samples are examined."

"You've answered my first question. Now for my second. What are we going to do with the dead man in the next room?"

"What did you have in mind?"

"I don't know," I admitted. "Call the police? From my experience, they're all a bunch of lazy crooks who could never find out who besides them commits a crime."

"You got that right," Oliver said. "So what's Plan B?"

"Dispose of the body somewhere." The words were rolling around in my mouth before they came out and sounded somewhat like the bleating of a sheep.

"This isn't Pulp Fiction," Oliver declared. "We're not squashing a prominent lawyer into a pile of junked cars. As if no one will notice he's missing. Not to mention our pretty young friend saw the body. She won't be pleased if we deny him proper funeral and cremation."

"Didn't you tell me you thought Wassana would do anything for a visa?

"Never said that," Oliver explained. "My statement to you was that because she wants the visa you might have a chance. Wooing her maybe, shutting her up if we deny Panchen his proper Buddhist rites, never. She'd tell someone. And who could blame her?"

Oliver was right. My suggestion made no sense. It wouldn't help us find out who killed Panchen and would make matters worse. My ideas needed improvement.

"What would you do?" I asked.

Oliver shook his head.

"That's no way to think, mate. I won't be available for consultation when you're tangling with those Russians. Better start thinking for yourself. Right now. "

Couldn't argue with that logic.

"Give me a few minutes and to come up with something," I told him hoping it was true.

BEFORE I COULD reveal my plan to Oliver, he told me that his contact in the Ministry of Forensic Science had sent him a message confirming that based on Oliver's photos and observations, the most likely cause of Panchen's death was a poison injected into his neck. The frozen look on his face, the needle mark and the absence of any theft pointed to murder by toxic substance.

"Wants to see the hair and nail to confirm that this was murder," he stated as a matter of fact. "They will have them in a few hours."

"We should find out if Panchen has any next of kin who might take control of the funeral and cremation," I suggested. "Let the world think he died a natural death while we try to find out why he was murdered."

"Your girlfriend Wassana may be able to help us out with the first part," Oliver said.

"How would she be able to help?"

"She seemed quite distraught over this death," Oliver explained. More so than one would expect from an assistant manager over the death of a tenant. My suspicion is they had some sort of personal relationship. It's up to you to find out. I'll give you ten minutes."

Wassana was soon back with us. While waiting for her I studied the few paintings on the walls. Panchen had been partial to abstract modern art, shapes and colors that left much to the imagination. His taste was similar to mine. Someone was going to inherit a few very good paintings.

We all sat down after Wassana arrived. Oliver began.

"*Khun* Glenn has a few questions for you. It might help us find the people who did this to *Khun* Panchen." He glanced at me. It was my turn to speak.

"We have no doubt that *Khun* Panchen did not die a natural death. It seems clear that he was murdered as *Khun* Gordon told you earlier. We are in contact with the Thai police and they ask that we keep this between us until they are ready to release this to the public. Do you understand this?"

Wassana nodded yes. Her eyes were red.

My first question was about any next of kin or close friends Panchen may have had.

"He never mentioned any and on his condo registration forms he listed his law office as the place to call if anything happened to him," she informed us.

"I never saw any friends visit him," she said in response to my next question. "He was a very private person," she added. "He was either working or at home."

My third question was the most difficult for both of us.

"We are not trying to violate your privacy. However we do need to know your relationship with *Khun* Panchen. It may help us to understand why this would happen."

There was silence in the room for what seemed like a long time but a glance at my watch told me it was at most a half-minute.

"I don't see how this is important," she said, looking down at her feet.

"If it were not important, we would not trouble you with the question. Solving mysteries is what *Khun* Gordon and I do for a living. Trust me, Wassana, this is important."

Oliver interrupted.

"Allow me to come straight to the point, Wassana. Were you having a relationship with *Khun* Panchen?"

Wassana smiled weakly.

"Oh no, *Khun* Gordon. *Khun* Panchen was not like that. He was gay."

Oliver looked at me.

"I was like a daughter to him," Wassana said. "He was very lonely and he had no one else to speak with when he wanted to say what was on his mind."

"What was on his mind?"

"Mostly work," she replied. "He told me about his clients, the hard work, and all the worries. He said he regretted that he was too old to be open about his being gay because then maybe he could have had a partner in life."

"He wanted to leave me money after he died," she added. "But I refused. I did not want people to get the wrong ideas. He did so much for me already."

"Such as?"

"Whenever I had a conflict with my boss, or trouble with a boyfriend or my family, he would always listen and he always gave me good advice. We often spoke in English to allow me to learn to speak it better. You know he was educated in your country and he loved America very much. I am not surprised he worked for your embassy, even if he never told me. I understand it must be secret and will honor your request. Panchen would want me to do so."

"Did he ever tell you he was afraid of anything?"

"Never," she said firmly. "He did not have an enemy in this world. And he was very brave."

"You have helped us very much," I told Wassana. "You may go now. We will be in touch about the funeral and cremation. Will you be able to help make those arrangements?"

"He was a serious Buddhist," she said. "We often went to temple together. It would be my honor to see that all arrangements are made." She rose from her seat and left the condo.

So Oliver was right about how Wassana felt about the death rites. He does know everything.

"You're not quite old enough to replace Panchen as a father figure," Oliver said, interrupting my thoughts. "So you two might need to work out a different relationship."

"She seems like a very good person." I said.

"Won't argue with that," Oliver replied. "Maybe too good for you."

BEFORE WE LEFT the condo Oliver made one last sweep of all the rooms while I waited by the door. He returned carrying several items in his hands. One was a small plastic pill bottle.

"Sleeping pills," he informed me. "Like a few? You might need them if things keep going as they have been."

"No thanks," I said. I understood then what kind of pressures

Panchen must have faced, mentioned by both the late lawyer and Wassana. I was content to smoke weed. Oliver favored alcohol. Panchen relied on physician-directed medication instead of our self-medication.

"Also found this," he said, showing me a cell phone bill.

"Will help me find out who he has been talking to," Oliver explained. "I've got contacts at True," he added, referring to the cell phone company.

"Why not just take his cell phone?"

"Because whoever did this can probably track the cell phone. Especially if we have to turn it on to find see the call logs. Not what we want," Oliver explained. "No one is going to notice a missing cell phone bill."

The uniformed security guard saluted us as we walked through the lobby.

"Rank has its privilege," Oliver said as we walked toward Sathorn Road.

We hailed a cab and Oliver insisted the driver to throw the meter. Traffic was light and we were soon in front of my condo.

"Care to come up for a fat one?" I asked.

"No thanks, Oliver replied. "Got to get to the Club. There's an audience waiting," he added. "Can't allow Ray to steal my thunder, you know."

"You can take it from here," he instructed. "Not that you have a choice."

I smoked a joint so far down that it burned my fingertips, then went back to work.

"I NEED TO see you and Billy as soon as possible," Rodney Snapp heard me say as soon as he answered his phone.

"You know it's we who call you," he said. "So just sit tight until we do."

"I'll sit tight for another four hours and we don't meet by then maybe it's time to just get up and leave. There's a problem we need to discuss."

After a brief pause, Rodney said that he and Billy Sloane would be at my place in four hours.

Wassana received my next call as soon as Rodney was off the line.

"It is now time for you to arrange for *Khun* Panchen to have his funeral and cremation. We understand how important it is. We don't want to cause any unnecessary pain to you or any others who cared about him."

"Thank you for your kindness," she said..

"If you need any money for this, please let me know," I added.

"Thank you for your kindness, *Khun* Glenn," she said. "*Khun* Panchen long ago made all such arrangements through his law office. I will call them at once."

"This must be very difficult for you," I said, "but remember that no one must know of his work with us or how he died. You understand why."

"Yes," she answered.

"If you need help for anything, please call me. You now have my number on your phone."

"You are so kind, *Khun* Glenn," she said.

"I hope we can meet again in happier times."

"Yes, that would be very nice," she said.

It certainly would be, I thought.

BILLY AND RODNEY were right on time. They were on my couch facing me in my reclining chair. I opened the meeting.

"You guys promised me that all these actions against Noi were going to end if I did what you asked."

"And we kept our word," Billy Sloane said.

"That's not what her lawyer Panchen says. He tells me everything is still pending and it's only his appeal that has slowed things down."

"Panchen told you that?" Billy asked. I felt the shock in his voice.

"You know him?" I asked.

"Of course," Billy replied. "His name was on her appeal and we saw it when we made the file disappear. So he's wrong."

"When did you speak to him?" Billy asked me.

"Just a few minutes before my call to Rodney demanding this meeting so you could explain it to me."

Billy's eyes darted quickly in Rodney's direction. I saw Rodney catch their movement but did not register in any visible way. Then it was if it never happened and they both focused their eyes on me.

"You're sure it was Panchen?" Billy asked.

"Of course. When you a pay a lawyer you tend to remember their voice. It was Panchen."

"I have no idea why Panchen would say something like that," Billy said. Our lawyer at the Embassy has informed Panchen that the American case was gone and not a trace remained. The request to the Thai government was withdrawn and he knows we made that disappear too."

"I'd like to believe you. But what reason would Panchen have to lie to me?"

"Is it possible you are mixed up as to when he called," Billy asked. "Maybe all that weed you smoke has altered your sense of time. "

The bait was resisted. They weren't going to get me to talk to them about anything other than this kidnapping mission. They knew of my weed use but how they learned was a mystery. Maybe they were watching me, maybe Charlie had told them. It didn't matter anymore.

"Panchen spoke with me a few minutes before my call to Rodney. No doubt about that. When he told me nothing had been done for Noi I had to call your partner."

"We will look into this," Billy said. "We are men of our word and Noi is completely in the clear. We can put you on the phone with the Legal Affairs Officer at the Embassy and the Thai prosecutor if that will satisfy you. We can reach them right now."

"No need for that. Panchen can check again. There is no doubt you are men of your word. Maybe whoever Panchen spoke to had not gotten the news. I'll call him again as soon as we are done."

Billy announced that they had to leave and he and Rodney rose from the couch and headed towards the door where we said our goodbyes and they made their way to the elevator around the corner. As soon as they were gone I called Oliver and told him I would meet him at the Club in five minutes.

OLIVER WAS SEATED at the bar, a dozen regulars clustered around him, his voice booming above the clatter of dishes glasses and utensils. The two Joes and Edward were among the throng. Phil Funston sat alone at a table. I did not see Noi. A rugby game blared from a television set on a shelf at the far end of the bar. Ray the bartender began working on my martini as soon as he saw me walk through the door. He was abiding by the unwritten rules of the Club, and once Oliver had completed his story it would be Ray's turn to entertain the crowd. The audience was being treated to back-to-back tales by two master storytellers.

Oliver was finishing up a yarn he had told at the Club a few years back about a Russian gangster in Pattaya who thought he could muscle in on some drug trade run by the local Thai mafia. He figured he would send a message by killing one of the Thai drug dealers.

"A few days later they found his head on top of a garbage can on Walking Street and his pecker nailed to his front door," Ray shouted at his entranced listeners. "Rest of him probably fed to the fish.End of that war."

"You think that's true?" Phil Funston snarled in a voice just loud enough for me to hear. "No one messes with those Russians. Certainly not a Thai," he added.

That's what I thought, until Wang chased those Russian toughs out of the Club with nothing more than a stare. After all these years in this country, it was finally becoming clear to me that a *farang* should never underestimate a Thai.

As soon as Oliver was finished, Ray segued into his vignette. Something about a Chinese tour bus driver going the wrong way on a oneway street. It would have been fun to hear the full tale, but Oliver motioned for me to take my drink and bring it to a table that had the benefit of being as far from Phil Funston as possible.

"Enjoy your one drink, mate, and then we'll clear out of here," he said. "The Joes haven't said a word about our little game and let's make sure none ever gets out."

"So why didn't you tell me this when we spoke? We could have met you somewhere else."

Oliver shot me one of his withering looks.

"There was an audience to think about," he replied. "What am I supposed to do, walk away in the middle of a story? Have you no sense of artistry?"

"No, but I do have a sense of business. You're working for me. And being well paid."

Oliver threw me another glance that could kill.

"Is money all that you Yanks ever think about?"

"You know for me this is not about the money." I hoped my voice showed the contempt I felt for even implying there was a pecuniary motive involved.

"Okay, mate," Oliver replied. "It has nothing to do with one million dollars cash. You'd risk having all your closest friends killed just for the hell of it all."

"You know that's not true. It's for Noi."

"Calm down, mate," Oliver told me, patting me on the shoulder. "Can't you tell when someone is just playing with you? But maybe you can tell that to Noi when she gets back from her overnight date."

His remark stunned me into forced silence before a few deep gulps of air enabled me to speak again.

"Noi is on a date? An overnight date?"

"Isn't that what you just heard me say? And why not? She's an attractive lady and now that she's in the clear, isn't she entitled to celebrate?"

"An overnight date with some guy?"

"We never knew Noi to like the ladies," he remarked, "but these days anything is possible."

"This is unbelievable. After all, I thought…."

"Doesn't matter what you thought," he interrupted. "You won't be the first idiot who misjudged a woman and you won't be the last.

"Look at the good side," he continued. "You're looking at a ton of money and you met a wonderful young lady. Plus you get to work with me."

"Every silver lining has a cloud," I said as we got up to leave.

17

A FEMALE PRESENCE hung over Oliver's apartment like a summer fog over San Francisco. Lipstick-tinged cigarette butts lay in an ashtray, a makeup compact sat perched on the television stand. Several empty beer bottles and an empty bottle of gin lay scattered about the living room.

"Maid off this week?" was my question to Oliver as he threw himself on his couch.

"She was otherwise engaged. Girlfriend is still in her province."

"Amazing you ever get any work done," I said with admiration and envy.

"Any time you want to stop being a sanctimonious idiot, just let me know and I'll fix you up," Oliver replied. "Meanwhile, would you like a fresh one?" he asked, glancing at the empty bottles.

After seeing my head shake no, he walked to the refrigerator and returned with a solitary beer bottle in hand, moisture glistening on its sides. He spoke after a long pull on his beer.

"Glenn, you look worried and with good reason. There's no denying a connection between Panchen wanting to speak to you and his being poisoned before the sun came up the next morning. The question is what did he want to tell you? What was important enough for someone to kill him so he never got the chance?"

"My gut tells me Snapp and Sloane were behind it. In fact, it's almost certain Sloane was involved," I said. Oliver listened to my account of my meeting with them and how Sloane reacted when he heard me claim to have spoken with Panchen after the lawyer's killers would know he was dead.

Oliver leaned back, closed his eyes and clasped his hands behind his head for a few seconds. He reopened his eyes and relaxed his hands before he spoke.

"There's a very small universe of people who know about this kidnap plot. Besides us and your government, there are the two Joes. As far as we know, Panchen was unaware. So what he wanted to tell you is quite mysterious. As is the reason someone felt he had to die."

My gaze was fixed on the large window as Oliver's words resonated within me. He was right. My visit to Panchen's office was before Billy Sloan and Rodney Snapp had made their unannounced appearance in my condo. I never told Panchen anything about my deal with the agents. If he knew of my arrangement with the CIA, how did he find out?

"Maybe he learned something as he poked around for information on Noi's case." Something to do with her case perhaps."

"Now you're thinking like a smart guy," Oliver said, flashing me a thumbs up sign. "I was beginning to wonder how you ever made it as a criminal lawyer in America."

"And Panchen's cell phone records might give us some idea of what happened." Oliver nodded in agreement with my words.

"Let me see your phone," Oliver ordered. After handing it to him he pulled a paper from his pocket. "Courtesy of my connection at True," he explained, referring to the Thai cellular provider.

As Oliver scrolled my phone and glanced at the sheet of paper, my gaze returned to the window. It was a clear evening and the traffic six stories below on Sukhumvit Road, creeping along at a snail's pace, was easy to follow. It was relaxing to watch the movement at slow motion.

My peace of mind was interrupted by a loud noise. Oliver laughed when he saw me rush out onto the balcony.

"Ambulance chaser's instincts?" he asked.

"My practice was criminal defense."

I looked down at the street. A van had hit a bus but it didn't seem like the damage was great. The drivers were talking in the middle of the road, one gesticulating as the other listened. A figure moving across the street past the two drivers grabbed my attention like a shark grabbing a swimmer's leg off the coast of Northern California.

It was Rodney Snapp. This was certain even from six stories up. He had on the same clothing he had worn at my apartment a few hours ago. He reached the side of the street where Oliver's condo sat and then disappeared from sight. I told Oliver.

"I don't like this," Oliver said. He had never before shown such worry in his voice. He grabbed the television controls and turned on set, settling on the closed circuit channel that showed the lobby of his building.

"We'll see if he tries to get in here," he said softly.

We watched for several minutes. When Rodney did not appear on the screen, Oliver shrugged and returned to examining my cell phone.

"My contact got me that list of all incoming and outgoing calls for Panchen's cell phone over the past week," he said. "E mails and messages too, but there were none of those that would be pertinent to this matter. Take a look at this number," he instructed, pointing his finger to a place on the bill listing numbers called.

"Now look at this one," he said, calling my attention to the same number on the call list on my phone. "Confidential number," he added. "Even my contact could not tell me the identity of the subscriber."

"Recognize it?" he asked.

"That's Rodney Snapp's cell phone," I replied.

"Panchen dialed it the morning of the day he met you on the

street," Oliver told me.

Fear tightened my chest like a vise. Whatever this meant, it was not good.

"Take a look at this number," Oliver continued. "You know who Panchen was calling?"

"Haven't a clue," My voice was starting to sound more like a croak.

"What else is new?" Oliver said. "This is the number for the chief legal counsel at the Thai Ministry of Justice. The liaison with U.S. law enforcement. Panchen spoke with him right before he called Snapp."

A beer seemed like a good idea with that revelation. Then a better idea crossed my mind

"Any chance we can roll a joint?"

"Maybe we ought to finish this little talk first."

"I checked this fellow out," Oliver continued. "Classmate of Panchen's in law school. Thammasat Faculty of Law. One of the very best law schools in Thailand. Many of the top government leaders are graduates. Our late friend Panchen appears to have been well-connected."

"So you think Panchen learned something about Snapp and Sloane from his friend?"

"Now you are becoming less stupid," Oliver said. "There's hope."

"My bet is that this fellow at the Justice Ministry knew a lot and shared it with Panchen," he said. "Thai to Thai. Gave up Sloane and Snapp as quickly as your pal Charlie served you up to them."

The doorbell rang. Oliver put a finger to his lip. I kept silent.

The doorbell rang again. Oliver went to a cabinet and withdrew a pistol. He released the safety and walked towards the door.

"Open the door," a familiar voice called out. I had heard it over the phone and in person all too often the past few days.

"And put down the gun," Rodney Snapp added.

Oliver opened the door but kept the gun at hip level, pointed up at an angle.

Rodney entered the apartment.

"You can put down the gun, Oliver" Rodney repeated. "If it was my intent to do you harm you would be dead by now." He stared at Oliver, who stared back. Oliver lowered the gun and slid the safety back on.

"You can put it away now, Oliver," Rodney said. "I'm here as a friend. Let's talk."

We went back to the living room. Rodney and I sat down as Oliver returned his gun to the cabinet before joining us.

"How did you get past the guard?" was my first question when composed enough to speak. "We were watching the lobby the whole time." Rodney did not answer.

"How did you know we were here? And how did you know about Oliver?"

Rodney scanned the room as he spoke.

"People like Oliver and me make it our business to know these things," he said. "Isn't that correct?" he asked, looking at Oliver, who nodded. My shoulders tensed up and it must have been obvious.

Oliver placed a hand on my right shoulder. "Calm down, mate," he said. "Let's hear what the man has to say."

Rodney folded his hands on his lap, and leaned forward, staring at me.

"This visit is a mission of mercy," he said. "To save you from problems you don't want or need. The kind of problems that can get a man killed."

"You have already created a problem that could get me killed!" The throbbing in my temples grew fiercer with my shout.

Rodney held up a hand and lowered his head for a moment.

"With all due respect, Mr. Cohen," he began, "you are to be paid one million dollars in cash for your troubles. You are in a position to reward your closest friends. There are risks in everything but here the risks can be managed if you are careful. And let us not forget that as a result of your well-paid services, your friend Miss Noi is walking away from some very serious criminal charges. So all in all, it looks like you are being well rewarded for the risks you are taking."

I started to rise and lunge toward Rodney but Oliver grabbed me by the neck and pushed back into my seat. It didn't stop me from shouting at Rodney again.

"How dare you drag Noi into this? You guys framed her just to force me into this insane kidnapping plot."

Rodney smiled as he looked me straight in the eyes.

"Once again, with all due respect, Mr. Cohen, no one has framed anyone. Your friend Miss Noi has been engaging in some very disturbing criminal activity. Money laundering to facilitate criminals to hide their illicit funds from two governments, not to mention tax evasion and currency exchange violations. We've all seen the same affidavits from American agents and that's only the tip of the iceberg. I've seen stuff you haven't. They have her dead to rights. Her own bank records will eliminate any doubt. The charges would hold up in any court of law in any country. She was looking at a very long time in prison here or in America, maybe both, one after another. You could have walked away, let her face the consequences of her actions, and there isn't a thing we could have done to you."

"Am I right?" Rodney asked, looking in Oliver's direction.

"He has a point, mate," Oliver said, directing his comment to me. "But that's not why you're here, Mr. Snapp," he continued, mimicking the way Rodney had addressed me. "So why don't you just get right to the point and tell us?"

"Fair enough," Rodney replied. "Just what I told you I'm here as a friend. On a mission of mercy. Quite likely to save your life. All you have to do is stop looking into Panchen's death. It's no concern of yours and will lead you nowhere except danger and a potential unfortunate demise. Not everyone in my agency is as tolerant as me."

"What are you trying to hide?" I asked. "What did you and Sloane have to do with Panchen's death?"

Rodney stood up and walked to the window. He had his back turned to us for a few seconds and then turned to face us.

"Should have considered that you might be at the window and would see me coming," he said. "Goes to show everyone is learning all the time."

"Glenn," he said softly, "take my advice. Forget Panchen. Complete the job we're paying you to do. You and your friends get rich, Noi keeps her money and her freedom. We'll even protect your new friend Wassana if that's a concern." He saw the angry look of on my face and smiled. "Just make sure she keeps quiet about Panchen," he added. A chill surged through my body and it wasn't the air conditioner.

"Oliver will tell you that it's the wise choice," he added.

"The man does make sense," Oliver said. He told Rodney that he would speak to me.

Oliver was a good three inches taller than me and broader and at least as strong, but I grabbed him by the collar of his sport shirt and tried to shake him. He didn't move at all while I screamed at him.

"He's telling us we should let him get away with murder. A man died because of me. He just made a threat against Wassana. Can't you see who we're dealing with?"

Oliver gently removed my hands from his shirt and then made the timeout sign.

"I see it with perfect clarity," he said. "You will do as he asks. Have you given a moment's thought as to why he came here alone? Do you understand who or what you are dealing with? Why that Sloane character is not here with him? Rodney is not making threats against anyone. He's giving sound advice that will make sure no one has any problems. He is not lying when he said he comes as a friend."

"Well, let me ask him," I replied, turning to face Rodney.

He was not there. My eyes scanned the room. He was nowhere to be seen. Searching every room and closet yielded no sign of Rodney Snapp. I ran to check the television and its picture of the lobby.

"You're wasting your time," Oliver said.

"How did he get out without us hearing a thing?"

"I told you don't know who or what you're dealing with," Oliver replied.

"Now let's roll that joint," he said.

18

WASSANA SOUNDED RELIEVED when I called her and told her that a mistake had been made, Panchen had not been poisoned but had died a natural death. She did not ask how I learned this.

"I am so happy to hear that," she said. "I knew he was a good man, but I feared maybe he had done something bad in a past life and this was his karma. But I am so glad to know that is not true." Lying to Wassana was unpleasant but it meant that she would not be placing herself in any danger by letting on that she knew the truth. No doubt she would honor her promise to remain silent. but it would be easier for her if she did not think she had anything to hide.

Wassana explained that Panchen's body had been washed in accordance with Thai Buddhist tradition and many people had come to pay respect before his cremation. The visits did not sound all that different from the Irish wakes in San Francisco, with a different kind of food served. She explained that the next day he would be cremated. Asking her if it was appropriate to pay my respects crossed my mind, but explaining myself to other mourners would be risky. I promised to say a prayer for him, which of course as an agnostic would not happen, but it seemed what a Thai would expect a *farang* to say. She thanked me.

Rodney called not long after this conversation with Wassana. He said he would drop by for a brief meeting and ten minutes later he was there. He never mentioned Panchen or his visit to Oliver's condo. He wanted information on the two Joes, as we had discussed their working with me. He did not ask about Oliver. He was strictly professional but I was wary.

As soon as Rodney left, I called Oliver and told him about my conversation with Wassana and the meeting with Rodney. He made no comment on the former but was complimentary about the latter.

"You were right to tell him what he asked for," Oliver said. "These guys would have gotten what they wanted anyway. You just saved them some time. Maybe they'll be grateful."

"Do you think our friends the Joes are going to have problems with Rodney and Sloane?"

Oliver said he didn't think so.

"Checking them out to make sure they're not working with the Russians. Or someone else. Can't be too careful in their game. Which is now your game too."

Staring with longing at my stash box sitting on the coffee table, there was one more question that had to be asked of Oliver.

"Tell me honestly, what kind of men are Billy Sloane and Rodney Snapp?"

"You already know," Oliver replied. "See you at the Club."

He was right and that realization drove my hands to the stash box.

WHEN I GOT to the Club, Noi was there. I pulled a chair up to her table and spoke with her while waiting for my martini to be brought to me.

"You must be feeling good about having this case go away."

Noi seemed distracted and at first it seemed as if she had not heard me. Then she looked at me with her eyes signaling unfathomable thoughts. She placed a hand on my forearm. A strange blend of excitement and depression overtook me as her fingers touched my skin.

"Thank you so much for bringing me to *Khun* Panchen and speaking with him on my behalf," she said. "Your kindness and your friendship will never be forgotten." The way she said the word friendship caused my heart to sink a few inches. Her long black hair brushed her shoulders as she spoke.

"I was so sad to hear of *Khun* Panchen's passing," she continued. "He was too young. Not all that many years older than you," she added.

My heart sank a few inches lower. It would fall into my intestines if this kept up.

"Being a lawyer causes great stress. That's why I stopped being one."

Noi smiled as she removed her hand from my arm.

"Being a lawyer is like being an alcoholic," she said. "You never stop being one."

My drink arrived. It disappeared in three long sips.

"Are you okay?" Noi asked. "Is there something happening in your life that you want to talk about?"

"No, everything is fine. Dealing with your problems reminded me of being a lawyer in America and I don't like to think about those days."

"Then don't," Noi replied.

She cast her eyes down to the table and then raised them up to look at me.

"There's something I need to tell you," she said.

She's going to tell me about the guy she's been dating, was my thought. Oliver had already shocked me with that news.

"I'm leaving Thailand to live in your country," Noi said.

It felt as if my heart had stopped. I placed a hand against my chest to confirm that it was still beating.

"Are you sure you're alright?" Noi asked.

"Positive," I squeaked. "Put down that martini a little too fast." Noi smiled.

"There is finally a good time to tell you," she said. "I met a nice guy last year, an American like you, but as long as there was that money thing with Edward we couldn't become too involved. Too much risk, too much trouble. It would not be fair to him.

"Now thanks to you and Panchen, I am free to be with him," she continued. "Your country's embassy gave me a fiancée's visa. It was so easy and so quick. I didn't even need an interview. We'll be getting married when we get to America. We're leaving tomorrow."

I could not look at her. My life was at risk, and the death of a good man may have been my fault, all for Noi. Now she was going off to America to get married.

My eyes scanned the club. Wang stood at the kitchen window, moving his arms rapidly as he prepared someone's meal. The General was speaking with Edward. Sleepy Joe watched a rugby match on television through half closed eyes. Rhode Island Joe was tackling a plate of spaghetti. Phil Funston was annoying a waitress. Both Joes could be killed, because of my love for this woman, who had just given me twenty-four hours notice that she was moving out of my life before she made it in.

"Do the others know?" That was all I could think to say.

"I told everyone yesterday," she said. They wanted to have a party for me but it doesn't feel right with Panchen not cremated yet. My goodbyes have been given to everyone. Even Phil," she said with a smile. She rose from her chair.

"I must leave now," she said. "Have to finish packing for my trip. Thank you again for all you did for me. For being the best friend anyone could ever have. We will always be in touch."

She looked at me for a long moment. It seemed like the time for a farewell hug. Instead she gave me a deep *wai*. It was the first time she had ever done that to me.

"Goodbye, *Khun* Glenn," she said. "May you be safe from all harm. May only good things happen to you."

Not likely, I thought, watching her body sway as she walked away. I knew I would never see her again.

19

OLIVER SAUNTERED INTO the Club after Noi departed. He made his way to my table, stopping to greet everyone he passed. It reminded me of the President of the United States walking through Congress on his way to deliver the State of the Union address. He wedged his large muscular body into the seat next to mine.

"You look like you've seen a ghost," he said.

"A few of them actually."

"I guess you just learned about Miss Noi taking off for your country to marry her beloved," he said as he waved to Joy the waitress for a drink. He offered to buy me a martini but Coca Cola was my choice. "Sorry that you were the last to know. Kind of unfair, all things considered."

"I feel like a total idiot."

"That's because you are a total idiot," Oliver replied. A short laugh followed.

"Somehow I'm missing a lot of things that should be obvious."

"That's because you're not looking," Oliver said. "You're seeing what you want to see, not what is really in front of your nose."

The waitress brought our drinks and we sat in silence for a few minutes.

Oliver broke the quiet.

"You are going to have to learn faster than you like. So first you need to forget."

"Forget what?"

"Forget Noi. Forget Panchen. Forget the easy life you enjoyed before you decided to play Sir Galahad to a money-laundering manipulator who played you the way Casals played cello."

It surprised me that Oliver knew about Pablo Casals. But knowing things was his game.

"Easier said than done," was the best I could think to say.

Oliver motioned for refills and soon a fresh glass of Coke was set before me.

"Listen up, mate," he began, "when you're playing footsie with those Russians in Pattaya, thinking about that stuff could be the death of you.

"Have you given any thought as to how you're going to blend in down there?" he asked.

"Not really, Rodney gave me a map."

"A map?" Oliver said, his tone rising. "Did someone ask for directions?"

"Have you figured out how you're going to dress?" he asked again. "You still haven't answered that question." When he heard me say I planned to wear the same clothes as usual, he was not pleased.

"Oh, let's see," he snapped. "Mosey up to some Russian gangsters in a Pattaya bar wearing clean pressed Dockers and Lacoste. Well-shined loafers to boot. Even the hooker won't fool them if that's how you look. Maybe easier to wear a sign saying CIA agent around your neck. Make things easier and less painful. It will be over before you know it and you won't feel a thing."

I had more pressing questions.

"Rodney told me to get a woman from a bar so Polinov would see me as just another guy out for a good time. But he said I don't have to sleep with her."

"Heaven forbid," Oliver said.

"I've never done anything like that before."

"Never done what?" Oliver asked. "Sleep with a woman?"

"Of course I have. I mean never took one from a bar."

"So how do you intend to commence your new life as a sexpat?"

"Rodney can fill me in on the details of taking hookers from bars. I'll ask him when I see him."

"Fat lot of good that'll do. How much time you think that fellow has spent getting girls in go-go bars?" Oliver asked. "These guys always carry and there's no way they're taking off their clothes and letting a whore see their weapon. Or let these gals crawl all over them and maybe feel that piece. No bar wants cops coming in unless they are local guys coming for their payoffs. That's why he told you to go get a broad but didn't tell you how. He's got to know you're a virgin when it comes to that stuff. Just like him."

A new knot was forming in my stomach. There was so much I did not know or understand and my ignorance could be fatal.

"You know who you have to talk to," Oliver said. "Look around the room."

Edward and the General were still in deep conversation. Sleepy Joe had moved next to Rhode Island Joe and they were watching the rugby game. Joy was walking toward the kitchen to retrieve a plate of food from Wang. Then it struck me.

Phil Funston was arguing with a man, a new customer. Phil's bald head bobbed up and down as he gesticulated and shouted. In the midst of this he managed to signal Joy for a beer. It became clear. As a lawyer in America, my job required doing many distasteful things. Representing child molesters and snitches, trying hopeless drunk driving cases were high up on the list. Working hard for too little money was another unpleasant aspect of my life back then. But none of those compared to the revulsion that attached to this task.

The knot in my stomach became a knife slicing my intestines. Oliver saw the discomfort crossing my face.

"Best teacher you could ever have, but not necessary," he said with a twinkle in his eyes. "This Aussie can tell you all you need to know."

The stabbing pain in my gut disappeared. I rested my head in my hands, elbows pressing into the table. My fingers rubbed the stubble on my face, a reminder to shave next time I was in front of my bathroom mirror. The last few days hadn't left much free time. When Oliver said it wasn't necessary to deal with Funston, the stress it had caused was relieved.

Over the next ten minutes, he told me everything a man needs to know to pick up a hooker in a go-go bar and look the part. It wouldn't be necessary to dress like a refugee from an Australian drinking party, but looking like my usual permanent crease was out. Oliver recommended t-shirt and shorts, but when I balked we settled upon worn jeans and a tatty sport shirt. He told me to talk with only one woman at a time, buy drinks only for her, and stick to soft drinks for myself so I don't get drunk. He explained the "fine" the bar charged for taking the lady, and how much to offer for her services. "Make sure you slip her the money before you send her away as you get ready to grab Polinov," he said. "You can afford to be a sport. That's way she won't make a scene about losing a fee."

"It's well worth whatever you wind up paying me," Oliver remarked when we were done. "And you're not coming out of this too shabby either."

"I didn't get into this for the money. You know that as well as I do."

Oliver chugged the last of his drink.

"Well, mate, that may be true, but right now the money is all you've got."

20

WHEN I ARRIVED at the restaurant, Wassana was already seated. It was an upscale Japanese place on Ekamai. When *farangs* meet Thais for dinner, aside from local food, Japanese is the default. It is one cuisine which they both enjoy.

It took me three days, six false starts, and two huge joints to summon up the courage to call Wassana. After my unrequited feelings for Noi, I had no faith in my abilities with women, especially Thai women. Three former girlfriends could testify to that, one from Isan, one from Bangkok, the third from Trang. My romantic failures were a map of Thailand.

Wassana rose and gave a *wai* when she saw me. My smile and my defective Thai told her she was lovely. She smiled back either because she understood me or found it humorous.

My efforts to engage in small talk were no better than usual. She told me a little about her day and I listened quietly. She must have sensed me being outside my skill set, so she shifted to asking about me. Women seem to understand that men prefer talking about themselves.

"Did you come to Thailand because your government sent you?" she asked.

It was a struggle to find a response that was neither a lie nor the full truth.

"I was a lawyer in the United States and came here seeking a change in my life. After moving here my government offered me a job to which I just couldn't say no." That part was more or less true.

"Why could you not say no?" she asked. As I pondered how to answer the waiter came by with menus and rescued me.

"Let's choose our food and then there will be time to explain." We never returned to the topic.

I ordered salmon teriyaki while Wassana studied the menu. I looked around the restaurant, appreciating the minimalist Japanese decor. A few simple carvings and pictures hanging on the wall, a few statues placed in corners or against walls. The simplicity and space of the interior design relaxed me.

Wassana gave her order to the waiter in Thai. When the waiter asked about drinks, there was a pause while we waited for Wassana to order. She asked for a diet soda, so I did the same.

I hadn't been on a date in over a year unless you count one-night stands, and there were only two of those. Wassana's charm captivated me and made me want to be a normal guy with a normal relationship. It had been a while since my heart had felt any real interest in a woman other than Noi. Wassana was thirty-one years old, came from Isan like Noi, went to college in Bangkok, and her first and only job since graduation was with the condo company.

"I started as a secretary and worked my way up to assistant manager of a major property," she said with pride. It was nice to be with someone who was confident about what they were doing, because that sure as hell wasn't me these days.

I was careful about disclosing much to her. It was true about my having been a lawyer in America and that it made me unhappy, so I moved to Bangkok. Like many Thais, she assumed that all American lawyers were wealthy and had no problem picking up stakes and moving to Thailand to enjoy a life of luxury.

Towards the end of our dinner, I asked Wassana the question that had lingered since we met.

"I hope you don't mind me bringing this up, but the first time we met you asked about me helping you get a visa to America. I was just wondering why you wanted one. You seem very happy here in Thailand."

Wassana giggled.

"Oh, *Khun* Glenn, that was not for me. As you said, I am quite happy with my life in Thailand. Maybe someday I will visit your country, but not now. The visa was for someone else."

"A friend hoping to find a rich American?" I asked, then realized that might sound insulting. Fortunately, there was no sign that Wassana viewed it that way.

"Not for a friend," she replied. "For a client of *Khun* Panchen."

"Did you work with *Khun* Panchen in his law practice?"

Wassana told me that she did not have anything to do with Panchen's office, but that he sometimes discussed his cases with her.

"He told me of a lady he was helping. He thought that she should go to America. She was having some problems here and he thought she would be safer in your country. I asked him why couldn't he just call one of his influential friends. He said that in her case it had to be done in secret. When I met you and learned that you worked for the embassy, it seemed maybe you could help *Khun* Panchen. He did not know of our discussion. I hope that was not wrong of me to ask."

"Not at all. Do you know the name of his client?"

"Yes. He once referred to her as Miss Noi."

WASSANA HAD AN apartment in the same building where she worked, one of the perks of being an assistant manager, or maybe she just didn't like commuting. We took a cab and I escorted her to the lobby where she gave me a slight *wai* before we parted. I thought briefly of Panchen but my thoughts quickly returned to Wassana.

"Hope to see you again," she said softly as she said night and glided across the lobby to the elevators. As the doors closed behind her an alert sounded on my phone. There was a message from Sleepy Joe asking if he could stop by the next day. I told him to be there at one p.m.

After arriving home, I sat out on my balcony watching the lights of Bangkok, from gargantuan buildings crowding the evening skyline, to the crawl of headlights in the thick traffic clogging the streets below. Even ten stories up, one could detect the cacophony of horns honking, motorcycles with defective mufflers, and the Skytrain cruising above Sukhumvit. Above it all, Wassana's voice was in my head as was her face, bathed in the evening glow.

I longed to see her again. It was a pleasant surprise how quickly Noi was put aside and my failed relationships forgotten. My mind conjured visions of bliss and happiness, with Wassana and me together. In other words, fantasy and yearning. These are fatal traits of men from time immemorial.

There was another reason to see her again, though secondary. The revelation that Panchen wanted to obtain a visa to America for Noi through secret channels hung over me like a mushroom cloud after a nuclear explosion.

Why would Panchen want to do this, I wondered. Noi had never shown the slightest interest in going to America, and if she really wants to, she had an American fiancé.

One of the last calls Panchen had made before he was murdered was to his friend at the Thai Ministry of Justice, the liaison with U.S. law enforcement. Why wouldn't he use his influence to help Noi? Why wouldn't Panchen want his friend to know?

Why did Panchen call Rodney Snapp right after he spoke with his friend? How did he get Rodney's number? Through his friend at the

Ministry or elsewhere?

There were answers to all of these questions but my fear was that they were not going to be pleasant. Oliver could help me figure this out in the morning. I went back into my apartment and was soon asleep.

I WOKE UP at the crack of nine and made coffee. One part of life in America that followed me to Thailand was love of the bean. I know where in Bangkok to buy the best and maintain a shelf of fine equipment: grinder, French press, measures, filters with holders as backups. Over the years, coffee consciousness in Thailand has grown exponentially, which brought me great pleasure. I make occasional short trips to Chiang Mai, the Northern Thai city with the best coffee culture in all of Southeast Asia. It is worth the trip just to sit in its coffee houses.

Feeling expansive, I broke into my treasured stash of Black Ivory Coffee, the most expensive and best brew in the world. The beans are grown in the North, fed to elephants after being mixed in a special blend of fruit, and then roasted in Chiang Mai after the elephants eliminate the product. It may sound unappetizing, but don't be fooled. The elephants' digestion does something that gives a flavor unparalleled by any coffee I have ever tasted. The process is labor intensive and costly, especially hand picking the beans once the elephants make their deposit. A half-kilo of beans sets me back over five hundred U.S. dollars, but well worth the money. On top of that I shelled out several hundred dollars for a French made syphon, which is the old-fashioned way of brewing recommended by Black Ivory. It looks like the scales of justice except instead of two weighing plates, one side has an opaque vessel and the other a clear one.

They are joined by narrow piping. The clear one is for the ground coffee and contains a cloth filter. The opaque vessel sits atop a tiny tank for methyl alcohol. I carefully poured some alcohol into the tank, careful not to spill any. I then measured out six scoops of the precious beans, ground them by hand in my small wooden grinder, and carefully measured the powder into the clear vessel. I poured exactly three hundred fifty milliliters of mineral water into the opaque vessel, lit the wick and stood back to watch. When the water reached boiling after a minute or so, the heat caused it to be siphoned over to the ground coffee in the clear vessel. Once the brew had cooled ever so slightly, it was magically siphoned back into the opaque vessel. During the four minute seeping period, I called Oliver. He told me he was in Koh Phangan and would be returning to Bangkok in two days.

"In the meantime," he said "use those brains that served you well when you were defending people back in your country. Treat this like a problem in one of your cases. Dust off those skills you still have somewhere inside you. Hard as it may be to believe," he added.

I wondered if that advice would show up on his bill.

As usual, Oliver was right. Countless times in my days as a defense lawyer I faced what seemed like an insurmountable obstacle. Evidence piled up and it always pointed to guilt. There were no obvious holes in the prosecution's case, no exit from the impending crash, no alternative routes. There appeared to be nothing to say at trial to even look like a skillful defense of my client.

Somehow ideas always appeared after long hours of study and concentration. The story about the transvestite charged with drug sale was one such example. Many times these ideas worked, and my client was not convicted. Other times they failed, but the jury stayed out for days, what we defense lawyers called a "moral victory." On occasion I would run my defense past the prosecution and get my client a better deal, sometimes even a dismissal. Never give up is the criminal defense lawyer's code. It helped me through some very challenging cases.

Sitting at my desk with a steaming cup of the world's best coffee, black of course, and a small writing pad and pen, I flipped open to the first blank page and wrote down the names of everyone involved in the case.

Noi
Charlie
Billy Sloane
Rodney Snapp
Panchen
Wassana
Oliver
Sleepy Joe
Rhode Island Joe
Polinov

I looked at my list before getting up to pour my second cup. Upon return other people whose names I did not know but were part of the story joined the list:

Panchen's friend at the Foreign Ministry
Noi's fiancé

I took a few slow sips of my coffee and leaned back in my chair. There was one other person who belonged on the list:

Panchen's killer (might be one of the above)

I then wrote out a rough chronology. When preparing a defense in America, that was always the starting point. Hard to follow a trail if you don't know its order.

First came Sleepy Joe's arrest. Snapp and Sloane had mentioned how my handling of the problem gave them confidence in me.

Next was the subpoenas for Noi's bank records, which led to hiring Panchen.

After that, Charlie's call telling me he had volunteered my services to the U.S. government and he was taking a cut of the fee.

Then the unsettling visit by Billy Sloane and Rodney Snapp when they coerced me into this insane scheme to kidnap a Russian gangster.

The chance encounter on the street with Panchen came next.

My heart sank when writing the next entry, Panchen's mysterious death discovered during the visit to his condo. My spirit was uplifted when meeting Wassana was added.

Learning that Panchen had been in contact with Rodney.

The warning from Rodney to stop looking into Panchen's death.

Noi leaving for America.

I poured my last half-cup of Black Ivory and read what had been written. My head was filled with questions and a list of them was prepared:

Charlie told me that he gave Sloane my name when Sloane told him about a problem he had in Thailand. Was that true? If Sloane worked in top-secret operations outside the normal rules, why would he casually confide this to Charlie? What would make him think Charlie had a contact? Had Sloane already been following me when he asked Charlie? Did he know that Charlie knew me, and if so, how?

It was becoming increasingly doubtful that Panchen's encounter with me on the street was sheer coincidence. Panchen had been killed right after he said he wanted to warn me of something. He had intended to find me and set up a meeting where he would reveal what worried him. The next morning he was dead. It was a straight line from hiring Panchen to help Noi to his being killed. But why?

Noi had never mentioned any desire to go to America nor an American boyfriend, let alone a fiancé. Her claim that she was moving to the U.S. to marry this guy did not jibe with Wassana's report that Panchen was trying to get her a visa through backdoor channels. She wouldn't need Panchen's help if she had the fiancé. One of those stories was false. My money was on Noi lying to me. But for what reason?

Rodney had warned me to stop looking into Panchen's death if I wanted to stay alive. The implied threat was that Sloane would have me killed. Why was Rodney betraying his partner? Sloane was well aware of my suspicion that he was behind Panchen's death. My ruse in smoking him out and catching his surprise when claiming to have spoken to Panchen after his death should have told him that much. Sloane was one experienced operative who wouldn't overlook something that obvious. He wasn't concerned just because of my suspicion that he had been behind the murder but he was afraid of me finding out the reason for it. Another straight line, this one running from Sloane learning of my knowledge that Panchen had been murdered and ending with Rodney warning me to forget about it.

How did all of this tie in with the need to kidnap a Russian gangster without the U.S. government leaving any fingerprints?

Everything was connected, that was certain. How or why was unknown.

This journey to make sense of what was happening around me felt eerily like the practice of law, struggling to find a way to save a guilty client from their just desserts.

Only this time it was myself I was trying to save.

I looked at the clock hanging on my wall. It had no numbers, just marks where the hours should have been. The hands told me it was already 11 a.m. Sleepy Joe would be there in two hours. That allowed time for the fitness room in my condo, with a run on the treadmill for a while and lifting some weights. Lose some stress and keep off the fat. Thinking of Wassana, I didn't want the marijuana munchies and my daily martini to build a belly like Phil Funston's.

Of course that might make me look more like the sex tourist I was going to impersonate. The things a man must do for his country. It was necessary to follow through if I wanted to find the answers to my questions. My heart told me that was the real reason to go through with this. As angry and frightened as I felt, the truth had to be found. Whatever truth meant these days.

MY TIME AT the fitness room calmed me and tired me so that it was too much effort to worry. I went back upstairs to my condo, took a shower and watched the news on CNN until the intercom buzzed. The guard sent Sleepy Joe upstairs.

Sleepy Joe had a joint rolled and he lit it as he sat down on my couch.

"Get the word on when we go?" he asked as he passed the joint to me.

"It's just a matter of time until our friends tell us Polinov is ready to be taken." That wasn't entirely certain but it sounded authoritative.

Joe craned his neck over the back of my couch and exhaled a mouthful of smoke.

"I've been doing a lot of thinking," he said.

"You told me that your American friends knew about my arrest and how you got me out," he continued.

"It's fair to presume that they knew all about me and that includes my being ex–Special Forces," he added.

That seemed right.

"So then why didn't they just come to me?" he asked. "No offense, mate, but you hardly seem cut out for this kind of work. Could get a bit rough, you know."

He had me there.

"They must have figured on my bringing you in on the deal," I said.

"Maybe," Joe replied. These boys are sharp and they've been watching us for a while. Doesn't take a CIA spy to figure out who you would turn to when you needed a crew. But it wouldn't be clear if you didn't know about my talents. You didn't until very recently. I don't crow about them and don't exactly look like a man who can kill with his bare hands."

"Then maybe they did want me for the job," I said with wounded pride.

"No offense, mate, but what's special about you that they would pay you all that dough? Trust me, there are people out there who are under the radar and better made for this kind of work than you. Like me for example." I passed the joint back to Sleepy Joe. He skillfully placed it between his thumb and forefinger.

"What are you getting at?" I asked.

"It doesn't make sense that they would want you," Joe said. "We could be in a whole world of trouble. And we need to know why."

I explained my attempts to unravel this and showed him my notes.

"Not a bad start," Sleepy Joe said after he had scanned the list. "But there are a few names you left off."

"Like who?"

Sleepy Joe took another drag on the joint and put it down in an ashtray.

"How about the General?" he asked. "Or our friend Edward."

"What does the General have to do with this? And how on earth does Edward figure in?"

Sleepy Joe clasped his hands and brought them up to chest level as if he were about to *wai*. Instead he put his hands down.

"Who had me arrested?" he asked. We knew it was the General. "And wasn't it my arrest that Sloane and Snapp said brought you to their attention? If they didn't know the General, how would they find out?" "If you recall, it was Charlie who gave them my name," I reminded him.

Sleepy Joe gave me a strange look.

"How would Charlie know about the arrest? Every trace was wiped off the books. Unless someone spoke to you or me, the General or those cops, there was no way of knowing. You hadn't spoken to Charlie since you came here seven years ago. He didn't know anything."

Sleepy Joe continued to prove that marijuana does not dull the brain. With he and Oliver around, *Khun* Glenn was the third smartest guy in the room.

"We'll run this by Oliver and see what he thinks," I said. "Even if the General is mixed up in this, how does Edward figure in?"

Sleepy Joe picked up the half-smoked joint, which had gone out, and relit it. He took a long drag and passed it to me. I waved it off.

"Edward was Noi's partner in crime," he said. "It was the dirty money she ran to Laos for him and his friends that Sloane and Snapp used against her. The charges were filed to pressure you into agreeing to get involved in this mess. Obviously these boys investigated you and Noi. Think they didn't know about Edward? Maybe he was the one who told them you had the hots for the lovely Miss Noi."

"Because unless someone who knew me told them, they wouldn't know."

"Exactly," Sleepy Joe said as he took another long drag and placed the stub in the ashtray. "Charlie didn't even know Noi existed. But the General and Edward know how you felt."

Sleepy Joe's words resonated within me. My heart beat faster and I swore my pulse could be heard as well. Then these feelings subsided and my mind became clearer. It was as if a veil was lifted from my eyes or a curtain drawn back on the window from which I looked out onto the world. For the first time it was understood that these events were not happenstance, ill fortune or payback for something in a past life. They were a series of connected dots, intentionally drawn to create my path.

"We need to start asking questions," I said when my pulse rate returned to normal. "Seems like it would be easier to start with Edward."

"I'll have him over here in no time," Sleepy Joe said.

"How can you be so sure?"

"He's a customer," Sleepy Joe said. "A good one, too. Almost as hooked as you, but not quite," he added.

"But then he's going to know that I'm a customer too."

Sleepy Joe shook his head and frowned.

"Mate, have you considered that you might have bigger problems than Edward knowing you smoke weed? Assuming he hasn't figured it out already? Like why are you and me so tight? We're an odd couple, aren't we? You look like you stepped out of the pages of *Gentleman's Quarterly* and me? Well, it's a different a different image, you might say." Everyone in the Club must have figured that out long ago. Once again something I hadn't caught.

EDWARD EYED ME sheepishly when Sleepy Joe led him from the door to the living room. He seemed as uncomfortable as I about being outed as a pothead.

"Small world, isn't it?" he said as he sat down.

"And what is it you have for me?" he asked Sleepy Joe. "Sinsemilla? Cambodian buds?"

Sleepy Joe stood in front of Edward and stared at him.

"This time it's what you're going to give me," he said.

A puzzled look crossed Edward's round face. A few days' stubble gave him a touch of shabbiness.

"What could that be besides the money for your stuff?" he asked.

"Answers to some questions," Joe said. Starting with this one: "who have you been speaking to about my friends Glenn and Noi?"

Edward cleared his throat.

"What are you talking about?" he asked. "Speak to who and say what? Who would even ask?" His voice quivered and his eyes widened.

"Exactly what you're going to tell me," Sleepy Joe told him.

"There has to be some mistake," Edward said.

"We'll try this one more time," Sleepy Joe told Edward. "Have you spoken to any Americans who wanted to know about my two friends? Don't lie to me, Edward, I know all about your deal with Noi. We're not fucking around here, Edward. This is real."

Edward started to rise.

"You're crazy," he said. "I'm out of here."

When Edward was up on his feet, Sleepy Joe placed an arm across his shoulder and pushed him around to face my balcony.

"Let's get some air," he said as he guided Edward towards the sliding door. Sleepy Joe was not tall, same size as me, but he had several inches on Edward. As they moved toward the balcony, Sleepy Joe's lean body and Edward's pudgy build reminded me of Laurel and Hardy.

The two of them stepped out onto the balcony, Sleepy Joe guiding the hesitant Edward with the arm he had draped across his shoulder. As they approached the railing at the edge and Sleepy Joe warned Edward that this was his last chance to tell the truth.

"There's nothing to tell," Edward called out. The fear in his voice infected me.

The next sound was Edward's screams as Sleepy Joe dangled him over the ledge. I did not see him go over but when I made it onto the balcony Joe held one of Edward's legs in each hand. No one would ever suspect that this spindly fellow who looked like a walking string bean had such strength.

"Ready to talk now?" Sleepy Joe called out looking down at the dangling Englishman. Edward's screams were muffled by the noise from the streets and the side of the building which he faced as he hung by his feet.

I heard a woman's voice yell out in heavily accented Thai English, "Another crazy *farang* want to jump? Why he have to make so much noise when I watching a movie?"

"Joe, stop this right now! He could be killed!" I screamed.

"His choice, mate," Sleepy Joe said as he released a foot and brought his hand back over the ledge."

"Don't struggle so much," Joe called down to Edward. "I've only got you by one hand."

Edward told Joe he was ready to talk.

"Get me back up!" he cried. "It was two Americans. A black guy and a white guy. They wanted to know about Glenn and Noi and you."

Sleepy Joe grunted as he grabbed Edward's loose leg with his free hand, moved backward, and dragged him back over the ledge. Edward hit the floor with a thud, face down. When he rolled over his face was beet red, tears were flowing from his eyes, and snot streaming from his nostrils. His eyes were large and round and the look on his face recalled the look on the face of a victim of a serial killer in a second rate horror movie.

Sleepy Joe helped Edward stand up and gently walked him back to the couch. He asked me to get Edward a glass of water. Joe pulled up a chair facing Edward and was questioning him. Edward took the glass of the water and gulped it down. He handed me the empty glass and wiped his mouth with his hand.

Joe spoke in a measured tone as he questioned Edward. He made no threats and it was clear he did not have to make any after what

Edward had just experienced. Edward spoke in a weak but steady voice, pausing several times but his answers seemed to satisfy Joe.

Edward said that a few weeks ago he arrived home to find the two men there. They said they were American agents but did not give their names. No doubt they were Billy Sloane and Rodney Snapp. They were pleasant and professional but made it clear that failure to cooperate was not an option. They told him they knew of his money laundering and who he worked with, but so long as he told them what they wanted to know, they had no interest in his business.

"They wanted to know about Glenn," he said. "Who he associated with, his habits, where he went, what he did." I told them that he had been a lawyer in America, that he was close with Sleepy Joe and Rhode Island Joe, and because of Sleepy Joe, everyone figured he smoked weed. When they found out I was a customer of yours, they said that was not a problem. They asked me about Noi, and I said Glenn and she were good friends but that was all. But Glenn was in love with her. Everyone at the Club knew that," he said, looking at me apologetically with sadness in his eyes.

"Did they ask about the General," Sleepy Joe asked Edward.

"No, they didn't even mention him."

"Did they leave you any contact information?"

"No," Edward said. They said they would contact me if they needed.

"And did they?" Joe asked.

"One time," Edward said. "The black guy called me and he and the white guy came to my place and said they were sorry, but my business had to stop. They didn't deny their promise to leave it alone if I told them what they wanted but said things had changed. The white guy gave me some money to make up for my losses. It was all quite pleasant but they said never to tell anyone about them. I haven't heard from them since."

Sleepy Joe asked how much they had given him. Edward said fifty thousand U.S. dollars in cash. No wonder Edward thought it was pleasant.

"You can go now," Sleepy Joe told Edward. "No hard feelings, just business," he added.

"And of course, you won't say a word about this, will you?" he asked, turning his head towards the balcony. "Me either."

"Of course not," Edward said.

Sleepy Joe smiled.

"Remember, just business," he told Edward. "We're going to keep doing business, I hope. Your money was always good and now you have even more. So call me when you run low. And here's a present for being a good customer," he added. He handed Edward several large joints. Edward grabbed them and stuck them in his pocket. He thanked Sleepy Joe and promised to call. He was out the door seconds later.

"They didn't ask him about the General," I said, looking at Sleepy Joe in awe.

"Didn't have to," Joe said. "You can figure that one out yourself."

"I have. The CIA has someone in whatever organization the General is involved with and that's how they found out about Sleepy Joe's bust. Don't see the General telling that to two strange agents who show up out of the blue."

"Sounds right," Sleepy Joe said.

"But the little shit Edward ratted me out. Ratted out Noi, too."

"Edward's okay," Joe said. "Just not cut out for this kind of stuff."

"Neither am I."

"But you don't get to walk away," Joe replied.

We stood there silently for a brief moment. Joe's voice interrupted my thoughts.

"Netflix has *The Big Lebowski*, right?"

I nodded yes and headed towards my television.

21

RODNEY SNAPP AGREED to meet me in the restaurant at Foodland on *Soi* 16. I arrived ahead of him and grabbed a table close to the entrance. While drinking coffee and reading the Bangkok Post I looked up and noticed him seated across from me.

The restaurant was filled with office workers from the Asoke area and expats who lived nearby. Two foreigners having coffee in the middle of the day would not attract any attention and there was little chance anyone would eavesdrop on us.

There was no mention of the interrogation of Edward or Wassana's revelation that Panchen wanted to obtain a visa for Noi outside normal channels. My words went straight to the point Sleepy Joe had made.

"The deeper my involvement, the clearer it is how unsuited I am for this job.

"You and your psychopath partner did due diligence on me, you've made that clear. So you must know by now you made the wrong choice. Why on earth did you ever choose me? No matter what you wanted, there are far better people than me, many of them. That must be obvious to you and Billy."

The waitress came with my coffee and Rodney ordered a cup for himself before answering. If my derogatory reference to Billy Sloane bothered him he did not show it.

"You sell yourself short," he said. "You are a very smart guy. You are loyal and brave. You're an organizer and a leader, skills which are not common, especially here."

He saw the puzzled look on my face and explained himself.

"Look at the way you put together your little team. You drew on people you know and trust, each with some special skill you need. Oliver is what in my business we call an intelligence officer. Invaluable man to have at your side. Your strange friend Sleepy Joe is expert in what we call special operations. He is a real find and you are going to be grateful to have him with you. You could not have made a better pick. And when you needed help to save Sleepy Joe, you were sharp enough to recognize that the General was what we would call an asset like Oliver. You figured all of this on your own. This confirmed our belief that you were the right man for the job. We have a lot of experience recruiting people and we are totally convinced you are the right guy.

"To be frank with you, Glenn," he continued, "if you ever want to work with us, I'll make sure we grab you in a hot flash."

"Thanks, but no thanks. When this is over, you'll never see me again."

It was someone he had not mentioned that bothered me.

"You haven't said anything about Rhode Island Joe."

Rodney's coffee arrived and he took a sip before responding.

"There's not much to be said," he replied softly. "It's your call, but in my opinion he has no place here. He offers nothing and he's at risk of getting himself killed."

Rodney caught me off guard by this dismissal of my loyal and goodhearted friend.

"You don't know him at all. He's got guts and street smarts. He stands up for defenseless women at the Club. He once caught a pervert in a schoolyard when the cops wouldn't act. Used a disguise and a stakeout."

Rodney smiled.

"Think how ridiculous you sound, Glenn" he said. "He brings nothing to the table that you don't have already. Rhode Island Joe is your friend, and loyalty is an admirable trait, but when you get down to it, telling off a buffoon in a bar or catching a child molester in a schoolyard is not the same thing as possible hand to hand combat with the Russian mob. This one won't be played out in a bar or a schoolyard."

"I don't care what you think. He's in and he's getting a cut. If my back is to the wall, there's no one who will defend me with more heart than Rhode Island Joe."

Rodney took a few seconds to consider my words. He stared his coffee with rapt attention before he spoke. It was as if he were searching for an answer in his cup.

"You've already got Sleepy Joe and in my professional opinion he is worth a hundred Rhode Island Joes.

"I can't order you on this one," Rodney continued. "So long as no one is compromised we leave the team makeup to you. But here's some advice for you. Tell him the deal is off and thank him for his willingness to help."

Rodney's words stewed in my mind and heart for a minute while we finished our coffee. When my brain took control of my emotions it was undeniable that Rodney might well be right. He was a professional who did this work every day of his life. I was an amateur swept up in a cyclone beyond my control or understanding. Rodney had called Oliver an asset. If Oliver with his knowledge was an asset, Rodney was at least his equal, and his recommendations couldn't be cavalierly dismissed, because several lives could depend on what he was saying, mine among them.

Our empty cups sat on the table like a pair of eyes taking in the scene.

"If it makes you feel safer, then bring him along," Rodney finally said. "We understand how comforting it might be to have familiar faces surrounding you, especially one you trust and believe in. But I strongly advise you to bring in someone who can better protect you. Good as Sleepy Joe is, he alone may not be enough. He can protect himself or he can protect you but things get out of hand maybe not both of you. No way he protects all three of you. If anything happens to your friend Rhode Island, we don't want you blaming us. It will be on you."

"I'll think about it," was my only concession.

The waitress came and Rodney paid the bill. We left Foodland and walked towards the nearby BTS stop. He had explained in part why the government had chosen me to carry out a task for which I appeared most unqualified. My other questions still burned within me like hot coals. It wasn't yet the right time to pose them to Rodney. It wasn't certain he could be fully trusted. As we approached the stairs to the train I summoned the strength to ask the question that consumed me the most.

"You told me to forget about Panchen for my own good but I can't. A good man may have died because of his involvement with me. I can't let that go. I have to know the truth no matter what it may be. You have my promise to go through with this no matter what the answer.

"Was Billy Sloane behind the murder?"

"No," Rodney said as we reached the bottom of the stairs. "Now go back to forgetting and don't ever ask again. I only have so much pull with my partner."

A group of people rushed past me on their way up to the platform and obscured my view of Rodney. When the last person passed me Rodney was gone.

RHODE ISLAND JOE sat with me on a bench facing the lake in Benjasiri Park. We were only a hundred meters from Sukhumvit but we couldn't see or hear the traffic. I often sought solace in this pleasant green space amidst the concrete and noise of Bangkok. Joe had a bag of potato chips and a can of soda at his side. He diverted his attention from his snack long enough to hear me out.

"I just want to make sure you're still good with coming down to Pattaya with me on this thing we spoke about. It could get a little rough. There's good money in it for you, but if it's the money you're thinking about, don't worry, you will get some no matter what. No need to put your life on the line."

A look of disappointment came over Joe's face. His lips formed a rare frown.

"It's not about the money, Glenn and you know it. First of all, you're my best friend in this world. I'm not letting you face this alone, man. You're really not made for this rough stuff. I'd be kind of worried if you tried to pull this off without me."

"Besides," he continued. "Life's easy here and it's good, but it's become kind of boring. I need a little something to make it interesting. Like when I caught the perv." He clapped me on the shoulder.

"I don't know how you got dragged into this," he added, "but it doesn't matter. Once you were in, both of us were in. That's how it works, you know."

Joe had not been told about Noi or Panchen. It wouldn't have mattered to him. All Rhode Island Joe needed to know was that his best friend was in a tough spot and he wanted to help. My mind was made up and Rodney was wrong. This time there was no doubt about my judgment.

RODNEY SNAPP WAS right about my putting together a good team. Oliver told me everything we needed to know and pushed me to use my own skills. Sleepy Joe was my secret weapon. Rhode Island Joe made me feel safe and secure. He would take a bullet for me though I prayed it would never be necessary. His strength and single-minded determination to help would be necessary when we had to lug a drugged-out Polinov through the streets of Pattaya.

Oliver was not going to be present for the rough stuff. I was pretty useless on that end, my *Muay Thai* and gym routines notwithstanding. I didn't have the killer instinct of Sleepy Joe and didn't revel in catching bad guys as did Rhode Island Joe. A good chunk of my life had been spent on the side of the bad guys.

Rodney thought there was a need for someone else if Rhode Island was on the team. My first feeling was confidence in the two Joes; if they couldn't make it happen, doubtful a third person would make any difference. Besides, there were no others who could be trusted like these two guys. They were more than good friends; they were brothers.

That was why Rodney's concerns about Rhode Island Joe had me worried. Rodney was quite clear that despite my own self-doubt, he was confident in my abilities. Oliver was not going to be in the danger zone. As for Sleepy Joe, there was no question that he was well suited for this kind of adventure. Rodney just didn't think Rhode Island was of any use, might even be a detriment. I wasn't going to drop Rhode Island despite that professional opinion. If there were anyone else who could be trusted they should be brought on board and paid for their time, as this would maximize Rhode Island Joe's safety, not to mention my own. The question was who was that person? I made a mental list of every friend and acquaintance in Bangkok and came up empty except for one name.

Rodney complimented me for recognizing assets. The General owned a private security company and went around with bodyguards. If there was anyone who could find reliable and skilled protection, it would be him. Then I remembered that the General had taken advantage of me and inflated the price of the bribe paid to save Sleepy Joe. More ominously, on top the money, he had demanded a future favor. If already indebted to a man Oliver had called a "pirate," was it wise to ask for his help again ?

There was but one way to find out.

IT WAS A few minutes after 1:00 p.m. The General's Hummer was parked outside the Club, one of his security guards at the wheel. It was the surly fellow who had greeted me at the General's house the morning Sleepy Joe was in custody. We ignored each other.

I joined the General at his table. His other security guard moved over to allow me to pull a chair next to his boss. The General seemed pleased to see me.

"It's been a while since we had the time to sit and chat," he said. "When you come here you always seem to be engrossed in conversation with Noi or Oliver or one of your Joes. What's the matter, you don't have any more time for your General?"

I gave him my best version of a wai, which felt proper, as he was older than me and clearly of higher status. This was something I rarely did, certainly not well. The General smiled at my awkwardness and seemed pleased at the respect shown.

"I've been tied up with all sorts of things and am still in a state of shock about Noi going off to America. And still worried about Sleepy Joe getting in trouble again."

"Forget Noi," he said sternly. "If there's one thing you have no shortage of in Thailand it is Isan girls." That last comment rankled me. All too often one hears affluent Thai people speak in derogatory terms about people from Isan. The General, being affluent and powerful, reflected that kind of thinking, and he knew I did not agree.

"Go out and find yourself a woman who wants to be with you and you won't think of Noi," he advised. "Just give me the word and I'll introduce you to one any time," he added. "My *mia noi* has many friends who would love to meet a rich American lawyer. They know all about you."

"You'll be the first to know when the urge overcomes me. But right now my reason for being here is to talk business."

The General cast a glance at his guard who moved ten meters behind his boss, keeping him in his direct line of sight.

"So you enjoyed our last joint venture," he said.

"Not as much as the police, but it showed me who to turn to when I had a problem."

"What's your problem this time?" he asked. He called Mai the waitress and ordered two martinis.

My explanation was that an old colleague had called from America and asked me to help him on a case. He was defending someone in an American court and needed some sworn statements from Russian gangsters in Pattaya. They could help prove that my friend's client had not been involved with them in their criminal activities and they didn't even know him, and this would help clear him. Never having dealt with such people before and not knowing Pattaya made this risky. I wanted to help out my old friend, because he needed this case to stave off bankruptcy, but not if it meant being surrounded by Russian criminals in Pattaya all by myself. Since the General had a security company, perhaps one of his people was available to serve as my protection. Money was no object, as my friend's client would pay the bill.

"Maybe it's not such a good idea to get yourself mixed up with the Russians," the General said. "They keep to themselves and don't bother the rest of us but if you start dealing with them you might be asking for trouble."

"I'm just going to take some information, put it into a declaration, get them to sign, and send it back to America." My ability to lie so convincingly was becoming impressive. "They have agreed to help out a friend in trouble back in the States. But you're right that you never know what could set these guys off, which is why having some protection would make me feel better. Someone to be near me when with the Russians. Someone armed, though guns shouldn't be needed. Really just insurance." As I said that Mai arrived with our drinks.

The General waited until our drinks were placed before us and then responded.

"You can never be sure what will happen when you deal with Russians. I have to make sure my good friend Glenn is safe. Relax, I'll call you tomorrow and let you know it's handled. We can work out how much it is going to cost. In the meantime, cheers." We clinked our glasses and enjoyed our Martinis. Mine was as good as always. Ray never fails.

22

OLIVER MET ME at a Mexican place on *Soi* 23. He had just enjoyed a massage on that street and called to ask me to join him for lunch. When he mentioned the restaurant I told him to expect me in ten minutes. One thing I missed from California is good Mexican food. There are a few decent places in Bangkok and this was one.

"How was your massage?" I asked him when we were seated.

"Excellent," he replied. You really ought to get one yourself, Glenn. Might help alleviate the stress you've been under."

While waiting for our food, I updated Oliver what had transpired since we last spoke. He must have detected the pride in my voice while recounting how Rodney praised my instincts and skills and called me CIA material.

"Wouldn't let it go to your head, mate," Oliver said. "Part of the psychology they use to manage agents. Makes the agent feel powerful and necessary. Whether it's true or not."

"Just playing with you, mate," he explained when he saw my look of confidence deflate and my body slump. His comment restored me. My questions to him followed.

"Why did Rodney and Billy Sloane give Robert fifty grand to end his money running scheme? They could have just ordered him to stop. What choice would he have?"

"It's not clear what their principle motive might be," Oliver said. "But it's safe to assume that they were not concerned about Edward talking because he is afraid of them as he should be."

"Even though he told Sleepy Joe the whole story?" I asked. Oliver laughed.

"We don't know if it is the whole story. All we know is that he told you what you wanted to hear. Stuff you had already figured out. But it's good that he confirmed that you were right about the CIA doing their background checks on your team. Good work, mate."

"So what is the reason they paid him all that money?"

"This is the CIA we're talking about," Oliver said. "They've been known to have a need every now and then to move money around without a paper trail leading to them. Who better than Edward if such a need arises in this part of the world?"

"Think of it as a retainer," he added.

That made sense to me.

When told what Rodney had said about Rhode Island Joe and my own confidence in him, Oliver agreed with Rodney.

"Joe's a good man with a good heart," he said. "Love the way he shuts down Funston. But he's basically a lumbering elephant and you need swift gazelles."

"I don't care what anyone thinks, "I replied. " It is my decision and Rhode Island Joe is in."

"I respect your loyalty," Oliver said, "though it may not be wise."

That was almost exactly what Rodney Snapp told me.

"There is a compromise that should please doubters," I told Oliver and explained my discussion with the General and his promise to find protection.

"I was afraid to tell you in advance. Thought you might not like it. You called the General a pirate when he overcharged me for the bribe to get Sleepy Joe out of trouble."

"And indeed he is a pirate!" Oliver exclaimed. "But a pirate who loves you. He wouldn't have gone out of his way for just anyone, especially to spring Sleepy Joe, who was trying to sell weed without giving the General his cut. He did it for you, Glenn, just like he's providing this protection. You Yanks have such funny thinking when it comes to money.

"And he knew Sleepy Joe was going to pay you back, so not one baht was coming out of your pocket in the end.

"This is quite good thinking by you. You're getting better and better. You stood up for your friend even when the professionals said otherwise and you came up with a solution everyone can live with. You even had the guts to go to the General thinking I would disapprove. That Rodney fellow is right. You are becoming a leader.

"Have to give me some credit for pushing you," he said.

"Surely it will appear on the bill you send me."

Oliver assured me that it would.

AFTER LUNCH, OLIVER suggested we walk off the tacos and enchiladas with a stroll to the Club. "We'll be there when Ray starts his shift. Love hearing his first story of the evening."

Sukhumvit between Asoke and Thong Lor is a beehive of street action. It is always a joy for me to walk in Bangkok, a pastime which most Thais and *farangs* alike seem to reject. The heat does not bother me and I carry a small umbrella during the rainy season. Most of what I know about Bangkok was learned from observing life on the streets. When we passed the little stand where the old man changes watch batteries, I made a mental note to bring my fancy Citizen watch to him.

I was deep in thought, and Oliver was making comments about the attractive women we encountered along the way. In Bangkok there are many of them so there was an endless stream of observations. We approached a narrowing of the sidewalk where a concrete pillar emerged from the ground on our right, leaving the sole passage a narrow pathway on our left. When we went through a familiar face greeted us.

Billy Sloane stood in front of us. A toothpick protruded from his mouth. His gut looked bigger than I recalled. He could have passed for a Southern sheriff.

"Well, well, look who we have here," he said in a jovial voice. Oliver frowned.

"I know who you are and what you are, Mr. Sloane," Oliver said. He spoke with a coolness he had never before used in my presence. He stood stiffly erect and glared at Sloane.

Sloane removed the toothpick from his mouth and dropped it on the sidewalk. He stepped out of our way and the three of us walked along Sukhumvit.

"Very good, Oliver, You're everything they say you are and more."

"Lucky to have this man helping you," Sloan said looking at me.

"Why are you here?" I asked.

"Just wanted to say hello," Billy said.

"Tell us what you need to say and leave," Oliver told him.

"If you want to be that way, let's just get down to business," Sloane replied

"You're leaving for Pattaya in two days," he said. "You will be on the 9:00 a.m. bus out of Ekamai. The others will take the 7:00 a.m. bus. We've reserved hotels in your name. Just show your passport when you get there and that's it. Booked a room for you at one place and rooms for the Joes nearby. We'll text you the hotel names the morning you leave.

"When you get there we'll let you know when and where to find Polinov. If things go right as we all expect they will we hand you a million bucks cash later that day. Now keep walking and don't look back."

"With pleasure," Oliver said.

"HE'S A PSYCHOPATH, isn't he?" I asked Oliver when we were a hundred meters past Sloane.

"And worse," Oliver replied. "Trying to send us a message but it's one we received a while ago."

"Why couldn't he just call me or arrange a meeting?"

"Just to show us he always knows where we are," Oliver explained. "To make us more afraid of him than of the Russians."

"Should we be?"

"Probably."

We entered the Club. Ray saw us. I gave him the thumbs up sign and he reached for the martini shaker.

When we were at a table Oliver spoke.

"You're right about Sloane being involved in killing Panchen. I just don't know the reason. Sloane's not being completely straight with us, that's for certain. It's not just Panchen warning you that tells me this. It's also Rodney's warning. Something is not right. Something to do with Sloane. It's tied in with Panchen's death. Let's not get rattled but let's stay on our toes."

"Why are you so certain Sloane was behind the murder? Seems like it was only days ago you were agreeing with Rodney that I ought to forget the whole thing."

"They aren't inconsistent," Oliver said. "We should take notice that Sloane is a dangerous character and was probably behind the murder of a respected Thai lawyer. Having said that, it is in your best interests to refrain from attempts at proving this. Everything my contacts tell me about Sloane persuades me he is a man who solves problems by killing people. I don't want you to become one of his problems."

"Panchen deserves justice. And my country deserves better than

Billy Sloane."

Oliver shook his head.

"Glenn," he said, "any justice for Panchen is not coming from the courts or law enforcement. And as for whether America deserves Billy Sloane, last time I checked he was an authorized agent. Pretty high up as matter of fact. Maybe your country is getting what it deserves. Your government could rid itself of its Billy Sloanes any time it wanted. Don't see them doing so anytime in the near future."

There was nothing more that could be said. Oliver was right.

"Let's get the team together for a final wrap," Oliver said after we were silent for a moment. First let's get hold of our friend Rodney for a few details.

"Seeing as how Snapp and Sloane seem to pop up without warning, let's use a meeting place for our team that they won't invade," he said.

Joy brought over my martini and Oliver's beer, a pint of Foster. He raised his mug and I followed with my glass.

"*Chokh dii khrup*," Oliver called as the link of glass touching rang out. Good luck, the popular Thai drinking salutation.

We were going to need good luck.

BY THE TIME my martini glass was empty Ray was beginning his first tale of the evening. His lilting Irish brogue carried above the chatter of conversation spread about the bar. Soon such buzz had ceased and all attention was directed towards Ray. It had to do with a guy who made his first visit to a go-go bar and wound up looking like a fool, being cheated and humiliated. Every move the poor sucker made was wrong and dragged him deeper into a hole. We listeners realized it was going to end in disaster for the poor guy, but there was something inside each of us that reveled in hearing of his disgrace. Not the ideal story for me to hear.

"Pay attention so you don't make those same mistakes," Oliver said as he clapped me on the shoulder.

23

RODNEY SNAPP AGREED to meet with me. When told that Oliver would be with us, he said it made sense.

We met in the lobby of Oliver's condo the next morning at nine. When we entered the apartment the smell of freshly brewed coffee tickled my nostrils. Oliver knew how much a steaming mug meant to me in the morning.

"Want to keep you happy, mates," he said. "Can I offer you a cup?" Rodney politely declined.

We sat down in the living room, Oliver and I sipping from our mugs of coffee while Rodney sat and watched us.

"It's crunch time," Oliver said. "We have a few questions that need to be answered before anyone leaves for Pattaya."

"Ask and if they can be answered, they will be," Rodney replied.

Oliver asked about the chemical spray we had been promised, the one that would disable Polinov.

"It will be in Glenn's hotel room when he arrives," Rodney said. "It takes one spray in the face to put someone out for four hours with no harm to them.

"Worst that might happen is they don't recall the events immediately preceding their being incapacitated," he added. "Or they get all mixed up about them."

"And where and when does Glenn get the money?" Oliver asked.

"When Polinov is under control, he calls and we tell him where to go to hand him over. He gets the money when we meet," Rodney explained.

"Can we trust Billy?" Oliver asked.

"You can trust me," Rodney said. "Let me worry about my partner. Bring us Polinov and Billy will be fine."

"Last question," Oliver said. "What's the plan if anything goes wrong and my friends are in trouble?"

"If Sleepy Joe and the new guy you brought on can't help, we'll do what we can and intervene if we can do so safely. But there are no guarantees. My best advice is don't let anything go wrong. If you stick to the plan, nothing should go wrong."

Oliver laughed out loud.

"Rodney, if things did not go wrong, you would not have a job."

"You got that right," Rodney said.

RODNEY HAD ME recite the plan to make sure I understood what needed to be done.

I would check into my hotel, find the spray that would knock out Polinov, and wait for the text message telling me where to go to find the Russian. Before that, there would be a visit to the go-go bar of my choice where I would leave with the lady of my fancy. We would we stop for dinner at the restaurant where Polinov would be found. I would ask for a table by the water, near our quarry. That was a must. A nice bribe should work.

"If the bribe fails," Rodney said, "use the spray on the maître d' and grab the table."

"Are you serious?"

"Of course not. The bribe will work, don't worry."

My narrative continued.

The two Joes and the new security provided by the General would arrive separately and sit apart. After being seated near Polinov, the young lady would be sent on her way with an excuse, regrets, and some money. Then my real job would begin. After luring Polinov into conversation, when the moment was right, the Joes would overcome Polinov's guards. The spray would disable him and we would spirit him out of the restaurant and bring him to where Rodney directed us.

Rodney and Oliver listened intently. When my presentation was done, Oliver gave me the thumbs up sign.

"Impressive," Rodney said. "Shows we were right about you. Just a few pointers. When you start speaking with Polinov, let things run their course. React to what he says, not to what you are thinking. Don't rush things. Believe me, everything will happen as we planned. We've profiled Polinov and in spite of his being a murderer and a gangster, he can be quite sociable and friendly under the right circumstances. You can exploit that trait. If that weren't the case we would never have you meet him. You will recognize the right moment to act and remember, it is that moment only. Keep him engaged until then. Arrange a signal so your team knows when it is time to move. They should keep their eyes on you the whole time. Just remember we are nearby and watching. Keep your cell phones on all the time. Once you have Polinov out cold and under your control, get the hell out of wherever you are as quickly as possible and call us. We'll be waiting with your money."

"It will be you, right?"

"Absolutely. The government would never trust Billy with that kind of dough," he added with a grin.

"Can't blame them," Oliver added.

AFTER EVERYONE LEFT, the General called me on my cell phone.

"I've got you covered. Best around. All you need to do is call me when you leave for Pattaya and give me the name of your hotel as soon as you know it."

"Shouldn't I meet this guy?"

"No need," the General said. "You don't need to know who it is. He will know who you are and he will watch and protect you, don't worry."

"And what will I owe you for this service?"

"We'll work that out when it's all over," the General replied. "Surely you don't think for a second that I would ever take advantage of you?" I wasn't sure if it was a question or a statement of fact.

He ended the call before I could get an answer.

WE GATHERED AT my place the next afternoon, the two Joes, Oliver, and myself. Oliver assured me that neither Sloane nor Snapp would interrupt us. "They never break into to the same place twice," he said and then laughed. An open pizza box and several empty beer bottles covered my small table. The following morning all but Oliver would leave for Pattaya.

The two Joes listened as I ran down the plan. Sleepy Joe had a question.

"Shouldn't we test that knock out spray before we use it on the Russian?" he asked. "Wouldn't put it past them to trick us with water."

"And how are we going to do that?" I asked.

"Test it out on some unwitting motorcycle driver or bar girl," Sleepy Joe said, "Let them have a pleasant snooze and leave a thousand baht note for them."

"You'll be more confident when you have to use it on Polinov."

"If we have time," I said.

Oliver told us even though wouldn't be in Pattaya he would have his phone at his side every second we were down there. "Glenn needs anything from me, he gets it, right away," he said. Then he shared some final advice with us.

"When we first heard about this, it seemed insane. Maybe it was. But now that we have thought it through and set it up step by step, it isn't so crazy anymore. There is danger but you are ready for it.

"Sloane and Snapp will track you by your cell phones. You need to keep them on and stay in touch with each other. Anything goes wrong and you have to run, meet at midnight at the Aussie Pub across from Jomtien Beach. Any motorcycle taxi driver can find it. Ask for Harry, who runs the place. He will get you out of there unharmed."

Sleepy Joe interrupted again.

"Can we really trust these CIA guys? Everything I learned in Special Forces tells me no."

"Trust is not a concept that applies to people like them," Oliver replied. "I'd say they need us and that we are more trouble for them dead than alive. Easier to pay us and bury the story than to have people in our countries wondering what happened to us."

"Do you really think they will be waiting there with a million dollars?" Rhode Island Joe shouted. "That's a lot of money."

"Chump change for that outfit," Oliver said.

Sleepy Joe cried out another question.

"What happens if that magical spray turns out to be just tap water?"

Oliver shot him a stern look.

"Then you'll all be dead and I'll miss you all dearly," he replied.

Rhode Island Joe wiped pizza sauce off his mouth and spoke.

"Glenn's on top of this whole deal, am I right about that, Oliver? We're in good shape if we follow him, aren't we?"

"That's right, Rhode Island," Oliver answered. "Glenn is your leader. You must obey his instructions to the letter. If there is a problem he will decide how to handle it and you do as he says."

"I'd follow him into hell," Rhode Island said as he reached for another slice. Oliver continued.

"We should all be confident of success, but in this business anything can happen and we must be prepared for the unexpected. If you are cut off and alone, use your best judgment and make your way to that Pub.

"At the restaurant make sure you can see Glenn every second. He will decide when to make your move. When he scratches the top of his head with his left hand, that's the go ahead sign. The guards have to be taken out by force; there will be no chance of using the spray on these three men, only Polinov. You're not required to kill the guards, just disable them." He looked at Sleepy Joe.

"But if you have to kill to save your own lives, you do so.

"If any of you gets hurt, do what you can to help each other. But don't get yourself killed. You might have to leave the injured mate and call for medical aid. The CIA guys can come up with a cover story that works.

"See you in Bangkok when it's all over."

When Oliver finished, we gave him a round of applause. Then we raised our drinks and toasted each other, as well as the mysterious protector the General was sending.

OLIVER AND RHODE Island Joe left my place but Sleepy Joe remained. I rolled a joint while he trolled the television stations for a movie about to start. "We're in luck," he shouted. *The Day the Earth Stood Still*, 1951, Michael Renne and Patrica Neal. Hugh Marlowe and Sam Jaffee. Directed by Robert Wise. Twentieth Century Fox. The real one, not the rip-off remake from 2008.

"*Klaatu barada nikto*!" he shouted, mimicking the words Michael Renne, playing Klaatu the alien, had instructed the human Patricia Neal to tell his robot, Gort, in the event he was injured or killed. Science fiction lovers have been using the terms as a greeting or exclamation for over sixty years.

"How many times have we seen this, Mr. Memory?"

"This will be number twenty three," Joe said as he lit up the joint.

SLEEPY JOE WENT home after the movie, leaving me to my thoughts.

It was necessary to think positive and plan on success. After this was over and done with it would be possible to return to life as it had been before being sucked into this black hole of spy craft and intrigue. It dawned on me that the best way to set the groundwork for this goal was to make a date with Wassana for when I returned. Give me an extra motive to survive. She had said she hoped to see me again. After our first date my thoughts and my hopes were that we both knew we were destined to become a couple but neither of us knew when.

I called Wassana. When she answered I told her how enjoyable my time with her had been and asked to see her again in a few days. There was a long pause before she replied.

"I am sorry *Khun* Glenn, but that will not be possible." Her answer stunned me. My heart fell to somewhere in my spleen.

"Was there something I did wrong? It seemed like we had a good time. You said you hope to see me again."

"I was trying to be polite and thank you for a nice dinner," she explained. "But it did not mean seeing you in the way you are thinking. More like my relationship with *Khun* Panchen. He was a lawyer too. You are much older than me and you are a foreigner. And the work you do scares me."

There was nothing that could be done to change any of the points she raised. I told her of my regrets if this call made her feel uncomfortable and wished her the best of luck.

"No need to feel bad," she said as an ending. "It was interesting to meet you and good luck to you *Khun* Glenn as well."

Once again I had met a Thai woman, one who displayed all of the character and traits I so admired in their culture. She had class and brains to boot. Once again the woman rejected me.

24

MY ALARM SOUNDED at 6:45 a.m. I stumbled to my coffee station and ground enough high caffeine blonde beans to fill my large French press. I showered and shaved while it seeped, to make sure it was as strong as possible. One push down on the plunger of the French press and minutes later my first cup of black coffee was ready to be poured and savored.

The caffeine worked as expected, and soon the blanket of sleepiness had fallen away. After checking my e-mail and skimming the newspapers on line, it was time for a second cup, this time with milk and Equal, an artificial sweetener significantly stronger than sugar. I sat in the living room and watched the news on CNN. Obama and the Republicans were in full gridlock mode. The UK was making noise about leaving the EU. Another Japanese car company had been caught covering up defects. I turned off the set and poured the last cup of coffee.

My overnight bag was packed. It contained a change of clothing and two issues of the New Yorker. My passport and several one thousand baht notes were pushed down in the pocket of the jeans I would wear. On my bed an old Lacoste knockoff that was previously used at the beach lay next to the worn jeans. I put them both on and went back to finish my coffee.

It was eight fifteen. The twenty minutes walk to the bus station would leave me enough time to buy my ticket and some snacks for the trip. A half hour later I was at the Ekamai station, a ticket to Pattaya in my shirt pocket and a bag of Thai pastries in my hand. Being one of the first people on the bus enabled me to take a window seat which made it easier to read my magazine.

My one and only visit to Pattaya had been six years ago but the scenery along the way had not changed. Highways and flat expanses dotted with housing, industry and overpasses. I read one issue of the New Yorker and ate my pastries. The ride was only two and a half hours but it seemed like all day.

I dozed off somewhere in the middle of the ride and was awoken by the driver calling out North Pattaya through the address system. A quick scan of my messages showed that the name of my hotel was the only new one. I called the General and gave him the name and then texted it to Oliver, then grabbed my bag from the overhead rack and left the bus. Emerging into the glaring bright sunlight engulfed me in a swarm of people coming and going from buses. No one was wearing the business suits and ties or smart casual dress of Bangkok. In Pattaya, it was almost exclusively shorts, t-shirts or tank tops and flip-flops, men and women alike.

I made my way out of the terminal to the street where a chorus of cab drivers called to me. I entered the nearest cab and told him the name of my hotel.

"Good hotel," he said. "Right near Walking Street. Good time for you."

The cab slogged through traffic that was worse than Bangkok. The streets were filled with small restaurants, more bars than Phil Funston could visit in a lifetime, cars, motorcycles, buses, trucks, pedestrians walking wherever they felt, street vendors, hordes of fat *farang* men, and flotillas of red pickup trucks with benches along the sides of the beds, called *songthaews* everywhere else in Thailand but known as baht buses in Pattaya. With virtually no public transit system, they carried most people from place to place. The cab driver cursed a few times when one of them swerved in front of us to pick up a passenger.

The cab pulled up in front of my hotel. It was a small place right off of Walking Street. There were all manner of bar and massage parlors as far as the eye could see in either direction. After handing my passport to the young lady at the front desk, she checked her computer screen and she handed me a key and a form to sign. The wisdom of using real names had never been discussed but in the end it would not matter. Either we came out of this alive or our names would make no difference to us anymore.

My room was on the second floor. There was an elevator but I walked up. The room was small but neat and clean with flat screen television, a small bathroom and a queen-sized bed. After dropping my bag on the bed and turning on the air-conditioning and the television, the alert on my phone sounded. There was a message saying "Look under mattress, left side." I did and retrieved a small paper bag. Inside was a device that looked like an asthma inhaler. It was the chemical spray that would disable Polinov. Sleepy Joe had suggested we test it but there wasn't going to be any chance to do so.

It was a few minutes after noon. I sent text messages to the two Joes to see if they had arrived and one to Oliver simply saying "here." Within minutes the Joes answered yes. Oliver sent a smiley face.

It seemed like a good time for a walk around Pattaya. I had memorized the street maps Sloane and Snapp had given me and knew that the main areas of interest for the job were all a short walk from my hotel. My journey started by checking out Walking Street, right around the corner.

It didn't seem like the busy stretch of honky tonk of lore. Oliver had explained that during the day the Street was relatively quiet, but it sprang to life after dark, when vehicle traffic was banned and sex industry workers and their customers mingled with gawking tourists, performers and vendors. There were several fat foreign men on the street, many accompanied by bored looking young Thai women in scanty clothing. There were a few people walking briskly as if they were in a hurry to get through unscathed. Trucks and vans were unloading goods at restaurants, bars, and curio shops. It seemed like all the go-go bars were closed, their neon lights dark in the bright afternoon sun. Walking Street was clearly an evening venue.

The maps that Rodney had given me emphasized Walking Street and the Bali Hai Pier at its harborside end. With a shrewd suspicion that we were going to have to make it the pier at some point I decided to walk there to familiarize myself with the area. It couldn't have been more than a kilometer from one end of Walking Street to the other, but the narrow sidewalks were difficult to maneuver, and with all the vehicle traffic on the narrow street, walking off the sidewalk was not a reasonable option. There wasn't much to look at along the way as nearly all businesses were closed. My walk eventually brought me to the pier, where people were lined up to take ferries to neighboring islands. There were some smaller private docks off to the sides of the main pier.

I had walked for almost three quarters of an hour and was hungry. My eyes caught sight of a pleasant looking Thai restaurant on Walking Street just before the pier. There were several *farangs* eating there, including *farang* couples, a welcome relief from the mismatched twosomes that had been seen up to then. Upon entering, a hostess escorted me to a table and handed me a menu. I studied it, trying to decide if the dishes offered would look anything like the pictures. A waitress hovered by my side.

"You ought to try the diced chicken with basil," a voice with an American accent, vaguely Northeastern, called out from behind me. "Seasoned with herbs, not too spicy, tastes great over rice."

"Sounds good to me." I gave the order to the waitress and turned around.

The man who had addressed me was about my age, somewhere

in his late forties, salt and pepper hair cut short, and slightly overweight, judging from a mild double chin and a paunch that pressed against the edge of his table.

I thanked him for his recommendation. He asked me where I was from. I told him New York and he said that he was from Philadelphia. He had been coming to Thailand for two weeks vacation every year the past ten and spent it all in Pattaya, a different woman every night.

"I'm only up to number one twenty eight total because a few nights I was just too drunk," he explained. Another Phil Funston on my hands it seemed. Then what Rodney had said about my being able to recognize people who were assets came to mind.

"So what bars would you recommend for a first timer like me?"

The words were barely out of my mouth before my new friend rattled off a half dozen names, extolling each and detailing the women, the rates and the kind of crowd that went there. Upon my request he repeated his list and at least four were committed to my memory.

There was nothing more to say to my benefactor. We exchanged names and most likely his "Al" was as phony as my "Tom."

Whatever his name might be, he was right about the chicken with basil. I cleaned off my plate, thanked him, and headed back onto Walking Street. It hadn't changed at all during my meal, so a return to the hotel and waiting to hear from Rodney seemed wisest. There were no messages from anyone yet and it was a little before four in the afternoon. I would have to get a woman for my cover as a sex tourist, and therefore would have to head out for a bar the minute that message from Rodney arrived. It was time to smoke the joint I had brought with me, stuck carefully in the pair of rolled up socks. No one had told me anything about smoking, so it was left to my discretion. After thirty years of almost daily pot smoking, one joint was not going to affect me in any measurable way hours later. I would drink some coffee later just to be certain.

I opened the bathroom window and smoked the joint facing the street, doubting anyone could see me through the little balcony and the gauze curtains I that had parted just enough to allow the smoke to escape.

After the joint was finished I turned on the television. It was tuned to CNN and I left it there and laid down on the bed listening to the latest political predictions for the off-year U.S. elections, the latest terrorist attacks, and international weather reports. Fortunately they gave the latest Golden State Warriors score. They won, which made me happy. I'm a basketball fan and love that team.

The next thing I knew my phone alert was waking me up. Good thing it was set to a loud beep instead of vibration. Falling asleep might have meant missing this message that read "Royal Arms Seafood, Walking Street, 9:00 p.m." It was 7:10 p.m. I called the General and gave him that name. "Don't worry" was all he said. Next the name and location was texted to the Joes to make sure they showed up. I wouldn't put it past Sloane and Snapp not to tell Rhode Island.

A quick shower woke me and washed off the sleaze from the streets of Pattaya. My two-day stubble was kept, thinking it would help me look the part. I made a cup of coffee with the little drip cartridge machine the hotel provided and drank it while watching a replay of the same newscast that had put me to sleep. It may have been CNN, not Sleepy Joe's weed, that had caused me to snooze.

After getting dressed, the canister of spray went into a front pocket. Sufficient cash was taken as well. My passport and the rest of my money were left locked in the room safe. I took a deep breath, left the room, and was soon back on Walking Street. By tomorrow at this time I would be back in my condo and would never have to come back here again. That was the plan anyway.

25

WALKING STREET WAS still clogged with traffic but there were now more people. They threaded their way along the narrow sidewalks and spilled over the curb. Some crossed the street, weaving between the slow moving stream of vehicles. It was starting to grow dark and the neon lights were turned on for most of the go-go bars, though it was difficult to see if there was any activity within. Some of the bars sported young women dressed in the briefest of shorts and the most revealing of halter tops standing out front, holding signs advertising drink deals. There were no men entering or leaving. Probably too early, from what I had been told, but the only way to find out was to enter one.

Off to my left a colorful sign announced the name of the go-go bar to which it was attached. "Happy Hour until eight thirty p.m.," it advised, "Buy one, get one free." What a markup there is in booze. The name on the bar was one that Al had recommended. Several scantily clad young women cajoled any single man who happened by their space on the sidewalk. "Welcome" and "Hello, handsome man" rang out over the noise of the crowds. A few of the women lunged at passing men and grabbed them by their arms. I avoided their grasp. Al had seemed authoritative, and, calling to mind all that Oliver had told me, I walked through the thick beaded curtain at the entrance.

Inside it was dimly lit and difficult to see more than twenty feet ahead. The place was large, with an elevated stage in the center upon which a dozen nubile young ladies, some wearing skimpy bikinis and some wearing only the bottoms, danced and gyrated, several clinging to poles in the center of the stage. Nearly all were tattooed, some quite heavily, with almost every space on their bodies covered. The cast continually changed as dancers exited stage and others clambered on. The floor of the bar contained many people in motion: dancers, servers, customers, but the place was nowhere near full. The sound system blared ear splittingly loud European techno. All of my fears about go-go bars were realized—loud and sleazy. I spotted a small round table with one chair near the stage and sat down. The beaded curtain entrance was to my back.

A young woman who couldn't have been more than twenty, wearing the shortest of shorts and a halter top showing her bare midriff, took my order of Coca Cola. As she walked away the tattoo of a cobra covering most of her back was visible. It was not clear whether she was only waitress or if she was available for other services, not that she interested me.

My thoughts were interrupted by a loud and angry voice coming from behind me. The Boston accent made clear exactly to whom that voice belonged. A feeling of nausea overcame me, as if I had swallowed something unpleasant. Turning around, my fear was confirmed. Even in the dimness, Phil Funston could be seen twenty feet away at a table covered with several empty beer bottles and cocktail glasses. He was arguing with two bargirls. No mistaking that lumpy shaved head bobbing and twisting as he alternated his shouts from one lady to the other.

Far more than the sight Phil Funston's bald and misshapen noggin filled my mind. I saw my life coming apart. There was no way to explain myself to him and no way to fulfill the mission with my cover blown. The lives of the people most important to me were now in jeopardy. It could no longer be certain Noi was safe in America. If

I somehow survived, the pain of hearing Funston announce to the Club that he outed me in a Pattaya bar would be more painful than death. My range of action was severely circumscribed. Leaving the bar meant having to pass Funston to get to the entrance. There were no other doors leading outside. If his lumpy head was turned in my direction he couldn't miss me. Staying in the bar meant it was only a matter of time until he saw me. He was far too close for comfort. My options ranged from none to disastrous.

Somehow there had to be a way to get past Funston without being seen and there was precious little time to do so. A feeling of being trapped and of hopelessness seized me.

I looked around me, seeking some avenue of escape. There were none. I looked at my watch. It was a little after seven forty. I still had not found the right woman and now Phil Funston sat no more than twenty feet from me. How much worse can it get, I asked myself.

My answer came as Funston rose from his chair.

"If none of you bitches is gonna get me a drink, I'll just go up to the bar and get one myself," he yelled at no one in particular. He started moving in my direction. I could hear my heart pounding and could feel the digestive juices roiling in my guts.

As Funston came closer I lowered my head and tilted my body to one side, hoping that he would not recognize me. Despite the arctic level air conditioning, sweat began to bead on my forehead. I closed my eyes as if that would cause me to become invisible.

It was to no avail.

"My God!" Funston shrieked when he stood a foot to my side. He swayed slightly. "Of all the people to find here! Glenn Cohen, Mr. Clean! What the hell are you doing here?" His speech was slightly slurred. He was close enough that I could smell the alcohol on his breath.

"As if I need to ask," he added. In the dimness of the bar I could see the wide smirk on his face. A rotating red spotlight flashed across his face. It seemed as if his bald and lumpy head was on fire.

This is it, I thought. I'm not going to be able to get to Polinov. If I somehow come out of this alive, every day of my life at the NJA Club will be spent as the butt of jokes by Phil Funston and I would have to keep quiet as to why I was in that bar. What could ever be said to explain myself? I looked at my watch. Another minute had passed.

I felt Funston's hand on my shoulder. He was so close that I almost choked inhaling the alcohol that he had poured into himself.

"Since you're here, let's be friends," he said. "You wanted to play games before, no problem. What matters is now you're here. With me.

"Forget these bitches," he said, using my body to support himself. "Come on with me to a little place I know where they'll treat us like rock stars. Long as you're with me you're getting first class treatment.

"I don't hold any grudges," he added.

My body felt as if it was on fire, as if a burning fever had suddenly been sparked within me. There did not seem to be any way out of this nightmare and the clock was not merely running; it was approaching the speed of light. The Joes would be at the restaurant looking for me. Looking in vain. And Funston would ruin my name at the Club.

"Let me buy you a drink before we blow out of here," he shouted. I couldn't spare the time it would take to come up with a way to excuse myself. Funston did not seem likely to let me get away. He still had a hand on my shoulder to keep himself upright.

Then I recalled how Rodney and Oliver had seen something in me that persuaded them of my ability to rise to the occasion; now was the time to prove them right.

Sleepy Joe wanted to test the spray. This was that chance.

I felt for the small canister in my pocket and wrapped my fingers around it. Without anyone being able to see, the canister was palmed in my left hand so that it was not visible, and positioned so the plunger on top could be pressed with my thumb. I quickly adjusted my position so that I was facing towards Funston with the exit behind him. Phil was speaking in a loud voice but the words did not register. My mind was focused on my hand and thumb. My left hand aimed the nozzle of the spray at his face and my thumb pushed down on the plunger. Even in the dim light a thin mist could be seen shooting from my hand. Funston's face froze and his hand dropped from my shoulder. He stopped talking. I walked towards the exit as fast as I could and behind me heard a loud thud. At the beaded curtain I looked back and saw Funston lying on the floor. A rush of relief, excitement, and wonder filled every cell of my body as I passed through the curtain. Four hours of no Funston was now assured. Dealing with the inevitable blowback from his seeing me would have to wait until I returned to Bangkok. Once back on Walking Street the spray was shoved back into my pocket. A most pleasant and warm feeling flowed within me. Oliver would be proud when he heard about this. I just hoped he heard from me before he saw Funston.

Disaster had stared me in the face and I had frightened it away. There was nothing more to fear. Then it dawned on me that the next time the spray was used would not be on Funston, but on a murderous Russian gangster protected by armed bodyguards. Then again, I would have the protection of Sleepy Joe and the General's guy, whoever he may be. And the Russians might be able to kill me but not to humiliate me at the NJA Club.

It was now seven forty-five. There was little more than an hour to make it to the restaurant with a rented woman in tow. I scanned Walking Street, taking in the neon signs of the go-go bars and beer bars which fronted the street. Full nighttime darkness was approaching and there were many more pedestrians. Across the street, among the neon signs, my eyes spotted the name of another of the bars Al had named. Al was not responsible for Funston showing up in his first recommendation, so again I followed his advice and crossed the street. After passing through a steel door I found myself in a bar that was even darker, noisier and more crowded than the last. I wandered around before settling on a stool at the edge of a stage graced with more dancers than in the previous bar. I watched them, but only to play the role of sexpat to its fullest. After sitting there for less than a minute a woman wearing tight jeans and a V-neck shirt bearing the name of the bar on the front took my drink order of a Coke. When she turned on a small flashlight to write the order I saw that she had a pretty face and seemed somewhat older than the other dancers at this and the first bar. As she walked off to get my drink her trim and fit body passed under a spotlight illuminating the bar, and her well-shaped derriere, emphasized by the tight shorts, swayed like an erotic pendulum. Not wanting to act as if I was taken with her, I brought my gaze back to the stage.

There was no way to avoid watching the young women dancing suggestively on stage to an audience of mostly drunk, overweight, and loud *farangs* dressed for a day trip to the beach. It was incomprehensible how these women could bear the thought of being with these slobs. Even with my faded jeans and well-worn sport shirt, I was by far the most presentable man in the house.

Several dancers smiled at me from the stage. I remembered that Oliver had warned that a smile back would be a signal for them to leave the stage and sit with me. Two women sat next to me, one on each side. Each ran a hand across my thighs, arms, and hands. I gently removed their hands from my legs. "Where you from?" asked one. "How long you stay?" was posed by the other. When they found out I had already ordered a drink they smiled and asked sweetly if they could order for themselves. "Buy them a drink and you'll never get rid of them," Oliver had warned. I had to be certain that whomever I chose was suited for the role, someone who looked like a bargirl picked up by a sex tourist and who would not cause any problems. There couldn't be any other men in that bar looking for an employee, not a sex partner. My intuition would decide who was the right one and there was no time to waste. I politely said no and the two ladies scurried off.

The server returned with my soda. My eyes had adjusted to the dark and could see that she was indeed older than the dancers. I placed her somewhere in her thirties but as a Thai woman it was possible she was a bit older. She was unquestionably pretty. Her hair hung just above her shoulders. She wore a welcoming smile. No doubt the smile welcomed anyone who came into the bar.

As she placed the drink on the table her cleavage was visible below the top of her t-shirt. By speaking with her, other women would leave me alone while I figured out how to find the right one. There was a little more than an hour to make it to the restaurant.

She told me her name was Pim. I motioned for her to sit on the empty stool next to mine and she smiled and said only for a short time, as she had to take drink orders. When asked if she wanted a drink for herself she said yes and got up to get it. While she was gone, my gaze returned to the dancers. This time none smiled down at me nor did any approach my table. My hunch about focusing on Pim turned out to be right.

Pim returned with her drink and sat down next to me. "*Chok dii kha,*" she said, using the Thai version of "cheers" as we touched glasses.

"Where you from?" she asked. Claiming to be Canadian, I told her that my name was Tom—the same fake name given to Al—and that my stay in Pattaya began the day before and would last a few days. For reasons unknown even to me I added that there would be future visits.

Unexpectedly, we engaged in lengthy conversation. Pim's English was good enough for our conversation and she had a way of looking straight at me as if she were drinking in every one of my words. This pleased me despite the voice inside that warned me not to enjoy it. Several times she touched my forearm and once or twice my thigh. Part of her job I was certain, but to my surprise that made it no less pleasing. Clearly Pim was no ordinary waitress.

We spoke for fifteen minutes. She did not reveal her age but did say that she had a teenage daughter living with her parents in Isan, and she supported all three with her earnings at the bar. She had lived in Pattaya for ten years. She had worked at several bars and had been at this one for a year. She did not specify what jobs she had held, and, being ever the gentleman, I did not ask. I had not expected to find such enjoyment chatting with her. Talking with Pim was not all that different from speaking with Mai or Joy at the club, except Pim displayed her sexuality by dressing in a far more revealing manner and touching me with pleasant frequency. There was no denying the effect her smoldering appearance had on me. She left to refill our drinks and while she was gone it dawned on me that she might be the woman I needed that night. I just didn't know if she was available. Phil Funston, Al and Oliver would know if one can take the staff from a bar, but it was beyond my ken. There was now less than an hour left to get to the Royal Arms Seafood Restaurant and Polinov.

Pim returned and sat next to me again. She beamed when she heard me say how enjoyable it was to talk with her and I hoped it didn't cause her trouble if she was supposed to sit only briefly with a customer. She laughed and said as long as a customer keeps buying drinks, no problem. "The mamasan tell me she think you want bar fine me so no problem anyway," she added. Years of listening to Phil Funston had taught me that a mamasan was the manager of the hookers.

"It wasn't clear to me that you can go with customers. It seemed like you were just a waitress."

"I don't go with customer much," she said. "*Farang* men want younger ladies. But think you are different maybe. If you like I can go with you."

So it was that easy.

Oliver had told me to negotiate the lady's price before leaving the bar. "Get it out of the way right off and then you know how much to have ready to give her when the time comes to pay her and send her on her way," he said. Al had suggested a variable range of prices depending on how long the lady would be staying with me.

When I asked how much she wanted to go with me, Pim smiled and said it was up to me. I wasn't expecting that answer and would have to figure it out later.

I paid the bill for the drinks and the bar fine while Pim changed out of her work clothing. When she returned she was wearing a tight black t-shirt and a pair of shorts that barely reached the tops of her thighs. In the bright lights of Walking Street my attention was drawn to her well-shaped and smooth legs. No doubt she would pass for a hooker anywhere, and a very attractive one as well, good company for the short time we would be together. There was a clock visible through the window of a shop we passed on the Street. We had fifteen minutes to make it to Royal Arms Seafood.

26

PIM WAS QUITE surprised when told that before going to my hotel we would have dinner at the Royal Arms.

"*Peng maak*," she said, the Thai words for very expensive. I explained that many friends had recommended the place and this one night in town was my chance to try it. She grabbed my hand and we set off down Walking Street. I was confident that I looked like a sex tourist. As we walked, Pim told me she had often gone past the Royal Arms and admired it but had never been inside.

With all vehicle traffic now gone, Walking Street was an ocean of people. Darkness had descended and the scene had changed. There were still many overweight *farangs* with young women so small and dainty one would fear their being crushed in bed. Now there were other types on the street as well. Swarms of Chinese tourists marching in snaking lines, led by tour guides holding poles with stuffed animals or flags to identify them. Russian couples and families, many behemoth sized. Women stood in front of bars that had been closed earlier, hawking their wares, their wares being themselves. The massage parlors had even more women than before, enticing customers with "massage, mister" or "hey, handsome man." I doubted any man ever went into those parlors looking for an actual massage. Street musicians played their instruments, breakdancers leaped about and contorted their bodies to hip-hop music, other performers entertained the multitudes with mime and magic. A young girl covered with scorpions stood in the middle of the road and people dropped money into a basket set before her. Men wove among the crowd offering tours, companions, Viagra, and watches. A Middle Eastern man with a Salvador Dali mustache sold ice cream from a stand, scooping and making cones with theatrical flourishes. Tucked amidst the sleaze of the sex bars and massage places were souvenir shops, small eateries, American fast food chains, and on the side of Walking Street that faced the water, several attractive and expensive looking seafood restaurants. Aside from the working girls and the touts, there were no other Thais.

Pim pulled me towards the other side of the street. We made our way through the mob and were in front of the Royal Arms Seafood. Out front were several huge tanks filled with lobsters, crabs and deep-sea fish. A diner could select their entrée while it was still swimming. A long row of tables sat against a rail at the far end of the restaurant, nearly at water's edge. Polinov was seated at one, a bulky and mean looking Russian at each side. Two bottles of vodka and several shot and cocktail glasses were scattered about on his table. A chill clutched my spine and for the briefest of seconds I froze in place. Polinov was just as he appeared in Rodney's photos: a large, muscular man with short cut black hair turning gray, wearing a short sleeve black button-up shirt. He showed a slight smile. Polinov was big but did not seem menacing. The profile said that when he was not working as a gangster he could be friendly, even gracious. I knew that criminals could be complex people. He was no more than fifty feet from me studying the menu. My heart began to beat faster. Two deep breaths slowed it down.

At the entry to the dining area stood a small reception area. A young Thai man in a suit and tie approached us. He looked like the maitre d'.

"Two for dinner?" he asked.

"Yes," I replied. "And we'd very much like a table by the water.

Right about where that gentleman is seated," I said, pointing to Polinov. There was an empty table for two right next to his.

"Sorry, sir," the maître d' said, "but all waterside tables are booked in advance. That table is reserved. I can seat you close to the water but not right at the edge, sir."

If Pim heard the discussion she did not react. Maybe she presumed all *farangs* lied and were crazy to boot.

My response was delivered in a calm but firm tone.

"I promised my girlfriend a table by the water. This is a special day for us. I really need that table. Surely you understand." My hand concealed a folded thousand baht note.

"We would be so grateful to you if something could be done," I said, pushing my hand towards his, touching his thumb. He looked down and saw the protruding note. "We won't be all that long," I added. He took the note from my fist.

"Right this way, sir," the maître d' said. Pim stared at me and her smile grew wider. By the way she took my hand I thought she approved. Was she was thinking this guy isn't as dumb as he looks? Maybe she just found it humorous.

We were seated so close to the water we could have fallen in. Pim sat across from me and Polinov faced me from behind her. Menus the size of small catalogues were placed in our hands. My stomach was spinning like a washing machine. I was going to have to try my best to down any food. The spinning did slow down after a few minutes.

An obsequious waiter dressed in black recited the specials in English and then spoke to Pim in Thai. I ordered the catch of the day and she ordered a Thai dish. Neither of us ordered alcohol.

The light in the restaurant was sufficient to allow me to confirm that Pim was attractive. Her eyes were bright, her nose and mouth perfectly proportioned, and her nearly shoulder-length hair was straight and glowing. She had dark skin, which has always appealed to me. There were no lines on her face, but in Thailand, where women age at a glacial pace, one must look elsewhere for signs. Pim had the noticeably worn hands of a woman in her thirties who had known hard work: calloused, not soft, but not hardened or gnarled. They weren't smooth like Noi's or Wattana's. She must have sensed my thoughts about age, because she asked me how old I thought she was.

"Thirty," was my answer, having learned long ago to always lie downward to a woman when guessing their age.

"*Mai*," she said,. "*Ayu samsip jet pi.*" Thirty seven. A couple of years older than I would have guessed. I owned up to almost forty-eight, one of the few truths I told that night. She smiled and said she thought I was younger, no more than forty. She squeezed my hand when she said this. I tried to hide my pleasure.

This part was not as terrible as feared. No one gave us dirty looks. The place was filled with fat foreign men and young Thai women. Even if Pim came from a bar she was still one of the most respectable women in the restaurant. No visible tattoos, no piercings, natural black hair. By the standards of Pattaya nightlife, she was almost middle class, though any Pattaya regular would know she was being paid. In spite of the incredible danger immediately ahead, and my own discomfort with the bar scene, I was having a good time. After running a streak of five straight failures with women, the last two outright rejections, I found myself having a good time in a fine restaurant with an attractive and personable woman. My fears that this part would be painful did not prove to be the case. I was at ease with Pim and felt she was too. Being with her stopped me from dwelling upon what it would be like at the Club when Funston told everyone about finding me in that bar. As the Chuck Berry song is titled, "You Never Can Tell."

I looked past Pim, at Polinov and his bodyguards. Polinov smiled at me and nodded his head. I took another deep breath, slowly so that Pim would not notice. I was, after all, here to have a good time with Polinov, not Pim.

The Russians were ordering their dishes and there were two new unopened bottles of Stolichnaya vodka on their table. Our food arrived quickly, before the Russians' orders were brought to their table. The maitre d' kept looking at me as if he wanted to have the table ready for whoever had been bumped. I ignored him, thinking of how to approach Polinov once Pim was gone. I would glance at him periodically, making it appear as if I were looking at Pim. Once I caught Polinov looking at me with a smile.

Pim and I chatted for another ten minutes, comparing life in Pattaya to Bangkok, giving each other brief, selective and edited bits of our lives. Mine were nearly all fake, and I supposed hers were as well. Neither of us had eaten much. The Russians had cleaned their plates and were in the middle of the second new bottle. The fun was going to have to end. There was work to do.

Looking at my phone, I shook my head while frowning and spoke to Pim.

"I'm really sorry," I said, "but a man who was supposed to meet me for business tomorrow just texted that he has to leave first thing in the morning so we have to meet right away. He's on his way over, so I'm going to have to be alone for a while."

A look of disappointment passed over Pim's face.

"But don't worry," I said. "This won't take more than an hour. Why don't you rest up and meet me after later tonight?" I gently placed three one thousand baht notes in her palm.

Pim smiled and gave me a *wai*. Then she took my phone from the table and punched in some numbers. The first few notes of a song played and I realized she had dialed herself.

"Now we have each other's numbers," she said as she stood up. "See you later tonight." She sounded sincere, but after Oliver's warning about women from bars, it couldn't be. She would take the money and forget me. That of course is what we wanted. I watched her walk away, surprised at how the movement of her body held my gaze as if being hypnotized. A vision of the two of us in my hotel room danced across my mind. The thought was by turn pleasant and disturbing. It had been fun, but it was best that she was gone forever and I was alone. That was my norm anyway.

27

WITH PIM OUT of sight, attention turned to Polinov. I was careful not to stare at him. He watched Pim leave, and the smile on his face and the way he leaned forward told me he didn't know what was happening but was interested. Diversion from his serious business perhaps.

This was what Rodney meant when he spoke about the right time to engage Polinov. There would not be another opening like it. If Rodney's profile was correct, the Russian would be sociable and amenable to chatting with a harmless fool from the West lost in the labyrinth of Pattaya. If the profile was wrong, Plan B was in order. Problem was we had no Plan B. The only option was to make my move and trust in Rodney's profiling skills. Suddenly, sounds became distorted and the soft music was off tune. I hadn't had a drink, and the weed I had smoked earlier had worn off. It was a fear that was emerging, roiling my stomach, burning my face, squeezing my lungs. I took a long deep breath. In my mind I saw Noi, then Wattana, and then Pim. What was Pim doing there, I thought. Any woman who ever speaks to me seems to wind up in my subconscious. They drove away the fear, so I shouldn't complain.

I looked at Polinov and shook my head.

"Can you believe that?" I asked. "Bar fine her and take her here for dinner before heading to my hotel. When do you think was the last time she set foot in a place like this? Never, right? Then she tells me she just got a text from a friend who was in a motorcycle accident and needs her to help her home from the hospital. Demanded payment now to see her later."

Polinov laughed. It wasn't a laugh that causes a chill, like Billy Sloane's when he surprised Oliver and me in Bangkok. The way Polinov laughed and shrugged his hands reminded me of sympathetic voices at the NJA Club.

"Not good idea," he said in a heavy Russian-accented English. So the background information that he spoke serviceable English and enjoyed using it was correct. "I don't think you see that lady again. She have your money. All she want." He laughed and drank half a glass of vodka without blinking.

"You think she scammed me?" I asked.

"One hundred percent," Polinov answered. "How long you been Pattaya?"

"Just got here last night," I said. "First time to Thailand. "How about you."

"I been Thailand many time," he said. "Know enough to not trust Thai hooker. Always like to cheat *farang*. That why Russian not use Thai girls, bring own from Russia, Ukraine, Belarus. Very beautiful and not cheat."

"Afraid," he added as he finished the rest of the vodka in his cocktail glass. His smile faded briefly and then returned.

I put on my best embarrassed face, hoping to resemble a beagle caught raiding the garbage.

"I feel like such an idiot," I said. "Come all the way to Thailand to get laid and can't even do that. Thanks for the tip though. Never fall for that again."

"Buy you a drink?" I asked. "Your friends too," I added, pointing to the two bodyguards who kept their eyes on me. "Happy to have some company right now. Maybe you can give me more advice."

Polinov smiled and waved his hand.

"You come sit here. You drink some Russian vodka and you feel better," he said.

My plan was to avoid alcohol to stay fully alert. But I was used to a daily martini and could handle one shot.

One of the burly bodyguards rose from his seat to take a chair from a nearby table and move it close to Polinov, who motioned for me to sit and then signaled the waiter. An extra shot glass was brought to the table. I was relieved that it was only a shot glass. Polinov filled it with vodka and then did the same with his own. He raised his and I followed suit. "To beautiful women," he said as we clinked. Polinov downed the shot in one smooth movement and I copied him. It burned a little as it went down but that was all. It was excellent vodka and it calmed me. But if offered another shot it would be politely refused.

"You are American, my friend?" he asked. Muscles in my stomach tightened.

"Canadian," I replied.

"Same thing," he said and smiled.

I told him my name was Tom and he said his was Alexi.

"So you come Pattaya for vacation? Have good time?"

"You got it," I replied. "Need a break from all the assholes I have to deal with back home."

"Know what you mean," Polinov said. "Same here. Why I like go out, eat good food, drink vodka, have fun. Need break, same like you."

Is he really all that different from me, I thought? Or the General? Or Rodney Snapp and Billy Sloane? All of us could be charming when it suited us, other times not so charming. Was Polinov really any worse than we were?

One of the bodyguards walked next to Polinov and whispered in his ear. His head was turned in my direction but it wasn't clear if he was looking at me. My chest contracted and I gulped for air. Polinov spoke briefly in Russian and the guard sat back down in his chair. My chest and breath returned to normal.

He reached for the vodka. I told him one shot was enough for now because I still hoped to find a lady for the night.

Polinov thought for a moment, spoke to one of his bodyguards in Russian then turned to me.

"You want have good time, no problem? You come with me. We go club for Russians. Most beautiful girls. I see that you have best one. Then after we drink vodka all night. I show good time to new Canada friend."

"I'm game," came from my mouth, thought it seemed as if someone else was ordering the words to flow. My heart was beating quicker but not like during the near encounter with Funston. Then it was only fear. Now it was fear and excitement. Polinov was so amiable it almost seemed a shame not to be enjoying myself. And the shot of vodka had largely quieted the volcano within me.

Polinov stood up and his bodyguards did the same. One guard walked in front of Polinov while the other stood behind me. Polinov dropped several bills on his table. We followed him out, me in the middle next to him, hoping my impersonation of a sexpat and the vodka masked my tension.

There was no sign of either Joe. Scanning the restaurant would have alerted one of the Russians that something was not right. Rodney had called these guys the best in the business. I certainly wasn't. Halfway between the table and the exit, I scratched the top of my head with my left hand as Oliver had instructed. Polinov bid goodnight to the restaurant staff at the exit and we went towards Walking Street. No doubt the staff knew him as a good tipper.

As we proceeded I turned around and the bodyguard behind me smiled. He knew where Polinov was taking me. I was still largely caught in terror. What if Polinov had figured me out, not buying the role I was playing? The veil of fear lowered when my eyes caught a glimpse of Sleepy Joe and Rhode Island Joe a few steps behind. They were chatting amiably and looking at each other, just as if they were leaving the NJA Club after a night of stories by Ray and Oliver.

We reached the fish tanks I had seen earlier by the curb. Walking Street was now thick with people, many more than before, packed to such density that all movement was in slow motion. My ears detected a soft sigh, followed by a thud. Sleepy Joe moved next to the bodyguard in front of me. As he passed me he mouthed the words "one down." Rhode Island Joe moved to the other side of the guard in front, a few inches behind Polinov.

Polinov's radar detected the loss of a bodyguard. He turned around in one swirling motion, moving feet, hips and torso simultaneously as if choreographed. His eyes grew wide when he saw his rear bodyguard lying still on the floor by a tank of lobsters. Polinov turned forward again in time to see his other guard struggling to peel Sleepy Joe's hands off of his throat. The guard tried to speak but only a few garbled words came through. Polinov stared at the sight without moving. The guard fell face forward as Sleepy Joe released his hand from his neck. I felt a jolt course through my body, not like an electrical shock, more like the immediate perk following four cups of high caffeine coffee in quick succession.

I reached in my pocket for the spray and placed my thumb over the activating plunger and pulled the device emerged from my pocket as I turned to face Polinov. The Russian's eyes had grown larger and his mouth was open. He was looking at me and moving in my direction. He was less than two feet away. Suddenly he stopped moving. Rhode Island Joe's powerful arm was pressed against his chest, holding him in place.

Polinov didn't see my hand as I sprayed him. He fell forward too quickly for me to see the look on his face. Rhode Island Joe kept him from hitting the floor and lifted him over his right shoulder. I grabbed my phone and pressed the speed dial button for the special number Rodney had given for this day. He answered and said only, "Walk to the pier." I motioned for the two Joes to follow me.

I led the way with Rhode Island Joe a half step behind me on my right, Polinov slung over his shoulder like a sack of potatoes. The Russian was almost as tall as Rhode Island but thinner. If carrying Polinov was a burden, Rhode Island Joe didn't show it. He was smiling. We looked at each other and he winked. Sleepy Joe was a step behind Rhode Island, one quick move from either of us.

Walking Street was clogged with pedestrians but we pushed our way through the crowd. It reminded me of my days as a subway commuter in New York City, playing fullback to force my way into the train.

"Are they dead?" I asked Sleepy Joe in a near whisper.

"No, but they'll wish they were when Polinov's partners find out they couldn't protect him," he replied. "Aussie Special Forces trick," he added.

I knew from my earlier reconnaissance that the walk to the pier was no more than half a kilometer. One *farang* carrying another unconscious *farang* might have attracted attention elsewhere, but on Walking Street a drunken foreigner being assisted by a friend drew little notice. One friendly Englishman called out to us to ask if everything was alright, and Sleepy Joe replied that our friend had a bit too much to drink and we were taking him back to his hotel.

As we pushed our way forward my cell phone alerted me to a message. I looked and saw that I had received a text message from Pim. "Don't forget me," it read. I put the phone back into my pocket and thought that she must be honorable. After all, she had the three thousand baht and could have easily gone back to work and made more money to send to her family in Isan.

As we walked I told Sleepy Joe about my encounter with Phil Funston. He laughed.

"We'll probably hear a slightly different version from him, sad to say," Sleepy Joe said. "Probably something along the lines of him being slipped a Mickey Finn by one of the girls."

"I'm looking forward to hearing that one," I replied.

"No you're not," Rhode Island Joe said.

I looked at Rhode Island Joe. He still had a wide smile on his face. He was enjoying this. I wasn't.

As we shoved and elbowed our way though the mob, two hard looking young Thai men appeared at our sides, one adjacent to each Joe. They looked to be somewhere in their twenties. One was muscular and the other wire thin. Neither was smiling. One look at them and my criminal lawyer radar told me they were up to no good. Then I saw that each held a knife in their hand, pointed at the Joe by their side.

"We'll take your friend," the muscular tough said. I figured them to be Polinov's people. The thin fellow motioned for Rhode Island Joe to pass Polinov to him. It didn't look like he would be able to carry the Russian but then again life had become one surprise after another. Then it hit me that we could be killed right then and there on Walking Street and by the time anyone knew it the two Thais would be off with Polinov.

My fear was interrupted by the sound of Sleepy Joe breaking he arm of the knife-wielding muscular man. I heard the clatter of the tough's knife as it hit the ground as well as his cry of pain. A gurgling sound came from the same direction and then it was gone. I did not see the muscular man after that. He must have followed his knife to the ground.

I turned to check on Rhode Island Joe. He still held Polinov over his shoulder. The thin thug to his side appeared to be moving forward as if he were being pushed and I looked down and saw that his feet and legs were not moving. I looked closer and saw what appeared to be an icepick or screwdriver sticking out from the back of his neck, the metal shaft halfway in. He was pushed ahead by the force of the crowd until I saw him slipping lower and lower before he disappeared. I heard a voice say "Move fast!" It sounded familiar but I just couldn't place it. I turned my head to look behind me and did not see anyone I recognized. The crowd behind me seemed to be all tourists. "I'm moving as fast as I can," Rhode Island Joe muttered. When he realized he didn't know who he was addressing, he called out, "What the hell just happened?"

"Someone just saved your ass," Sleepy Joe calmly replied. "I put my money on the General's man, whoever the hell he may be."

We were past the bars and massage parlors, and the crowd had thinned out enough so that I could see the entrance to the Bali Hai Pier a hundred meters ahead of us. A few high end restaurants and better hotels lined the sidewalks. There were many Russians and I saw signs on the nicer restaurants in Cyrillic characters. I saw two ferries docked at the main pier and many smaller boats docked in several smaller piers off the sides of the Bali Hai.

Rodney Snapp appeared in front of us without warning.

"Follow me," he said and led us down a narrow dirt path on the left side of the Bali Hai Pier. The path was poorly lit. We encountered no other people along the way. Sleepy Joe asked Rhode Island if he needed any help carrying Polinov. "Twenty years of lugging cases of beer, I can carry this sack of shit a little more," he replied.

"We're almost there anyway," Rodney said. "That pier over there," he added, pointing to one that looked to be a few hundred yards ahead.

I quickly asked Sleepy Joe if he had killed the Thai and he said "Maybe." If he had, it didn't seem to bother him. "He was about to kill me. You next." A quick wave of nausea passed over me and then it was gone as suddenly as it had arrived.

This was my last chance to ask Rodney the questions that had lingered in my mind. Perhaps our success would move him to answer, I thought. I had nothing to lose by asking.

"I think that now I'm entitled to some answers," I began. "We could have been killed just a few minutes ago. I deserve to know some things you didn't want to tell me.

"If you will answer a question," I said, "I promise not to ask again."

"One question," Rodney replied. "No guarantee I'll answer but you can keep trying."

"Why did Panchen call you right before he died?"

If Rodney was surprised or any held other emotion he did not reveal it. I had encountered my share of cool people as a criminal lawyer but few matched Rodney Snapp.

"He called to ask me to get his client Noi a visa to the U.S. as confidentially as possible. He was clear that meant Billy must not know."

"Did Panchen wanting the visa have anything to do with Billy?" I asked.

Rodney nodded lightly as if to say "he got it." "I was right about you," he said softly. "Sooner or later you figure it all out. Let me try to explain."

"Oliver? He's one of us. No worries there. You? You were a criminal lawyer, you're trained to keep your mouth shut. Sleepy Joe? Ex–Australian Special Forces. Not a problem we can see. Rhode Island Joe? Yeah we were worried at first, but he would rather die than let you down. Besides, he's a Westerner like the rest of you. Anything happens to an American or an Australian, questions are going to be asked, embassies will be poking around, smart cops from overseas will be called in, Western newspapers will be snooping around. Billy promised me nothing would happen to you guys.

"But it's not the same for Noi," Rodney continued, "As far as Billy was concerned, she's just another Isan girl no one will ever miss. And one who lied to everyone, you included, and could not be trusted. If she started telling people how she had these problems and they all went away, it would eventually lead to you and then to us. Sad thing is Billy was right. It's his solution I didn't like. Over here he could do whatever he wanted with her. Harder in America.

"I got her the visa. I don't always agree with my partner."

"How did Panchen get your number?" I asked

"Don't you think he had his own Oliver?" Rodney replied.

Of course, I thought. The friend at the Foreign Ministry. Who must have known what Billy and Rodney were up to. Who must have known about me. Who must have told Panchen.

"I promised you one question and I gave you three," Rodney said. He put up a palm and said, "No more questions."

No reason to disagree. He had told me all I needed to know.

Less than a minute later we were at the beginning of a small pier jutting what looked to be two hundred feet out on the water. It was dark but I could make out a small boat at the end. I could see the figure of a man standing at the edge. As we drew closer I saw that it was Billy Sloane.

"I was hoping I'd never have to see him again," I told Rodney.

"After this, you won't," Rodney replied. "The money is in the boat. I'll put our friend in there and hand you the fee you just earned."

When we were a few yards from Billy, he called out to me.

"Good job, Glenn, knew you could do it. Your country owes you a debt of gratitude." He walked up to Rhode Island Joe.

"Put this pile of garbage on the pier," he said and Rhode Island Joe complied. I saw a look of relief on his face even in the dim lighting as he rubbed his shoulder. Billy pulled a pair of handcuffs from a pocket, pulled Polinov's arms behind his back and slipped on the cuffs. Polinov was still out cold. Billy reached into the small boat and withdrew a small length of rope with which he expertly tied the Russian's feet together.

"Toss him in the boat," he told Rodney.

"Give me a hand," Rodney said to Rhode Island Joe. "I'll be back with the money," he added, looking at me.

Rodney grabbed the Russian under the shoulders and Rhode Island Joe took the legs. The boat was an open cruiser, maybe thirty feet long. There was a small covered area in front where the wheel was visible. The boat was tied right at the end of the pier and was a two to three foot drop from the pier into the vessel. I watched as Rodney and Rhode Island Joe lowered Polinov into the center of the vessel. Rodney then clambered in and appeared be securing Polinov to some attachment on the side with a length of rope. I saw Rodney reach under one of the benches in the boat and pull out an attaché case. He pulled himself back up one leg at a time. I wondered how an overweight slob like Billy managed to get in and out of the vessel.

"My pleasure. You earned it," Rodney said as he handed me the case. "Check it first, it's not locked. You can set a code later." He used the flashlight on his phone for illumination.

I opened the case and inside I saw neatly stacked hundred dollar bills, reminiscent of the money I had taken from my dead client and the bribe I paid to save Sleepy Joe. I counted one rubber banded set and it contained one hundred notes totaling ten thousand dollars. I counted ninety-nine more of the sets. Sleepy Joe stood by my side, peering over my shoulder as I tallied the bills.

"I'll take your word each one has the same," I said.

"It's been good knowing you," I told Rodney and extended my hand for a farewell shake. "I wish you two the best of luck in the future but if I never see either of you again, it will be too soon. My friends and I will be taking our leave right now."

I turned to look at the two Joes. A look of shock was pressed on Rhode Island's face. Sleepy Joe's eyes, usually permanent slits from decades of perpetually being stoned, were wide open. I turned back to look at Billy.

"You're not going anywhere," Billy Sloane said. I looked at him and even in the dark I could see that he held a large pistol with a clip on top. I had seen these guns in some of the cases I had back when I was a lawyer in the States. They were called machine pistols, basically a small machine gun. It was aimed at Sleepy Joe but I knew that one pull on the trigger and he could kill all three of us in a second. Sloane knew that if he didn't kill Sleepy Joe first, the Australian would take that pistol from him in a flash.

"What the hell are you thinking?" Rodney yelled. "Put that thing away and get in the boat, Billy. We have to meet the ship. Let's get going."

"As soon as I finish this little business," Billy replied. "You know I never leave any loose ends lying around."

"You made me a promise," Rodney said.

"This is one promise I can't keep," Billy said.

So I had been right and had figured it out. But that didn't seem to be doing me any good.

"I know what you're up to," I said, looking at Billy. "You think you can keep this secret by killing everyone you used along the way. You killed Panchen when you realized he knew the whole story, which he got from his friend. You must have been monitoring Rodney's calls and saw the trail. You knew he had spoken with Panchen and with me."

"Not bad for an amateur," Billy replied. "It's a shame it has to end this way because you have potential. But I can't take any chances. The world can have their suspicions, but unless someone talks that's all they have. My reputation and my career are on the line here. No one outside the agency can ever find out what happened. Sooner or later one of you would talk. I know your types.

"Panchen would have spoken out if anything happened to Noi, so he had to go. I can take care of Noi in America, no matter what my bleeding heart partner might think. As for you, Glenn, you were just starting to develop your natural talents. But you let Panchen's death overcome your common sense. You would never have let go and never stopped asking questions. I realized that from the minute you let on that you knew I killed him. If I killed only you, your buddies would not let me get away with it, not even for all that money. So I have to take care of you guys right here. Rodney may feel bad but he's with us, so he won't say a word. Am I right, Rodney?"

"You forget about Oliver," Rodney said. "These guys don't come back, he'll figure it out and sooner or later he'll have you killed. So put the gun away and get in the boat."

"That's why I'm getting in the boat alone and you're going back to Bangkok to take care of our Australian friend," Billy said.

"No I'm not," Rodney replied.

"Don't be a fool," Billy said. "No reason for anyone to die unless they have to, you included." He was about to say more when a shot rang out. I watched a hole open in Billy's forehead as he fell backward into the water. I ran to the edge of the pier and looked down. I saw no sign of a body.

"He was absolutely right about that," Wang the cook said as he walked towards us from the darkness thirty or so feet behind us, a pistol in his hand. "Don't worry, Rodney, I'm not going to harm you." Wang tucked the pistol into a shoulder bag he carried.

"So you're the guy the General sent to watch out for us," Sleepy Joe said when Wang was right next to us. "Not bad for the cook."

"Cook?" Wang said. "I'm the owner. General bought me the place years ago. Why the hell you think I work so hard?

"But keep that quiet," he added.

At least I had solved the mystery of who owned the NJA Club.

"I'll take the money," Wang said. When Rhode Island Joe gave him an angry look, Wang laughed. It dawned on me then that he spoke English far better than he had ever let on.

"Don't worry, after the General takes his fair share you'll get the rest. He won't be too greedy. He really likes *Khun* Glenn. Trust me, it's safer with me than you. General don't cheat you, just want to make sure it get back to Bangkok. With me, for sure. With you, who knows what happen. Better this way. Come to the General's house tomorrow at noon. Just Glenn."

The two Joes looked to me as if to ask if Wang could be trusted. I nodded my assent.

"You will be paid in full, I guarantee it," I said. "Whatever the General has up his sleeve, it doesn't include ripping us off. I think we can trust those who save our lives twice in one night."

I handed the briefcase to Wang. The cook smiled, turned around, and walked off into the darkness.

Then it all struck me. We were alive but were almost made dead. At least two men were actually dead, the Thai thug and Billy Sloane. Maybe the other Thai thug as well. My legs were wobbly. I wished there were a rail to grab onto. Instead I grabbed onto Rhode Island Joe.

"Those Thais were Polinov's people?" I asked Rodney.

"No way," he replied. Russian and Thais don't work together. They were freelancers who hang around Walking Street looking for angles. When they saw you guys with Polinov, they figured out something big was happening. They knew who he was. If they could snatch him from you, Polinov would have paid them well. Assuming he didn't think they were in on it with you and got greedy."

"What happens now?" I asked. "There are dead men all over Pattaya." I nearly choked on my words.

Rodney put a hand on my shoulder. His voice was calm.

"In this business, there are always dead people. "And you didn't kill any of them." He paused. "Well maybe Sleepy Joe did, but we won't know quite yet. Rest assured that because they are dead, many others will live. So go home, and get your money tomorrow."

"Won't these bodies raise questions?" I asked Rodney. "Like your partner maybe floating up on shore in the morning?"

"We'll take care of it," Rodney said. "Go home, Glenn." He patted me on the shoulder, turned around and walked to the boat. I saw him climb down and heard the engine start. I watched as the boat left the pier.

"You heard what the man said," Sleepy Joe said. "Time to go."

Then I heard my phone alert. I looked at the message. It was from Pim.

"Where are you?" it read.

"Who was that?" Sleepy Joe asked. "Oliver? The General?"

"No," I replied. That was the lady from the bar."

"You must have made quite an impression," Sleepy Joe said. "She was already paid but she still wants you."

"Considering the luck you've been having with women," Rhode Island Joe said, "maybe you ought to grab the chance while you can. You paid for the room for the night, right?"

"You guys can't be serious," I replied. "At least two men dead, and we were seconds away from boosting the body count, and you want me to jump in the sack with a bargirl?"

"Mate, couldn't think of a better reason to celebrate," Sleepy Joe said.

"Even if I felt in the mood, which I don't, I'm not Phil Funston. I don't pay."

Both Joes laughed.

"Oh, you don't?" Sleepy Joe asked. "Let me see. You were willing to get all of us killed for your Noi and what happened there? You would have risked our lives to help that young girl from the condo and where is she when you need her? What did this one want from you?"

"Actually she said it was up to me. I gave her three thousand baht."

"Sounds like the best deal you've had in a long time," Rhode Island said.

I thought it over for a few seconds. I saw Pim's smile, heard her voice, felt her touch. Did it matter how we came together?

"You know you might be right," I said.

28

I CALLED OLIVER on the walk back to my hotel. As soon as he picked up he said "Thank God you're okay."

My body was still dripping with the residue of fear and sweat. Hearing Oliver's voice evaporated much of the fear.

"Good job," he said after hearing everything. "I'll come by your place for my money after you meet the General. My bill will be ready."

"By the way, Sleepy Joe is right about the lady," he added. "He's starting to impress me more and more. But he is an Aussie after all."

"You guys can't say anything about this at the Club," I said. "Funston is going to be bad enough."

"Don't worry, wouldn't want to humanize you," Oliver replied.

THE ALARM ON my phone sounded at eight in the morning.

Pim was nowhere to be seen. A piece of paper lay on the pillow where she had slept. On it she had written "Hope to see you more. When you come Pattaya. Or I go Bangkok you like."

Remote possibility of the latter, was my thought. Zero chance for the former.

The idea of our meeting again was confusing. Not possible. It's just the residual shock of last night. That's all it is. At least that was what my logical mind told me.

There was a struggle taking place between my logic and my feelings. It had been undeniably pleasant and I hadn't enjoyed being with a woman that much for a very long time. Maybe it was relief at still being alive. That was all. But maybe not.

And whatever this all meant, there was the unpleasant encounter that awaited me when I had to face Phil Funston's revelation that he had found me in a go-go bar in Pattaya. The Joes and Oliver would understand, but no one else would. Not the staff, the General, Edward, or the other regulars.

It was the price I had to pay for success.

A cabbie was happy to drive me back to Bangkok. I dozed off ten minutes into the ride and woke up when we were passing Suvarnabhumi airport. During the half hour it took to reach my condo my mind could not stop running the movie of all that had happened the day before. As the hours built up distance, exactly how frightening it had been became clear. Up until then, I had only seen one person killed, and when that occurred my thoughts were more engrossed in stealing the dead man's money than in fear of being killed as well. This was not the same. I had played a role in Panchen's death, had seen Billy and a Thai thug killed. Polinov's bodyguards and the second thug might be joining Billy Sloane in the murky waters off the pier on my account.

For what? I asked myself. For Noi, who had lied to me and shut me out of her life with a weak goodbye? For Wassana, who was frightened of me? To make more money for the General Oliver, or myself? Didn't we each already have more than we would ever need?

Then my thoughts turned to Panchen. One of the smartest, most decent people I had ever met, certainly in the legal profession. I had been terrified of dying at Billy Sloane's hand, but watching him take a bullet in the head and fall dead off the pier brought pleasure as the scene replayed in my mind.

Who I was becoming? Someone who took vengeful joy at the death of another?

As a general rule, no. In the case of Billy Sloane, yes.

One thing was certain. The man I had been twenty four hours ago was no longer the same.

BACK IN MY condo a long, hot shower invigorated me. My Pattaya outfit went into the garbage. I arrived at the General's house looking as fresh and pressed as always.

The surly guard who greeted me when I came to help Sleepy Joe was on duty again and he was equally unpleasant. He brought me to the library, where the General was seated with the briefcase Rodney had give me. As I walked in, the General rose from his seat and extended his hand to me and we shook. The General's grip was firm.

"That's how we did it when I was a military attaché in your country," he said. We sat down.

The General, his smooth face as calm as always, saw the conflict in mine.

"You have to accept, Glenn, that the world is not perfect. We are not perfect. We do the best we can."

"And this is the best we can do?" My voice was rising. "At least three dead men, maybe another one, two or three. Kidnapping, assault, violating Polinov's right to fight extradition. Risking the lives of the people I care most about in this world. That's the best we can do?"

The General shook his head slowly.

"Glenn, you didn't kill anybody. You didn't even try to kill anybody. If I am not mistaken, a number of people tried to kill you and your friends. One of them killed Panchen, a good and honorable man. Had they not done those things, they would all be alive today. Any extradition hearings Polinov might have had would have been a farce and you know that. Would have depended on which foreign power put the most pressure on Thailand. Now he has to answer for his crimes against your country. What's so unfair about that, my good friend? "

I put my head in my hands and struggled to accept the General's words. He was right but it didn't make me feel any better.

"Let's have some coffee before you leave with your money," the General said. "Black Ivory this time," he added. He reached over to the edge of the table and pressed a button I hadn't noticed. A woman servant opened the door and the General spoke to her in Thai.

"She'll be back with our coffee in ten minutes," he said. "Black Ivory. On a special occasion like this, we deserve the very best."

It was obvious that Wang had told the General all he knew. He had been at the restaurant and seen me spray Polinov. He surely told the General how he had saved Rhode Island Joe and prevented the thugs from grabbing the Russian, and what had taken place at the pier, including Billy's admission that he had killed Panchen.

My hope was that because Wang had left the pier before my meeting Pim at my hotel, the General didn't know of my night with her. No such luck.

"It was a relief to learn that no matter how sickened you might have felt, it didn't keep you from your new girlfriend," he said.

The heat of shame burned on my face. The General must have seen it turn red.

"I was disappointed that after turning down my many offers to provide you with beautiful women, you spend the night in a cheap hotel with a bargirl."

Before my shock wore off, the General spoke again.

"You don't think I was going to leave you alone all night, did you?

Wang was outside your door the whole time. He left here just before you got arrived. Poor guy has to cook all day after babysitting you."

"General, it's not like you think," I started to explain while stammering and grasping for the right words if there were any. The General waved his hand and smiled.

"Just joking with you, Glenn. I was delighted to hear for once you thought like man. This old soldier can assure you nothing takes away the lingering fear of combat like a woman."

"I don't know about that."

"Yes, you do," the General replied. "And you don't have to be embarrassed around me. In my time as a soldier I paid enough women to build five houses in Isan. Just don't shout about it like Funston."

There was a knock on the door. The woman servant returned with a tray bearing a pot of coffee, cream, sugar, and two cups.

The General handed me the briefcase.

"Less than a hundred grand for me," he said. "Most of that is going to Wang. He deserves it. I'm sure you feel the same."

I nodded in agreement, then snatched the bag and left. It was in the cab that it dawned on me that I hadn't touched the Black Ivory Coffee.

~

WHEN I RETURNED home from the General, Rodney Snapp was sitting at my kitchen table, a small satchel set before him. His unannounced appearances no longer surprised me.

"Why are you here?"

"Have to bring Charlie's ten percent to him. Couldn't trust the General with that. I'm going back home tonight." I counted out ten packets of bills and handed them to him. He stuffed them in the satchel.

"Will you make sure nothing happens to Noi?" I asked.

"With Billy gone, she doesn't have any problems," Rodney said. "I'll send your regards to her and Charlie."

"How about you do me big favor and don't?"

"It's been a pleasure," Rodney said as he left.

OLIVER ARRIVED AT my place a few minutes before the two Joes. We sat on my couch. He handed me a bill typed piece of paper that said only "Professional Services: $100,000.00."

"Inflated but I'll pay," I said and counted it out from the briefcase at my feet. Oliver placed the bills in a gym bag he had brought. He patted me on the back and thanked me. The intercom buzzed and the security officer announced the arrival of Sleepy Joe and Rhode Island Joe. A few minutes later they were in my condo.

Each was handed a thick manila envelope. "One hundred fifty thousand U.S. for each of you," I said. They seized the packets and gazed at them as if they were staring at the Covenant of the Lost Ark.

Oliver and Rhode Island Joe left together. "See you later at the Club," Rhode Island shouted on his way out. Sleepy Joe remained behind. He produced a thick joint and lit it. "Best stuff I've ever had. Been saving it in my humidor for a special occasion. This is it."

He was right. It put me to sleep. When I woke up Sleepy Joe was gone.

IT WAS A joy to be back at the Club, the impending confrontation with Funston notwithstanding. The Club was my home and it contained my family, so this ordeal had to be faced. Ray had not yet arrived. Sleepy Joe was at his usual table in the rear. Rhode Island Joe was making his way through a hamburger and a pint. Wang was working in the kitchen and nodded at me as if nothing had happened. Phil Funston was arguing with a stranger. The General sat at his table and he motioned for me to join him. It felt good to be back in the life I was meant to lead. And four hundred thousand dollars richer to boot.

Best of all, my life was slipping back into the quiet and uncomplicated existence it had enjoyed before my world was turned upside down.

While making my way to the General, my phone alert went off. It was a message.

"So happy you call me go Bangkok. See you tonight. Pim." There was a little heart at the end of the message.

What was it Walt Whitman wrote?

"Do I contradict myself? Very well, then I contradict myself."

You aren't the only one, Walt.

As I approached the General, Funston rose and walked towards me. When he was within a foot of my face he let out a loud laugh.

Here it comes, I thought.

"You just won't believe this," he said. "I was down in Pattaya and some girl in a bar must have slipped me a Mickey Finn. Took a sip of my drink and next thing you know I was out cold for four hours. My cash was missing. Lucky I only had a few thousand baht.

"And whatever they put in the drink must have had a touch of LSD. At one point I thought I had seen you in the bar. Talked to you, close as we are now.

"No way that's gonna happen, not with Mr. Goody Goody."

Funston laughed and walked away. I felt as if I had just smoked the fattest joint sleepy Joe had ever rolled.

"Good to be back to normal," was my greeting to the General.

"Let's hope none of us ever have to go through anything like that again."

"Fully understood," The General replied.

"Now about that favor," he said.

THE END

Acknowledgments

It is not possible to adequately thank everyone who helped me as I worked on this novel. No conclusions should be drawn from the order or omission of a name.

Keybangers Bangkok, an English-language writers' group, has been my collegial anchor, the members having read, discussed and made sound editorial suggestions as the novel was in progress. The input of all members was invaluable, with particular recognition extended to Saranit Vongkiatkajorn (Sar) and Paul Bond, whose efforts went far beyond the call of duty. Thanks to Daniel Caro for helping set up my blog and toDavid Ring for introducing me to this wonderful group of writers. Special thanks to Delia, who holds Keybangers together.

Sheldon Penner of Pattaya Players and Pattaya Improv Group acted as an editor and as a guide to the intricacies of his adopted city. Many of his suggestions were incorporated.

My daughter Liz read, proofed and commented on the novel, and her insights were invaluable.

My artist daughter Melody designed the beautiful cover. She also devised the catchy phrase on the book cover.

My good friend MK "Ming" Chang read the very first draft of chapter one and helped steer me in the right direction.

Blake Dinkin, founder of Black Ivory Coffee, the world's finest, guided me through the intricacies of its production and perfect brewing.

My Thai language teacher, the charming Ajahn Mui, taught me not only the language and alphabet; she also enlightened me as to the ways and culture of the Thai people.

And of course, a heartfelt thanks to my dear wife, Josephine, for allowing me the time and space to realize my passion and create this novel.

About the Author

Stephen Shaiken practiced criminal law in for more than thirty years, the first four in Brooklyn and the rest in San Francisco. His decades as a criminal trial lawyer are often embedded in his writing. He is a graduate of Queens College and Brooklyn Law School, and earned an M.A. in Creative Writing from San Francisco State University. He currently splits his time between Bangkok, Thailand, and Tampa, Florida.

Stephen's short stories have been published in numerous magazines, and several may be read on his blog. Stephen's two novels are best described as exotic noir thrillers, but he also writes humor, literary, and occasional science fiction stories.

Bangkok Whispers is Stephen's second novel, featuring the same characters as his first, *Bangkok Shadows*. Follow Stephen on his blog and on Twitter, and sign up for his newsletter to receive advance notice of Stephen's future novels and short stories.

Click here to visit the *Bangkok Shadows* page on Amazon.

Follow Stephen's blog:
www.stephenshaiken.com

Follow Stephen on Twitter:
@StephenShaiken